AUNT BESSIE UNDERSTANDS

AN ISLE OF MAN COZY MYSTERY

DIANA XARISSA

For Denise.

AUTHOR'S NOTE

Welcome to book twenty-one in this series. I'm surprised and delighted to still be writing about Bessie and her friends. I expect, when I get to the end of the alphabet, to take things in a different direction, but I don't intend to stop writing about Bessie! I always suggest that readers start with the first book in the series and read through them in order. They progress alphabetically by the last word in the title. If you choose, you can read them in any order, but the characters do change and develop as the series goes along.

Bessie made her first appearance in my romance novel *Island Inheritance*. She'd just passed away and left her estate to her family in America. In the process of developing Bessie's character for that book, I found that I wanted to write more about her. This series came out of that desire. Because Bessie had passed away in the romance, the first cozy mystery was set about fifteen years before the romance novel. This series began, therefore, in spring, 1998, and the stories have progressed from month to month since that first book.

This is a work of fiction. All characters are fictional creations. Any resemblance they may bear to any real person, living or dead, is entirely coincidental. The businesses on the island are also fictional, and again, if they resemble any real businesses, that is also coincidental. The historical sites on the island are all real, but the events that take place at them in these stories are fictional.

Having set the books in the Isle of Man, a British crown dependency, I've used English (and Manx) terminology and spelling throughout the book. There is a short glossary and some other notes at the back for anyone who may be unfamiliar with any of the words used. I've been living in the US for over ten years now, however, so I'm certain that an increasing number of Americanisms are sneaking into my writing. If you notice any, let me know and I'll try to correct them.

I'd love to hear from you and have included all of my contact information at the back of the book. I have a monthly newsletter about new releases that you can sign up for on my website. There is also a free Bessie short story available there, if you are interested. Otherwise, find me on Facebook, Twitter, or Instagram.

CHAPTER 1

" *I*'m sorry to bother you, especially when you're so busy with Christmas at the Castle," Hugh Watterson said to Bessie when she answered her phone.

"Christmas at the Castle is going much better this year," Bessie told him. "We've a year's worth of experience and a better committee. It isn't nearly as much work now that certain people aren't helping."

Hugh laughed. "That's good to hear, because I need a small favour."

Elizabeth Cubbon, known as Bessie to nearly everyone, smiled. She'd known Hugh since his childhood, which had been a difficult one. His parents hadn't approved of his desire to join the police, and Hugh had spent many nights during his teen years in Bessie's spare bedroom. Having never married or had children of her own, Bessie had been happy to act as a sort of honourary aunt to the children of Laxey. Disgruntled teenagers always knew they could spend a night at Bessie's cottage on Laxey Beach, where they'd be given biscuits or cake and some very sensible advice.

Now Hugh was in his twenties, but Bessie often still thought of him as a small child. That was bound to change, as Hugh's pretty and vivacious wife, Grace, was expecting their first child in the next fortnight. Grace was a primary-school teacher. She'd been working in

Laxey and neighbouring Lonan as a supply teacher since September, but Bessie knew that she'd stopped working about a week earlier. No doubt Hugh's favour had something to do with Grace.

"What do you need?" she asked.

Hugh sighed. "I keep having this dream. Grace is home alone and she goes into labour. The power goes out and she can't find her mobile. She can't drive herself to Noble's, not when she's in labour, but she can't find her phone and the phone in the house won't work without power."

"What a horrible nightmare."

"It's awful. Grace just laughs at me when I tell her about it, but I can't get it out of my mind."

"I'm sorry. How can I help?"

"I'm trying to find people who can check on Grace," Hugh said, sounding slightly sheepish. "I don't want her to know what I'm doing, because she doesn't want me fussing over her, but I was wondering if you could have lunch with her one day next week?"

"I'd love to have lunch with Grace. Which day?"

"What works for you? When won't you be in Castletown?"

Bessie looked at the calendar next to her phone. It was unusually full due to the event at Castle Rushen. This was the second year in a row that she was helping Manx National Heritage with the fundraiser. After someone had been murdered during the planning stages of the first event, Manx National Heritage had almost decided not to continue with it, but Christmas at the Castle itself had been a huge success, raising a good deal of money for MNH and the other charities that had taken part. Bessie was spending a lot of her days in the lead-up to Christmas in Castletown, at Castle Rushen, helping with everything from planning to decorating as opening day for this year's event grew closer.

"I'm not in Castletown at all on Wednesday," Bessie told Hugh. "I could manage lunch on Thursday, as well, if that would be better. The committee isn't meeting until two on Thursday."

"Wednesday would be great," Hugh said, sounding relieved. "Doona is taking Grace out for the day on Monday, as she has a day off work. Grace is spending much of Tuesday with some of her teacher friends. You'll see her on Wednesday. I'm sure I can find someone to do something with her on Thursday. Her mum is coming to stay with her for the weekend. She'll drive up some time on Friday and stay until Monday. I'll worry about next week later."

"Maybe the baby will come this week."

"He or she isn't due until next week. I'm not ready for the baby to arrive, although I doubt I'll feel any more ready next week, or the week after, or ever."

Bessie chuckled. "You're probably correct. You'll never feel ready, but the baby will arrive when he or she is ready, and you and Grace will make it work."

"I hope so."

"You can't change your mind now."

"Yes, I'm all too aware of that," Hugh said. "Anyway, if you could ring Grace and invite her for lunch on Wednesday, I'd really appreciate it. Just don't tell her that I suggested the invitation, please."

"I'll ring her this morning. Was there anything else?"

"No, but thank you. I'll pay for your lunch, wherever you go."

"Don't be silly. I'm quite happy to have lunch with Grace and pay for my own meal. I may even pay for hers, as a treat before the baby arrives. It will be a nice break from everything else I'm busy doing at the moment."

Bessie put the phone down and then glanced at the clock. It was only seven, and probably too early to ring Grace. Her internal alarm nearly always woke her at six. She'd done nothing more than shower and get dressed before the phone had rung. Grace had mentioned some time back that she was having trouble sleeping, especially as she worried about keeping Hugh awake. If Hugh was up and out of the house already, hopefully Grace was sleeping late.

After a quick breakfast of cereal with milk, Bessie took herself out for her morning walk. It was a cold and crisp December morning and Bessie found herself walking briskly to try to keep herself warm. She'd pulled on a heavy coat, but perhaps it was time to get her heaviest coat out of the back of the wardrobe.

3

Once she'd begun to feel warmer, she didn't want to stop walking. Having the entire beach to herself made her feel as if she should walk for as long as possible. The row of holiday cottages that stretched along the sand next to Bessie's small cottage were always crowded during the spring and summer. This year they'd had guests staying in them into the autumn as well. While Bessie didn't really mind the holiday cottages, she did love having the beach to herself again.

Bessie often turned around at the stairs to Thie yn Traie, the large mansion that was perched on the cliff above the beach. Today she barely glanced at them as she continued her march along the water's edge. It didn't seem long before she spotted the new houses in the distance. This was the first December since the houses had been built and Bessie found herself wondering how the new residents had decorated for Christmas. Taking a look was as good an excuse as any for continuing her walk, she decided.

A few minutes later, she laughed at herself as she turned around past the last house. It was far too early on a Saturday morning for anyone in the houses to be awake. Curtains were tightly drawn in every single house, meaning Bessie hadn't been able to spot a single decoration. There were no signs of movement at Hugh and Grace's house along the row. Feeling relieved that she hadn't rung Grace before her walk, Bessie slowly made her way home. She waited until eleven to ring.

"Grace? It's Elizabeth Cubbon."

"Where has Hugh put you on the rota, then?" Grace asked with a sigh.

"The rota?"

"Oh, I'm sure he didn't call it that, but that's how I feel about the whole thing. He's rather obsessed with this idea that I'm going to go into labour and be unable to get help. I think he believes that my labour will only last about ten minutes and then I'll be all alone with the baby and no medical attention."

Bessie laughed. "I'm sure he knows better than that, but you should be grateful that he's so concerned about you and the baby."

"I am grateful. It's just odd, being so popular at the moment.

People I haven't spoken to in years have rung to ask me to lunch. My social calendar has never been so full."

"Enjoy it while you can. Once the baby arrives, I understand everything will suddenly revolve around him or her."

"Yes, I know. It's nice, it's just exhausting. I don't have enough energy to keep going out every day."

"You're more than welcome to come here one day," Bessie suggested.

"You must have been assigned either Wednesday or Thursday. Maybe you could come here and I won't even have to move off the couch all day."

Bessie chuckled. "It is Wednesday that I was ringing about. Why don't I bring something with me when I come? Chinese? Pizza? What sounds good?"

"Everything sounds good right now. I feel as if I'm eating for myself and maybe triplets. I know babies grow a lot in the last few months, but if I'm not careful I'm going to gain far too much weight."

"I'll bring Chinese. I'll get lots of healthy choices with vegetables and not too much rice."

"Perfect. But how will you manage without a car?"

Bessie had never learned to drive. For many years she'd relied on a local car service. The service was now owned by a Douglas company, but they were still happy to accommodate Bessie, who'd been one of their best customers for decades. "I can get a taxi to take me to the restaurant and then to your house," Bessie told Grace. "I do similar things all the time."

"I hate for you to go to all the expense. Why don't I collect you and the food?"

"Because you're meant to be resting. I have other things to do that morning, anyway. I'll be booking a car for the entire morning and having them take me all over the island."

"If you're sure it isn't a bother, I'll see you around midday on Wednesday." Grace said.

Bessie put down the phone and then picked it back up to ring the car company. She hadn't had any other plans for Wednesday before she'd rung Grace, but now that she'd mentioned it, she did have a great many errands to run. Having a car and driver for the morning made sense. Christmas was rapidly approaching and that always meant lots of extra running around.

By the time Bessie got to Hugh and Grace's house on Wednesday, she was feeling worn out. The day was overcast and grey, with the threat of rain or even sleet in the air. The smells coming from the box on the seat beside her had Bessie's mouth watering.

"Let me help with the box," the driver said as he parked in front of the house.

Bessie climbed out and then waited while he picked up the box. Then he followed Bessie to the house's front door. She knocked and then smiled as Grace pulled the door open. She gave Bessie a clumsy hug around her large tummy and then stepped back.

"Come in, come in," she said.

The driver carried the food into the kitchen. "Did you want me to wait for you?" he asked Bessie.

"Oh, no. I can walk home from here," Bessie replied. "Thank you so much, though. You've been wonderful." She handed him a large tip before he left.

"Have you had a good morning, then?" Grace asked as Bessie began unpacking the box from the Chinese restaurant.

"I had a very productive morning. I should have introduced you to Mike. He's new to the taxi firm that I use and new to the island. He went out of his way to be helpful."

"That's good to hear. As Hugh and I both have our own cars, we never use taxis, but it's good to know you're being well looked after."

Bessie spread all of the small boxes of food across the large counter. "This is a wonderful kitchen."

"Yes, we both love it. We're so fortunate to have been able to buy this house."

They'd only been able to afford the large new home because someone had been murdered in the house's dining room. The value of the property had plummeted after the murder, and Grace and Hugh had been delighted to get far more house than their budget would normally have allowed.

"I should have asked you what you wanted," Bessie said. "I got a little bit of everything."

"I'm not all that hungry," Grace replied.

Bessie raised an eyebrow. When they'd spoken on Saturday, Grace had said she was hungry all the time. As Grace passed Bessie a plate, she frowned and then put her hand out to hold onto the counter.

"Are you okay?"

"Just small contractions. I think they're just the practice ones that I've been having for months, but they seem to be a bit stronger today."

"Maybe you should ring your midwife?"

Grace shrugged. "Even if they are the real thing, they're too far apart to worry about."

Bessie didn't argue. She knew very little about pregnancy and childbirth. Grace was smart and sensible. If she thought she was in labour, she'd head for Noble's, the island's hospital in Douglas.

After filling a plate, Bessie took a seat at the small table in the kitchen. Grace spooned up a few things and then joined her.

"Did you want a drink?" she asked, starting to struggle back to her feet.

"Sit down. I can get drinks," Bessie told her. She got them each a cold drink from the refrigerator and then sat back down. Grace was frowning again and rubbing her tummy.

"I'm fine," she said when she looked up at Bessie. "Nothing is happening yet."

The sound of heavy rain on the roof startled them both. The large sliding door that opened onto the beach showcased the storm outside. Waves were crashing against the sand and the sky was nearly black. A moment later the power failed.

"It's Hugh's dream," Grace laughed.

"Where's your mobile?" Bessie asked.

Grace glanced around the room. "I probably left it in the bedroom, charging. Hugh's obsessed with my keeping it fully charged all the time."

"What about torches or candles?"

"There's a large torch on the counter next to the sink."

Bessie walked carefully across the dark room. There was enough light from the windows and sliding door to keep her from walking into anything, but it was very dark for midday. Switching on the torch helped a lot. Returning to her seat, she set the torch in the centre of the table and then resumed eating.

"This is fun," Grace laughed. Then she gasped and took a slow deep breath.

"Pain?"

"It isn't pain exactly," Grace replied a moment later. "It's just a tight feeling around my tummy. It's almost painful, but not quite. It does feel as if it's the prelude to something, though, more so than what I've felt in the past, anyway."

"We should ring Hugh."

"Goodness, no. He's working. I'll ring him when I'm sure this is the real thing, once I'm at Noble's and the midwives have told me I'm truly in labour. What's happening now could go on for days." As soon as she finished speaking, she made a face.

"Again?"

"They're like those waves out there," Grace gestured. "Although maybe not as angry as those waves are at the moment, not yet, anyway."

"Do you not want to eat anything?"

Grace pushed some food around on the plate and then took a small bite. "I'm not very hungry, which I suppose may be a sign that things are happening. It may also just be a sign that I ate too many pancakes for breakfast, though. Hugh decided to make them this morning, and I think I ate a dozen."

Bessie chuckled. "It may be a bit of both. We can put all of the food in the refrigerator and you and Hugh can have dinner for tonight, and probably for lunch tomorrow as well."

"Let's hope the power comes back on, or everything will spoil."

A moment later the lights flickered several times and then came back on. Bessie switched off the torch but left it within reach. She cleared her plate while Grace ate a few more bites, and then she helped her put the leftovers away. When that was done, Grace smiled at Bessie.

"You haven't seen the nursery, have you?"

"No. Hugh invited me, but he didn't want me to see it until it was finished, and I've been busy with Christmas at the Castle since you put the final touches on the room."

"I love showing it off. It's just perfect, mostly thanks to you and Mary."

Mary Quayle was one of Bessie's closest friends. Married to one of the island's wealthiest and most gregarious men, Mary was quiet and shy. She was also incredibly generous at every opportunity. Having helped pay for a wonderful honeymoon for Hugh and Grace as their wedding gift, Mary had been thrilled to then help Bessie plan a baby shower for Grace. The young couple had been shocked by the number of gifts they'd received for their impending new arrival, and Bessie was delighted to have helped the pair, who were struggling a bit financially after buying the house.

Grace led Bessie up the stairs, stopping once to take a few deep breaths. She led Bessie to the bedroom nearest the master and opened the door. "What do you think?"

Bessie looked around the room. It had been painted a soft grey that would be suitable for either gender. The wooden cot was against one wall, with a large baby-changing table on one side. "That's a lot of nappies," Bessie said, nodding at the carefully stacked piles.

"I'm told that's about a week's supply," Grace replied.

"Goodness," was all that Bessie could say.

Bessie's old rocking chair sat in the corner. A new cushion with a light pink cover was tied to the seat. "Pink? Does that mean you think you're having a girl?"

Grace flushed. "We don't know, but I've said all along that I think the baby will be a girl. Hugh thinks it will be a boy. Neither of us cares, as long as he or she is healthy, of course, but Hugh and I have a running debate about the baby. That pillow is just part of the debate."

She winked at Bessie and then crossed to the small built-in

9

wardrobe. Pulling it open, she took out another cushion. It was an exact match for the one on the rocking chair, except it was blue. "Hugh puts this one on every night when he gets home from work," Grace laughed. "I change it back to pink every morning. It's just our silly little thing."

Bessie grinned. "I think it's sweet," she said, touched by the small insight into the couple's marriage.

Grace nodded and then put her hands on her tummy. "Goodness," she exclaimed before breathing in slowly.

"Sit down," Bessie suggested.

Grace looked at the rocking chair that was three steps away. "Not just yet," she said before she took another breath.

"Maybe you should ring your midwife."

"Maybe," Grace shrugged. "I'm not ready to ring her. They said not to worry until the contractions are only five minutes apart."

"We should be timing them, then."

Grace nodded. "I'm ready to start timing them, anyway." They walked back down the stairs together, with Bessie's hand on Grace's arm. She was getting increasingly worried about the girl.

As she flopped onto the couch, Grace smiled at Bessie. "Thank you for lunch. I'm sure you have better things to do with your day than sit and time my contractions."

"I have other things I could be doing, but nothing I'd rather be doing. I'll at least stay until we've timed a few contractions."

The words were hardly out of her mouth when Grace gasped. "Here's one."

Bessie looked at her watch. The second hand didn't seem to be moving at all as Grace took several deep breaths.

"It's over," she told Bessie twenty-two seconds later.

"Now we just have to wait for the next one."

Grace sighed. "There must be an easier way to have babies."

As they waited, Bessie told her about the various charities that were involved with Christmas at the Castle that year. It was just over four minutes later than Grace made a face. "Here we go again," she sighed.

"That was only four minutes. Time for Noble's."

Grace laughed. "We need more than two that close together. We're meant to time them for an hour. If they keep coming that close together or get closer, then I'll ring my midwife. You don't have to stay, of course."

"Do you know where you left your mobile?"

"It's probably upstairs. Can you go and get it for me, actually? I'm sorry to be a bother, but it has the midwife's number and I'll never find it otherwise."

Bessie went back up and found the phone on one of the bedside tables. When she walked back into the sitting room, Grace took it gratefully.

"I had another one while you were gone," she said softly.

"They seem to be getting closer together," Bessie replied.

"Maybe. I'm told they'll speed up and slow down and that it will be hours before the baby actually arrives."

Bessie sat back down feeling as if she was in over her head. "Maybe we should ring your mother," she suggested.

"She had a committee luncheon today, otherwise she probably would have had lunch with me."

"Which committee?" Bessie asked, just trying to keep the conversation flowing. Maybe Grace would forget to have contractions if she were distracted enough.

"She's on the decorating committee for Mannanan's Kids this year. They finished decorating their room in the castle yesterday, so they were going out for lunch today to celebrate."

"It looks wonderful, too. I keep peeking at all of the rooms when I go in and out of the castle. Everyone has done a..."

"Contraction," Grace interrupted.

Bessie noted the time. "Maybe I should be writing the times down," she said after Grace told her it was over.

"Hugh has a special sheet for them," Grace told her. "He wanted to be prepared, so he made a chart. I think he put it in the desk drawer."

There was a small desk built into the corner of the kitchen. Bessie found what she was looking for in the centre drawer. "There are a dozen copies. Surely you won't have to time your contractions for that long."

"Hugh wanted to be prepared."

"He's going to be sorry he missed it, then."

"I don't think so. He's already incredibly nervous about the baby. I think it's better for both of us that he isn't here."

Bessie chuckled. "He'll be there for the part that counts, anyway."

"Oh, yes, he won't miss the birth. As I said, I'm sure I have hours to go." She sighed. "Another one."

Bessie noted the start time in the small box on Hugh's chart. A short while later, she added the end time to the next box.

An hour later, as contractions continued at roughly four-minute intervals, Bessie was ready to ring the midwife herself. Grace was oddly calm between contractions.

"Okay, let me ring her and see what she says," she agreed after a contraction that lasted nearly a minute. When Grace put the phone down, she smiled at Bessie. "She thinks I should go to Noble's and get checked. It could be the real thing."

"I'll ring for a taxi."

"I can probably drive," Grace began. As the contraction hit, she shook her head. "Taxi," she gasped.

While they were waiting, Bessie brought Grace's hospital bag down from the bedroom.

"I packed it a month ago," Grace said. "It seems a long time ago now."

As she and Bessie stood at the door, watching for the taxi, Grace hugged her. "Thank you for being with me. I'm suddenly quite terrified."

"Once we're in the taxi, you should probably ring everyone."

"Mum should be done with lunch by now. I don't want Hugh to leave work early unless he has to, though."

The same driver, Mike, arrived a moment later. He grinned as he helped Grace into the car. "Hang in there. I already know my way to Noble's far too well."

It turned out that Mike and his wife had four boys, and even though they'd only been on the island for a month, they'd already had to go to Noble's three times. "The oldest, he's ten, he fell out of the tree in our back garden," he said. "We were living in city centre Manchester and didn't have any trees. He couldn't wait to climb one, but he wasn't very good at it. He broke his arm. Then the baby tripped on the stairs and banged his head. We've had to put on stair gates, but I suspect he'll work out how they work before too long. He's very clever for two."

Bessie glanced at Grace. Girls sounded a good deal easier to Bessie.

"The twins were next. They're both six and they wanted to go down the slide together one afternoon. When the one in the front stopped, the one behind didn't. He just got a badly bloodied nose, but we couldn't get the bleeding to stop on our own."

Grace grabbed Bessie's hand. "I'm not ready for children," she whispered.

Bessie was relieved when they reached the front entrance to Noble's. Mike was just starting to tell them about his wife's first labour and delivery and Bessie was certain that Grace didn't want to hear another word. Grace was pale and shaking slightly as she climbed out of the car.

"It's going to be fine," Bessie assured her as they walked into the building.

An hour later, they'd put Grace in a room. There were four beds, but the other three were empty.

"I'll check on you every half hour," the midwife said cheerfully as Grace settled onto the bed. "Press the call button if you need me sooner. You're progressing, but slowly."

"Can you give us an idea of when the baby might arrive? Should she ring her husband to leave work early?" Bessie asked.

The midwife laughed. "She has a fair few hours to go. If he finishes at five, he'll have time to get dinner before he needs to get here."

Grace moaned. "It's starting to hurt," she said softly.

"I can give you something for the pain, but it could slow things down," the midwife replied.

"I'll wait until I really need something," Grace replied.

As the midwife left the room, Grace pulled out her phone. "Mum first," she said. "I know she'll want to be here right away." After her mother, Grace left a message for Hugh with Doona at the station. "Just tell him I'm at Noble's but it's going to be a while. He can come after work," she said.

When she put the phone down on the nightstand, she grinned at Bessie. "Doona is more excited than I am."

"Doona isn't the one going through all the pain."

Grace nodded and then took another deep breath. "It does hurt rather a lot, really," she said when the contraction finished.

When Grace's mother appeared, Bessie wandered out to the large lounge on the ward. An older woman, maybe sixty, was sitting staring at the television, which was tuned to some programme Bessie had never seen before.

"Getting a new grandbaby," the woman told Bessie. "My daughter is forty-two and far too old to be having her first baby, but what can you do? She doesn't want me in the room, but I can't go home, not when the baby could arrive at any moment."

"Good luck. I'm just here with a friend."

Hugh rushed through a short while later, stopping to hug Bessie and thank her for looking after Grace throughout the day. "Are you staying for a while?" he asked.

"I think I might. This is something new for me and I'm rather enjoying it."

Hugh's parents arrived and then joined Hugh in the room with Grace. Bessie wasn't so sure about staying as the hours slipped past. Having waited this long, though, she didn't want to go home and miss the best part. The other woman's daughter had a boy just before midnight. It was two hours later when Hugh finally walked back into the lounge.

"It's a girl," he said, sounding completely overwhelmed.

CHAPTER 2

"Congratulations," Bessie told him.

"Thanks." Hugh sank onto the couch next to Bessie, looking dazed and confused.

"Are you okay?"

"It was amazing," he said slowly, "but it all feels so much more real now. There's a real baby here and she can't do anything for herself. I'm terrified."

"It's going to be okay." Bessie patted his arm. "You and Grace are going to do an amazing job as parents."

Hugh nodded, but he still looked shell-shocked. "Do you want to see the baby?" he asked.

"If I won't be intruding."

"Not at all. Grace sent me out to see if you were still here and to invite you back. She wants to show the baby off to everyone, and as she said, you're practically family anyway."

Bessie smiled as she got to her feet, feeling grateful to Grace for saying such a thing. Hugh led her to a small private room at the end of the corridor.

"Grace's mum is paying for the private room," Hugh said as he pushed open the door.

Grace was in bed, holding what looked like a huge pile of blankets. As Bessie approached, she smiled. "I may have wrapped her up a bit too much."

It took Bessie a moment to find the tiny face among the layers. When she did, though, she felt a rush of affection for the tiny girl.

"She's gorgeous," she said.

"Thanks," Grace grinned. "She's fast asleep, but the midwife assures me that that's only temporary. I feel as if I could lie here and watch her sleep all night."

"Not if I have anything to say about it," Grace's mum interjected from the doorway. She smiled at Bessie. "I had to go out and ring a dozen people with the news, but now I'm back and I want to cuddle my grandbaby. Grace, you need sleep, anyway."

Grace looked as if she were going to protest, but then yawned. "You may be right," she admitted.

"I won't leave the room," Grace's mother promised. "You close your eyes for a few minutes and get some rest. Your body has just worked harder than it has ever had to work before. Hugh, you go home and get some sleep, too. It may be the last chance you get to sleep for more than a few uninterrupted hours for a very long time."

Hugh looked at Grace. "I should stay," he said.

"No, Mum is right. You go home and sleep. Take Bessie home, too. It's the middle of the night. I assume you've taken tomorrow off work?" Grace asked.

"Yes, and the rest of the week. I'm using holiday time and saving my paternity leave for after you come home with the baby."

Grace nodded. "So go and sleep for as long as you can. The baby and I will be fine here. They won't let me leave tomorrow, even if I beg, or so I've been told. As long as Mum is here, I'll be fine."

"And I'm not leaving," Grace's mother said firmly.

Hugh nodded. "Would you like a ride home?" he asked Bessie.

"Are you okay to drive?" she wondered.

"I'm tired, but I'm fine. I had a cup of coffee a short while ago. I won't fall asleep behind the wheel, I promise," Hugh told her.

Bessie gave Grace a hug and smiled again at the baby. "Congratulations," she said.

"Thanks."

She gave Grace's mother a hug, too, as it seemed that sort of occasion. Hugh was quiet on the drive back to Laxey. Bessie would have worried more about his driving if she hadn't been mostly asleep in the passenger seat. As it was, she didn't even notice where they were until the car stopped.

"You've driven home," she said, feeling confused.

Hugh looked at her for a minute and then shook his head. "I forgot about you," he said. "I'm more tired than I'd realised."

As he moved to restart the car, Bessie stopped him. "I can walk home," she said quickly. "I don't think you should be driving any further until you've had some sleep."

"I'll walk you home, then," Hugh replied. "Some fresh air and exercise will probably do me good."

The walk back to Treoghe Bwaane seemed to take forever. Bessie felt as if she were trying to walk through treacle as her tired legs dragged through the sand. Hugh stumbled over a piece of driftwood and nearly fell to the ground.

"Go home and go to bed," Bessie told him. "I can walk myself home."

"We're nearly there," Hugh replied. "There's Thie yn Traie."

They'd only gone a few steps further when Hugh put his hand on Bessie's arm. "I know I'm tired, but I don't think I'm seeing things. Is there a light on in that holiday cottage?"

Bessie looked at the last cottage in the row. From where they were standing, it did look as if there was a light on in the dining room.

"Does Thomas leave the power on all year?" Hugh asked.

"Yes, because he and Maggie do all of the maintenance during the winter months," Bessie explained.

Thomas and Maggie Shimmin had bought the cottage next to Bessie's some years earlier. Thomas had quit his job in banking as soon as they'd received planning permission to tear the small cottage down and replace it with the row of holiday cottages that now covered the beach.

"Could they have been working in that last cottage today?" Hugh asked.

"I didn't think they were going to do anything else in there until they found out about their planning application," Bessie replied. After someone had been murdered in one of the bedrooms, Thomas and Maggie had found it difficult to find holidaymakers willing to rent that particular cottage. Eventually, they'd decided that they would be better off tearing it down and building a new, larger cottage in its place. As far as Bessie knew, they were still waiting for a decision from the planning board.

"We can't ring them at this hour to find out," Hugh sighed. "I'm going to check the doors."

Bessie followed him closely as he walked up to the sliding doors that faced the beach. They seemed to be securely fastened. The front door, on the other hand, was partly open.

"I'm too tired for this," Hugh muttered as he pulled out his phone. As he rang the station to request assistance, Bessie heard a noise from inside the cottage.

"What was that?" she asked.

Hugh slipped his phone in his pocket. "We aren't going in until my backup arrives," he told her.

The loud scream that filled the air made him change his mind. "Stay here," he told Bessie as he pushed open the cottage's front door.

"I'll feel safer with you," Bessie argued, following Hugh into the building.

Hugh reached for the light switch right inside the door. "Police!" he shouted.

"It wasn't my fault," someone shouted back. "I didn't even know he was in here."

"Who is that?" Hugh demanded.

Bessie could hear sirens approaching.

"I was just looking for a place to get out of the rain," the voice said.

Hugh walked further into the house with Bessie on his heels. The lights in the sitting room were already on. "Where are you?" he called.

"In the bedroom," the voice replied.

Hugh looked into the first bedroom, where the body had been found months earlier. It was empty, the large bed having been removed as evidence. The second bedroom was only a few steps away. Hugh pushed the half-closed door open and switched on the light.

The man standing in the corner stood up with his hands in the air. "It wasn't me," he said desperately.

When Bessie spotted the body on the bed, she gasped. It was a man and he was clearly dead, a large knife still sticking out of his chest. There was a lot of blood on the victim, and also on the other man, who was still holding up his hands. He was shaking and looked terrified.

"Police!" a loud voice shouted from the front of the house.

"Back bedroom," Hugh called. "Ring for a crime scene team and as much backup as you can get. We've a murder victim and a very likely suspect."

"It wasn't anything to do with me," the suspect yelled. He looked around the room and then rushed to the small window. As he struggled with the lock, Hugh took his arm.

"You'll only make things worse for yourself if you try to get away," Hugh said. "I know who you are."

The man shuddered. "I was just looking for a place to get out of the rain," he repeated himself. "I never expected to find, well, that."

Hugh nodded. "Do you know the victim?"

"No, I don't think so. I didn't really look at him. I don't want to look at him."

"It's okay. We'll work it out later. Just calm down." Hugh said.

As the room slowly filled with various police officers, Bessie started to wish that she'd let Hugh drive her home after all. Someone told Bessie to wait in the cottage's sitting room, and she was asleep sitting up when John Rockwell arrived.

John was the police inspector who was in charge of the Laxey station. Bessie had first met him over a dead body a few years earlier and the two had become good friends in the time since. He was in his forties, and Bessie considered him one of the handsomest men she knew. His beautiful green eyes looked tired as he sat down next to her.

"Grace had a girl," she told him.

"So I heard. I'm going to send Hugh home as soon as I've taken his statement. He looks completely exhausted."

"He's not the only one," Bessie muttered.

"Which is why I'm sending you home now," John told her. "Before I do that, though, one question. Did you recognise the victim or the man in the room with him?"

"Hugh said that he recognised the man in the room. I'm fairly certain it was Callum Sharp, but I haven't seen Callum in a few years, so I could be mistaken."

"You aren't mistaken. I want to hear everything you know about Mr. Sharp tomorrow. He's going to be spending a few days with us while we investigate. What about the victim?"

"I didn't get a good look at him. Really, I just glanced at the bed. There was so much blood," Bessie said with a shudder.

"I may want you to take a look at him, but I'll leave that for tomorrow after I'm sure we have all the photographs that we need. We're probably going to need to clean him up before anyone will be able to identify him."

Bessie swallowed a lump in her throat. "Oh, dear," she murmured.

"Constable Tucker is going to walk you home and check that everything is okay at your cottage. I'll come and get your statement from you around midday. If you can, sleep until then," John told her.

Bessie glanced at her watch. It was nearly time for her internal alarm to wake her for the day, and she hadn't been to bed yet. "Don't worry if I don't answer when you knock. I may well sleep past midday."

"I'll ring before I come."

The walk home was something of a blur. When Bessie finally woke up at one o'clock the next afternoon, she couldn't even remember changing into her nightgown, but clearly she had. Whether she'd brushed her teeth or washed her face seemed inconsequential. Still feeling incredibly tired, she showered until she'd run out of hot water and then started a pot of coffee brewing.

Her answering machine light was flashing frantically. As she sipped her coffee, she listened to a dozen messages from friends who were excited about Hugh and Grace's new baby. At some point, the messages changed. The later callers wanted to know about the body that had been found in the holiday cottage and about the man standing over it who may or may not have been the killer.

Bessie deleted all of the messages and then poured more coffee into her cup. She had to make a difficult phone call.

"Mark? It's Bessie. I'm not going to be able to make it to the committee meeting today," she said.

"From what I've been hearing, I'm not surprised," he replied. "Did you really find a dead body last night?"

Bessie sighed. "Not exactly. I was with Hugh Watterson. He found the body."

"I'm going to reschedule today's meeting to tomorrow. We have a few important things to discuss, and we need everyone to be here. Will two o'clock tomorrow work for you?"

"Of course. I'm sorry to make you reschedule, though."

"It's fine. Mary couldn't make it today, either. I was already considering rescheduling."

Bessie put the phone down feeling guilty. She'd never missed a committee meeting, ever. The phone rang a moment later.

"Hello?"

"You're awake," John said. "I'm at the holiday cottage. I'd like to come over and take your statement, if you don't mind."

"Not at all. Although I don't know how much I'll remember. I was awfully tired last night."

"I'm sure you'll do your best. I'll be there in a few minutes."

Bessie hadn't had breakfast and it was past time for lunch. Not feeling at all hungry, she piled biscuits onto a plate for John. He knocked on the door as she refilled her cup again.

"I'm sure you need the coffee, but if you can spare a cup, I'd be grateful," John told her as he sat down at the kitchen table.

"I'm going to start another pot as soon as this one is empty. Have as much as you like." Bessie poured him a large mugful of coffee and then added the last little bit from the pot to her cup. John was silent as she refilled the coffee maker and set it going again. Once Bessie sat down across from him, he reached over and patted her hand.

"How are you?"

"Tired and sad. Too many bad things keep happening on the island."

"I know. When I applied for the job over here, I was told that drugs were the island's biggest issue, but that hasn't been the case here in Laxey since I've been here."

"In all the years I've lived here, I've never seen anything like this," Bessie sighed.

John patted her hand again and then sat back and pulled out a notebook. "Start by telling me everything that you did yesterday. What time did you wake up?"

"It feels a long time ago," Bessie began. She told John everything that she could remember, from breakfast through the sitting at Noble's waiting for news on the baby.

"Amy wouldn't go to bed until we'd heard," John interjected once Bessie had recounted Hugh's announcement. Amy was his teenaged daughter. "She's thrilled that they had a girl."

"So am I," Bessie admitted. "I'd probably have been just as happy for them if they'd had a boy, though."

"Then Hugh brought you home?" John asked.

"Hugh offered me a ride home, but then he forgot I was in the car and drove back to his house instead of here. Knowing how tired he was, I insisted he not drive any further and he agreed to walk me home." Bessie told John about seeing the light on inside the last holiday cottage and did her best to remember everything that had happened from there.

"Tell me about Callum Sharp."

"Where do I start? He's from Laxey. In fact, he grew up not far from where you live now. His parents owned one of the little bunga-lows on the next road over from you. He went to the local schools and then got a job in Douglas at the ShopFast in the town centre."

"How old is he?"

Bessie thought for a minute. "Around twenty-five, I believe. He worked for ShopFast for a year or so and then moved on to a job with one of the smaller shops in Onchan. From there, I believe he changed jobs fairly regularly, never quite finding something that he truly enjoyed."

"Do you know where he's working now?"

"I don't think he is working right now. Last I heard, he was sort of drifting from job to job and from flat to flat, staying with friends until they tired of him and then moving on to the next friend. His parents sold the house and moved to Rugby about three years ago. I've no idea why he didn't go with them, really."

"So he's unemployed and has no permanent address," John sighed.

"For what it's worth, I rather liked him when he was a child. He isn't terribly bright, but he was always kind. I remember him coming to my door one day to ask for a biscuit. When I gave it to him, he ran back down the beach to hand it to a little girl who'd dropped her ice cream and was crying. That was the sort of child that he was then, anyway. He may have changed, of course."

"What about drugs or drinking?"

"I've never heard his name in connection with any illegal drug issues, although I don't hear as much as I used to these days. With everything else that's happened in the past few years, I don't often get teenagers staying at my cottage any longer. As for drink, I'm sure he was in trouble for drink-driving at least once, but that was years ago now. Hopefully, he learned a lesson from the experience. I don't believe he has a car at the moment, so that would help."

"Known associates?"

Bessie gave John a few names. "I believe Callum was most recently staying with the last man I named. I suspect he'd worn out his welcome and decided to let himself into a holiday cottage for the night. He probably didn't see any harm in it. He may have been staying there for a while, actually. I'm surprised there aren't more break-ins during the winter months, now that I'm giving the matter some thought."

John nodded. "Thomas and Maggie have been very fortunate thus far. The locks on the cottages aren't the best and they rarely have them changed. Callum had a key to that last cottage in his pocket."

"Do you think he killed the dead man?"

"I don't, actually, although it would certainly simplify things if he had. He was drinking at the Cat and Longtail until closing time. Walking from there to the holiday cottages would have taken him some time. The coroner hasn't determined the time of death yet, but I believe it was some hours before Callum stumbled over the body."

"Unless he killed the victim and then came back for some reason," Bessie said.

John nodded. "Of course that's a possibility we're considering. I've only spoken to Callum briefly. I want him sober before I question him more extensively."

Bessie nibbled her way through a biscuit, her mind racing. "Who was the victim, then?" she asked.

"We haven't identified the body yet. Callum insisted that he didn't know the victim and no one on the scene was able to recognise him. I'd like to show you some photographs of the body to see if you know him, but it's possible, maybe even likely, that he's from elsewhere on the island or from further afield."

"How bad are the pictures?" Bessie asking, regretting the biscuit that suddenly felt like a hard lump in her tummy.

"They aren't good," John admitted. "I'll just show you one unless you think you might know him."

Bessie took a deep breath and then nodded. John opened the folder he'd brought in with him and flipped through a few photos. He pulled one out and put it in front of Bessie.

The face was pale, and at first glance Bessie felt relieved that she didn't know him. As she studied the photo, though, something stirred in her memory.

"I may know who it is," she said sadly.

"Let me show you another photo."

The slightly different angle made the victim look rather different. "This looks more like the man I think it is," Bessie sighed. "He isn't from Laxey, which is probably why no one recognised him last night, but he is from the island."

"Name?"

"I could be wrong, as I haven't seen him for at least three years, but it might be Phillip Tyler." Bessie spelled both names for John.

"Tell me everything about him."

After turning the photographs face down, Bessie took a long drink of her coffee before she replied. "Phillip grew up in Port Erin, but his mother was from Laxey. She met her husband at university in Liverpool and they moved back to the island after they'd both finished school, buying a small house in Port St. Mary. They moved to Port Erin right after Phillip was born."

"What was his mother's name?"

"She was Rebecca Palmer before she got married. Her parents had a house in the village. I used to see her mother fairly regularly, often at the Laxey Market. She was always happy to tell me all about Rebecca and her family. They had a little girl, too, called Madison."

John looked up from his notebook. "Do Rebecca's parents still live in Laxey?"

"No, sadly, they both passed away a few years ago." Bessie sat back and took a sip of her coffee. "It may have been as many as ten years ago, now that I think about it. Her mother had some sort of aggressive cancer. She was only given months to live when they diagnosed it, and unfortunately, the doctors were right. Her husband just seemed to fade away very quickly once she was gone. If I remember correctly, he was at least ten years older than his wife. I don't think either of them ever expected her to go first."

"What else can you tell me about the family?"

"Not much. Rebecca stayed home with the children for many years and then went back to work. I believe she works for one of the banks. Her husband works for an international shipping company and travels a lot, or at least he did years ago."

"Do you know his Christian name?"

Bessie frowned. "I think it's Peter, but I could be mistaken. I'm almost certain it begins with a P, anyway."

"Tell me more about Phillip, then."

"According to Rebecca's mother, he was a model baby who achieved all of his milestones right on schedule. He did well at school and then went to the same university across where his parents had met. While he was there, he developed a passion for helping others. That led him to pursue a career working for a series of different charities, mostly to do with cancer research. I think that may have been motived by his grandmother's untimely death."

"So he didn't return to the island?"

"He did return to the island for a while. He worked with a few different charities here, including Cancer Care IOM. I believe he was working for The Liliana Fund before he was offered a job across."

"The Liliana Fund?"

"It's a local charity that supports cancer patients on an individual basis. They provide support for all manner of things to individuals who apply through their grant programme. While they do help island residents, they also accept grants from people in the UK and even further afield, which is why they haven't been invited to participate in Christmas at the Castle, at least not yet."

"Oh?"

"We have limited space at the moment, although we are using more rooms than last year. After the success we had with the first event, we had two dozen charities apply for the ten rooms we'd planned to include this year. The Liliana Fund was one that we turned down, primarily because so much of their funding goes to people outside of the island."

John nodded. "So that was Phillip's last job on the island. Were they sorry to see him go?"

"I believe so. As I understand it, he was a hard worker and very good at what he did. He did a little bit of everything, too, from fundraising to event planning to courting donors. I can ask a few friends about him, though. I know a few people who are a good deal more involved in the island's charity circles than I am."

"Let's make sure the body is his before you start asking questions," John replied. "Tell me about Phillip's friends."

Bessie shrugged. "I knew his grandmother and had a nodding acquaintance with Rebecca. I haven't seen Rebecca in a great many years. She used to make odd visits to Laxey Beach with the children when they were small, but that was some years ago. Her mother told me about Phillip's achievements, but not about friends, or the women in his life, either."

"Which was my next question," John said.

"As I said, it may be ten years since Rebecca's mum died. Phillip was probably still at university at that time. He must have been around thirty now."

"That would agree with the coroner's initial estimate on the body. Do you know where he went to work across?"

Bessie thought for a while. "I'm not even certain I remember how I know he went across," she said eventually. "I suspect I must have talked to someone at The Liliana Fund who mentioned it, but I'm not sure."

"Did you talk to anyone there about Christmas at the Castle?"

"Not really. Mark dealt with the applications, although Oliver did do a presentation to the entire committee before we made our decisions. Mark did all of the notifications, though."

"Did Phillip leave recently?"

"You're really straining my memory, but I believe he left about two years ago, maybe a bit more or less."

John made another note. "Do you have an address in Port Erin for Phillip's parents?"

Bessie found her address book and flipped through it. "This is from about twenty years ago," she warned John. "I used to sent Christmas cards to just about everyone I knew, including Rebecca." She read out the address.

"I'm going to ring into the station to see if I can find anyone who knew Phillip Tyler," John told her. "I'd rather have a more definite identification before I ask his parents to look at the body."

Bessie nodded. "I can't be certain, not from the photographs."

"And it's been many years since you've seen him. Maybe I'll ring The Liliana Fund and see if anyone there remembers Phillip."

"I'm sure Oliver Preston will remember him well. Oliver runs the fund and has done since the beginning. He founded it in memory of his mother, Liliana Preston. It's only a small operation with two or three staff. He'll remember Phillip, who worked there for at least a year or more."

"Maybe I'll start with him, then, see if he can give me a preliminary identification. Thank you so much for your time."

"Good luck," Bessie said as she followed John to the door.

"I'm afraid I'm going to need it. This isn't looking the least bit straightforward."

"They never are," Bessie sighed.

After John left, she tidied up from their snack and drank another two cups of coffee. For the first time in a very long time she hadn't taken her morning walk on the beach. Knowing that the police would still be at the last holiday cottage, hard at work, made her feel reluctant to go anywhere.

"You need the fresh air and the exercise," she told herself sternly after she'd finished off the second pot of coffee. She knew she'd had far too much caffeine, as well. A long walk was exactly what she needed.

She'd been worried that crime scene tape might block off some section of the beach itself, but she didn't see any as she marched as quickly as she could past the holiday cottages. There were cars and people all around the last cottage, but Bessie deliberately stared at the sea and ignored everything else. She hadn't gone far past the last cottage when someone shouted her name.

"Elizabeth Cubbon, I knew you'd turn up eventually," a loud voice said.

Bessie made a face and then stopped. Dan Ross was younger than she was and would have no trouble catching up to her if she kept going. At least this way the police were nearby if she needed help.

"Mr. Ross," she said coolly, staring hard at the reporter from the *Isle of Man Times*.

"Care to make a statement about what you found last night?"

"I didn't find anything last night," Bessie countered.

"I was told you were with young Hugh Watterson when he stumbled across a murdered man in the last holiday cottage," Dan said. "That's the second dead body that's been found in that cottage. If I were Thomas and Maggie, I'd stop letting people rent that one out."

Bessie knew that neither victim had been renting the cottage in question, but she bit her tongue, refusing to let Dan's words provoke her. He knew as much about the situation as she did, after all. He was just trying to get a quote for his newspaper.

"No comment, Miss Cubbon?"

"I'm just trying to get my walk in before the rain," she replied.

"It does look as if it's going to rain," Dan agreed. "If it had been raining last night, no doubt young Hugh would have driven you home and you'd have missed out on finding your latest victim."

Bessie counted to ten and then started over again. The dead man wasn't her victim, and she wasn't going to let Dan see how much his words were upsetting her. "Hugh and Grace had a baby girl," she said after a long pause."

"Yes, I know. I believe my headline is going to be 'New Father Finds Dead Man' or maybe 'The Baby Was a Girl, but the Dead Body Was a Man.' Which do you prefer?"

"You know your audience better than I do."

Dan chuckled. "You're determined not to let me ruffle you, aren't you? Surely you must understand that the good people of the island have a right to know about the things that happen here. I'm just doing my job."

"I'm sure it's a very difficult job, at that. Perhaps you'd be better off looking for a new one. I understand ShopFast is hiring."

Dan stared at her for a minute and then began to laugh. "I feel as if I've just been insulted, but I'm not sure why."

Bessie just smiled and began to walk slowly away. After a few paces, she realised that she was holding her breath, waiting to see if the obnoxious man was going to follow her. It wasn't until she was past the stairs for Thie yn Traie that she let out a relieved sigh. She hadn't gone much further when she began to realise just how tired she still felt. After standing at the water's edge for several minutes, taking deep breaths and filling her lungs with sea air, she turned for home. She'd only just walked past the last cottage when once again she heard her name being called.

CHAPTER 3

"*B*essie? Oh, Bessie?" the words cut through the air.

Swallowing a sigh, Bessie stopped and waited for Maggie Shimmin to walk down the beach to her. "Good afternoon," she said.

"It's not very good, though, is it?" Maggie demanded. "You've only gone and found another body in that last cottage of ours. We were going to start clearing it out this week, you know. We want to make sure it's empty and ready for when we get permission to tear it down and rebuild it."

Bessie almost blurted out an apology. The dead man was not her fault in any way, though. "Hopefully the investigation won't take long," she said instead.

"Yes, well, it would go more quickly if they knew who the dead man was and why he was in the cottage. I don't suppose you recognised him?"

"I didn't even look at the body last night," Bessie said, not quite answering the question.

Maggie sighed. "You know I never complain, but this is another setback that we don't need. Thomas and I want to get that cottage torn down and rebuilt before the spring season starts. After the first murder, we never could rent it out again, well, aside from that week when that woman whose brother killed the fake vicar stayed there. Thomas hasn't been well and my back has been playing up, but we were determined to keep working in spite of all the obstacles in our path. Maybe it's time to admit defeat and sell the entire project to the developers from across who keep bothering us."

"Developers from across?"

"Oh, yes, there are two different groups of them who want to buy the cottages from us. They don't want the cottages, of course, they just want the land. If we sell, I'm sure they'll simply tear down the cottages and build condos or townhouses or something in their place. The island has become a very desirable place to live in the last year or so and there aren't nearly enough houses. If Thomas and I had seen what was coming, we'd have built proper homes on the land and then sold them all off as soon as they were completed. Those new houses down the beach from here went for silly money, well, all except the one where the man was murdered."

Bessie nodded. House prices on the island had skyrocketed. Maggie was right. If she and Thomas had built houses, they could have sold them for a considerable profit. They might have struggled to get planning permission for houses, though, as Bessie would have objected. The thought of a UK developer buying the land was upsetting. She could only hope that Maggie and Thomas stuck with the cottages they'd spent so much time and effort on thus far.

"The police won't tell us anything about what happened," Maggie continued. "I know you were there. What happened?"

"I've no idea. Hugh was walking me home late last night, after we'd returned from Noble's. We spotted a light on in the cottage, so Hugh stopped to check the doors. The front door was ajar, so Hugh went inside."

"I keep telling Thomas we need better locks on the cottages, but he keeps insisting that they're safe enough as they are. Maybe he'll listen to me now."

"Hugh rang for backup and then lots more police came. Eventually, someone walked me home."

"That's it? I heard you went inside the cottage."

"I went into the sitting room because I didn't want to stand by myself on the beach," Bessie admitted.

"I also heard that the murderer was still standing over his victim, a dripping butcher knife in his hand."

Bessie laughed out loud. "I spoke to John this morning and he didn't say anything to suggest that the case was all wrapped up, so I think you can discount that story."

Maggie frowned. "I was hoping it was true so that we could get back into the cottage later today. How long do you think it will be before they'll let us back inside?"

"I've no idea. You should ask John Rockwell that question."

"I would, if I ever saw him. He sent one of his constables to question us early this morning, some young man who knew nothing about anything."

Bessie hid a grin. Maggie enjoyed nothing more than complaining and gossiping. If the constable had said anything interesting, the entire island would have known about it by now. She had to wonder if John had sent a particularly thick constable or one who was smart enough to play dumb.

"I'm sure John will be in touch when he has anything to tell you," Bessie said.

Maggie sighed. "That's what Thomas keeps saying. He isn't nearly as impatient to get things done as I am. He's quite calm about the whole thing, really."

"Good for him."

"Oh, there's Dan Ross. I wonder if he knows anything," Maggie said. She rushed past Bessie, shouting Dan's name.

Bessie stood for a minute, watching the pair, and then turned for home. No doubt Dan would trade any information that he did have for a quote from the shocked and saddened owner of the cottage where the victim had been found. Both Maggie and Dan would end up happy from their exchange.

The answering machine light was blinking again when Bessie walked inside. She listened to a few messages from nosy friends before deleting them all. Now wasn't the time to ring anyone back; she'd take care of that later. What she wanted to do now was some research.

In her office, she pulled out the stack of papers she'd been working through. Marjorie Stevens at the Manx Museum Library had sent her several years' worth of letters from a woman called Onnee who had grown up on the island and then moved to the US at the age of eighteen. Onnee's scrawling handwriting took some time and effort to decipher, but after working her way through the first twelve months of letters, Bessie felt as if she was beginning to make progress.

A distant cousin had travelled with a friend to the island, and Onnee and the friend, Clarence, had fallen in love. They'd married on the island and then, just a few weeks later, set sail back to the US. The cousin had died on the journey, leaving Onnee on her own with her new husband.

The earliest letters had been full of sadness, as Onnee experienced homesickness quite badly. On arriving in the US, the couple had travelled to Wisconsin, where Clarence's family lived. Onnee had received an unenthusiastic welcome from his parents and the fiancée he'd left behind. Faith had been staying with Clarence's parents while he'd been away, and the letter he'd sent to inform everyone of his marriage arrived after Clarence and Onnee's own arrival.

After staying with Clarence's parents for a short while, Onnee had demanded that she and Clarence find their own flat, but Clarence had continued to spend nights with his parents and Faith even after they'd found the flat. Onnee had fallen pregnant almost immediately, but then, only a few months later, she'd lost the baby. Now, as the one-year anniversary of her rather impulsive marriage approached, she'd written to her mother to tell her that she was thinking of leaving Clarence and returning to the island.

Bessie sat down with a clean sheet of paper and a favourite pen, ready to transcribe the next letter. While she knew that Onnee wasn't going to leave the US, because Marjorie had told her there were fifty years' worth of letters to go through, Bessie was still incredibly curious as to what was going to come next.

"Dearest Mother," she said aloud as she printed neatly on the blank sheet.

Two hours later she'd finished the letter. Onnee still wanted nothing more than to move back to the island, but she was fairly certain that she was pregnant again and she wrote touchingly about her desire to keep this baby. Clarence had found a good job and they had enough money coming in to start thinking about buying a little house of their own. That he wanted to buy a house near his parents' home was a difficult issue. Faith was still living with Clarence's mother and father, although Onnee was happy to report that Faith had found herself a boyfriend. Onnee could only write of her hope that the relationship would result in marriage and that Faith would move away.

Bessie stood up and stretched. She'd been sitting still too long. A glance at the clock told her that she ought to be thinking about dinner. It felt more like midday than five o'clock, but that was what happened when you overslept. Sighing, she headed for the kitchen. Still not feeling terribly hungry, she heated some soup and ate that with a slice of bread. It was too late in the day for more coffee, even though it sounded good. She settled for a cup of tea with a biscuit and then tried to decide what to do with her evening.

Another walk was always an option, but when Bessie looked outside, it had begun to rain. That was all the excuse she needed to start looking for a good book. She was debating between Agatha Christie and Jane Austen when someone knocked on her door.

The tall brunette had clearly been crying. Bessie studied her for a moment and then smiled sympathetically. "Rebecca?"

The woman nodded. "We just identified the body," she said through tears. "They said you found him, and we know that you've found others. We didn't know what else to do, who else to talk to. The police won't tell us anything."

"Why don't you come in?" Bessie invited.

Rebecca hesitated and then nodded. She took a few steps forward, and the man behind her followed. As she looked around the cosy kitchen, she drew a sharp breath.

"It all looks the same," she said. "I remember this kitchen from my childhood and then again from when Phillip and Madison were children. You always welcomed visitors. Coming to Aunt Bessie's for a biscuit was part of the fun of visiting Laxey Beach."

Bessie nodded. "I always enjoy seeing everyone and watching the children grow up and later bring their own children."

"And now Phillip won't be bringing his children here," Rebecca said, bursting into tears.

As the man pulled Rebecca into a hug, Bessie found a box of tissues. She handed it to him, and then filled the kettle. Tea was definitely needed.

After several minutes, Rebecca cleared her throat. "I am sorry," she said. "I wasn't prepared for all of the memories, that's all. I didn't expect everything to be the same as it was all those years ago."

"I imagine my heirs will want to redo the kitchen, unless they simply sell the cottage. A developer will probably tear it down and build something new and modern in its place."

"That would be a shame," Rebecca sighed. Her companion cleared his throat. "I'm sorry," she said quickly. "I'm not myself. Bessie, this is my husband, Peter. Peter, this is Bessie Cubbon. Everyone calls her Aunt Bessie."

"It's nice to meet you," Peter said politely.

Bessie nodded. He was taller than his wife, but not by much. His hair had a sprinkling of grey through it and his eyes were green. He looked incredibly sad, as if the weight of the world had suddenly dropped on his shoulders in the past hour or two.

"As I said before, we just identified Phillip's body," Rebecca said. "It was the hardest thing I've ever had to do in my life, aside from telling Madison. That was actually more difficult. She idolised her older brother. He was five, nearly six, when she came along and I'm sure to her he was almost like another adult. We might have been here sooner, but we had to arrange things for Madison first."

"Is she okay?" Bessie asked.

"She's with her boyfriend and her closest friend," Rebecca replied.

"They've rung one of Phillip's friends to come around as well. They'll all support one another until we get home."

"And I'm supporting Rebecca," Peter added.

"Even though it's been a blow to him, too," Rebecca added.

Peter nodded. "I'm devastated, obviously, but I'm more focussed on wanting to know what happened than anything else. I want whoever hurt Phillip caught and punished. I'm just sorry that capital punishment is no longer an option."

Rebecca shivered. "I don't want to talk about that."

"No, let's talk about what happened. We understand you were there when the body was found. What can you tell us?" Peter demanded.

Bessie shook her head. "I was with the police constable when he found the body, but I didn't see or hear anything. I've given the police a full statement, but I doubt it will help with the investigation."

"The police inspector who questioned us said that someone was found with Phillip, but they don't think that man was responsible for his death," Rebecca said. "I don't understand."

"Did they tell you where the body was found?" Bessie asked.

"Yes, at the last holiday cottage, the one where that other man was killed a few months ago," Peter replied.

"I believe the police think that the man who was discovered with the body had simply broken into the cottage so that he'd have a place to stay for the night. They seem to think that he was as surprised to see the body as anyone."

"So you can't tell us anything," Peter sighed.

"I wish I could. The best thing you can do now is talk to the police. Tell them everything you can about Phillip. Give them every detail about his life, his friends, his jobs, everything that seems important and everything that doesn't seem to matter at all. The more they know, the easier it will be for them to work out what happened."

"We don't know much about his current job," Rebecca said. "He was working for a UK charity. They recruited him from the island. As far as I know, he was happy and doing well."

"Did he have a girlfriend across?" Bessie asked.

Rebecca shook her head. "He'd had a bad experience in his last relationship. He said he was going to wait a while before he was going to risk getting hurt again."

"His last relationship? Was that on the island?" was Bessie's next question.

"Yes," Rebecca sighed. "He was involved with a girl called Nicole Carr. He was getting ready to propose, actually. He'd even picked out a ring, but then he found out that she was seeing someone else behind his back. He was heartbroken. I don't know that he would have taken the job in the UK if it hasn't been for that, actually. He needed to get away and the job offer came at just the right time."

"Nicole married the man she'd been cheating with," Peter added. "His name is Liam Kirk, and they got married about three months after Phillip left the island. I don't know if they're still together, though. Knowing her, maybe not."

Rebecca sighed. "It was difficult for all of us. Phillip and Nicole had been together for three years and she'd become like a daughter to us. We were excited about them getting married, looking forward to grandchildren, even. When we found out that she'd cheated, we were all shocked and hurt."

"If she and Phillip had married, he wouldn't be dead now," Peter said flatly.

"We don't know that," Rebecca said quickly.

"We do. He must have been killed because of something that happened when he was across. It's her fault he went across in the first place. As far as I'm concerned, she's as guilty as whoever actually wielded the knife."

"I don't agree," Rebecca said, flushing. "I don't want to argue, though. Let's not fight, not now."

Peter shrugged. "I don't want to argue either. This is hard enough as it is."

"I hope you told the police all of this," Bessie said.

Rebecca nodded. "We told them everything we could think to tell them. We'll probably have more for them later, after it all starts to sink in, but we did our best."

"I told them all about Nicole and Liam," Peter interjected. "I suggested they take a good long look at Liam when they start looking for the killer."

Bessie nodded. She wasn't sure why Liam would want to kill Phillip, especially since he was the one who'd ended up with Nicole, but she didn't want to ask and risk starting another disagreement between the couple.

Rebecca clearly had the same thought. "Liam didn't have any reason to kill Phillip. He took Nicole away from Phillip. If anything, Phillip had reason to kill Liam, not the other way around."

"Maybe Nicole was trying to get back together with Phillip behind Liam's back," Peter suggested.

"Phillip would have told me," Rebecca replied. "If he'd heard from her at all, he would have mentioned it." She looked over at Bessie. "We spoke on the phone at least once a week. He knew I'd worry otherwise, so he indulged me. He told me everything that was happening in his life."

"Was he just on the island for a holiday, then?" Bessie asked.

Rebecca frowned and looked down at the table. "I don't know," she said in a low voice. "We didn't know he was here. He never mentioned that he was coming for a visit. I don't understand it. He always told me everything and he had to know how excited I'd have been if I'd known he was coming for a visit."

"Did he visit often?" Bessie wondered.

"Never," Peter snapped. "He'd been gone for two years and he'd not been back, not once. Rebecca used to cry after every week after she'd spoken to him, but he didn't seem to care, not at all."

"That's not fair," Rebecca said. "He did care and he wanted to visit, but he was very busy with his new job and his new life across. It took him ages to settle in and make new friends, but once he'd done that he got very busy. He also felt odd about coming back to the island because he was worried about seeing Nicole. We visited him a few times, though, which was lovely."

"And he never mentioned having any problems at work or in his personal life?" Bessie asked.

"Never. He loved his job and he felt as if he was making a real difference. He especially enjoyed being able to meet some of the men, women, and children that the charity helped. He'd not been able to do that with his last job over here and he missed it very much."

"I seem to remember he worked for The Liliana Fund before he moved," Bessie said.

"Yes, that's right," Rebecca said. She rattled off a short list of island charities. "He worked for all of them before The Liliana Fund. He enjoyed the work there, but it frustrated him that so many of the grant recipients were either across or elsewhere in the world. They do great work and he enjoyed being a part of it, but he missed feeling a real connection to the people he was helping."

Bessie nodded. "I can understand that."

"He was going to look a few of them up," Peter said. "I wonder if he ever managed to find anyone."

"He found one woman," Rebecca replied. "I told you about it at the time. Phillip found her in a Derby hospital and she couldn't stop crying when she found out that he used to work for The Liliana Fund. Apparently, the fund was paying for someone to look after the woman's daughter while she was in hospital. That is the sort of thing the charity funds, rather than actual medical treatment."

"I seem to remember Oliver Preston saying something about wanting to buy wigs for cancer patients who'd lost their hair and helping patients keep food in their cupboards," Bessie said.

"Yes, and they often pay for cleaning services to help patients keep their homes clean during treatments, or buy school supplies for patients' children, " Rebecca told her. "There are so many little things that people don't think about when it comes to fighting cancer and other serious illnesses."

"Who replaced Phillip at the fund?" Bessie asked.

"There was a young man, Dylan Collins, who was already working there part-time," Rebecca said. "He took on Phillip's responsibilities when Phillip left. I understand that Oliver hires temporary staff to deal with the things that Dylan was doing before he moved into Phillip's job."

A loud ringing noise startled everyone. Rebecca sighed. "That's my phone," she said. It took her a minute of digging around in her handbag before she found the device. It was still ringing loudly as she pulled it from her bag.

"Hello?"

"Yes, okay, we'll be back soon."

"I know, I know."

She frowned as she dropped the phone back into the bag. "That was Harry," she told Peter.

"What did he want?"

"Madison is upset and can't stop crying," she explained. "He thinks we should come home."

"You go. I'll stay here and see what else I can learn from Bessie," Peter suggested.

"I don't know anything," Bessie told him.

Rebecca shrugged. "Harry was Phillip's closest friend. I don't know if you ever knew Harry Holt?"

Bessie thought for a minute. "I don't believe so. Did he grow up in the south of the island?"

"He grew up in Douglas," Rebecca replied. "He and Phillip actually met at university, or rather on the ferry across before their first semester. They sat next to one another on the ferry and they were both delighted to find out that they were going to the same school. They were friends from that moment onwards."

"He's very upset, too, obviously," Peter said. "He wasn't happy when Phillip moved across. They had something of a falling-out over it, actually. I'm not sure they'd spoken in the past two years."

Bessie frowned. "That's a shame." She'd been hoping that Phillip would have told someone about his planned visit to the island. That seemed less and less likely. "Do you have any idea why Phillip was on the island?" she asked.

"I wish I did. He rang on Sunday, as usual. We had a lovely chat about a charity race they were planning for spring. I asked him about visiting, because I asked him every time he rang. He said he'd try to find time to fit a quick trip home into his schedule, but it would probably be after the race, because the planning for that was taking up a lot of his time."

"Excuses," Peter said bitterly. "He always had excuses. I don't know why he was staying away, but he was definitely staying away."

"Nicole broke his heart," Rebecca said.

"Two bloody years ago. He should have been able to get over that by now. Anyway, he didn't have to see Nicole if he came home. It's a big island, big enough for him and Nicole, at least for a weekend."

Rebecca shrugged. "I kept trying to be understanding," she told Bessie. "As I said, we visited him in Derby. Madison went more often than we did. She even hinted that she might look for a job over there, but, well, I'm afraid I got very upset when she mentioned the idea. She never discussed it with me again."

"But she was still giving the idea some thought," Peter said. "Apparently, Phillip was sending her information about jobs."

"I see," Rebecca said tightly.

"We have to let them go," Peter told her.

"If we hadn't let Phillip go, he'd still be alive," she shot back.

"We don't know that," Peter said. "We don't know anything yet, but we're going to find out."

Rebecca's phone rang again. She frowned as she answered it. "Yes, Madison?"

"We'll be home soon. We're trying to find out what happened to Phillip."

"I know that, but we're doing what we can."

When she put the phone back in her bag, she got to her feet. "We have to go," she told Peter. "Madison needs us."

Peter looked as if he wanted to argue, but after a moment he stood up. "If you think of anything that would help us discover what happened to Phillip, please let us know," he said to Bessie.

"I'll let the police know. Solving Phillip's murder is their job," she replied.

He nodded. "Of course, but you must understand that, as his parents, we have a need to understand what happened."

"If I can help in any way, I will," Bessie said. "Remember what I told you, though. The more you can tell the police about Phillip, the better the chances of them solving the case."

"They'll soon get tired of hearing me talk," Rebecca said. "I feel as if I could talk about him for hours and hours."

"Maybe you should find a counselor," Bessie suggested.

Rebecca shrugged. "Maybe." She headed for the door with Peter at her heels. "Thank you for your time. I wish I could have brought my grandchildren to Laxey Beach to play. Now, even if Madison does have children, I won't ever bring them here. They won't play on the beach where Phillip died."

She opened the door and walked out with Peter following. He gave Bessie an awkward wave as he shut the door behind them. Bessie sat at the table, staring at the door, for several minutes. Her heart ached for the couple, for Madison and for everyone else who had cared for young Phillip. Whenever she closed her eyes, she could see the bed covered in blood. Who had killed Phillip and why?

It was too early to go to bed, even though she felt exhausted. After pacing around the kitchen for several minutes, she decided to take a walk in spite of the rain. The last cottage in the row felt closer than normal as she went. There were still several lights on inside, and as Bessie walked past, she could see a pair of men working hard in the cottage's dining room. One of them noticed Bessie and waved at her. Waving back, she picked up her pace and walked on to the steps at Thie yn Traie.

As the rain began to fall more heavily, she turned back towards home. As she passed the last cottage again, she heard someone call her name.

"Bessie?"

She smiled when she spotted Hugh Watterson rushing towards her. "Hugh? What are you doing here?"

"Grace is still at Noble's, so I came over to do a few hours of work. I'm hoping to save as much as I can of my holiday time and paternity leave for when the baby is actually home. Besides, I found the body. I want to be a part of the case, baby or no baby."

"You aren't tired of the baby already?" Bessie teased.

Hugh flushed. "Not even a little bit," he said firmly. "Grace may be, though. I understand she had trouble feeding the baby today. When I suggested that we just give her a bottle, though, she nearly bit my head off."

"What did her mother say?"

"That breastfeeding is very difficult, but totally worth it if Grace can manage. And that it's too soon to give up. I love having Grace's mum there, but I rather feel as if she's taking over a bit."

"You should talk to her."

"I might, once Grace is home. I'm torn, really, though, as I'm terrified to do anything with the baby. She's so tiny and she seems incredibly fragile. Grace's mum is terrific with her and she's good with Grace, too. She made Grace sleep most of today, which is exactly what Grace needed. I don't know what we'd do without Grace's mum."

"But you'd like to find out?" Bessie suggested.

Hugh flushed. "Maybe, but maybe not in the middle of a murder investigation."

Bessie nodded. "The victim's parents came to see me."

"They did? You should ring John and tell him everything they said."

"I was going to wait until morning. It seems too late to ring him now."

"He'll want to know," Hugh insisted. "They were very upset when he spoke to them. They may well have told you more than they told him."

"I'll ring him when I get home, then."

CHAPTER 4

"Thanks, Bessie," John said when she'd finished recounting the time she'd spent with the bereaved parents. "They were very badly shaken when I spoke with them. I hope they take your advice and come back in to tell me more about their son. If they don't, I'll follow up with them in the next day or two."

"I was hoping you would solve this case quickly. Hugh is going to want to be involved and he should be home with Grace and the baby."

"He's going to start his paternity leave as soon as Grace gets home, but I believe they're keeping her an extra day. The baby has a touch of jaundice, I understand."

"Is that serious?"

"Not as far as I know. Hugh didn't seem worried, anyway."

"He didn't even mention it to me, and I just spoke to him a few minutes ago."

"I'm sure he has a lot on his mind. As I said, I don't think it's anything serious, just something the doctors want to monitor."

"I know Hugh wants to be involved in the investigation. The timing is unfortunate."

"That's the nature of the job," John sighed. "I was in the middle of a major drug smuggling investigation when Thomas was born. I missed nearly all of his first three weeks of life. Sue was furious."

"I don't blame her."

"I didn't either, but I didn't have much choice. I didn't have paternity leave in the same way that Hugh does, either."

They chatted for a short while longer about changing attitudes towards childrearing before Bessie found herself yawning in between her own sentences. "I think I need some sleep," she said apologetically.

"We both do. Ring me tomorrow if you learn anything else. Otherwise, maybe we should have a gathering at your house tomorrow night."

"You'll be more than welcome. I'm not sure we should invite Hugh, though. He should be home with Grace."

"If she's still in Noble's, Hugh will probably be happy to come."

Bessie put the phone down and headed for the stairs. There seemed to be many more of them than normal. When she finally reached the top, she gave her teeth a cursory brushing and ran a comb through her hair. Feeling as if she'd done enough, she changed into her nightgown and crawled into bed. She was asleep as soon as her head touched the pillow.

It was three minutes past six when her internal alarm woke her. She stretched and then carefully climbed out of bed. "Not too bad," she said to herself as she headed for the shower. She was still slightly out of sorts but felt almost back to normal, which was gratifying.

What she needed now was a very long walk on the beach, she decided. Perhaps she'd walk as far as the new houses, or even beyond. After a quick breakfast of cold cereal, she headed out, determined to walk until she was too tired to walk any further.

She'd only gone a few hundred yards when a loud voice shouted at her across the sand.

"Good morning, Maggie," Bessie said with a sigh.

"Not so good, really, but it is morning," Maggie replied. "Thomas is still tucked up in bed, but I wanted to come down and get some work done somewhere. I can't do anything with the last cottage, but there's plenty to do in the others."

"Good for you. I've always been an early riser, of course."

Maggie shrugged. "'I'd much prefer to lie in all day, but then nothing would get done, would it? Thomas has an excuse, of course, because he's been poorly, but now it's all down to me and I can't afford to waste the morning. Did you recognise Phillip Tyler, then?"

Bessie blinked at the sudden change of subject. "Um, no, as I said yesterday, I didn't look at the body," she said eventually.

"I was surprised to hear it was him. When he left he said he was never coming back."

"Did he? I didn't realise."

"Oh, yes, that Nicole Carr broke his heart and he never wanted to see her again. He told his friend, Harry, that he was moving across for good."

"Moving across for good doesn't preclude visiting," Bessie suggested.

"He and Harry had a big falling out over the whole thing, actually. Phillip said he wasn't even going to visit, not when there was always a chance that he'd see Nicole while he was here. Harry didn't understand the problem. He's never been in love, of course."

"Hasn't he?" Bessie asked, not at all interested in the reply.

"Harry Holt?" Maggie laughed. "He'll still be single when he's fifty. That's about when he'll realise that he's getting older. I imagine he'll find himself some twenty-five-year-old trophy bride around then."

Bessie raised an eyebrow. "You seem to know a lot about him."

"I rang a few people last night. More than one of my friends had a story about Harry. He's broken a few hearts, that man. It would have been better if he'd been the one involved with Nicole. He wouldn't have cared in the slightest if she'd cheated on him."

"But Phillip cared very much."

"He did. So much so that he swore he'd never come back to the island."

"Except he did come back."

"Yes, I have a theory about that. I think he was kidnapped across and then dragged back here against his will."

"Why?"

"Why what?"

"Why would someone kidnap him and bring him here?"

"So that they could kill him on the island."

"Surely it would make more sense for them to kill him somewhere else, somewhere where no one knew him, maybe. It would be to the killer's advantage if no one could identify the body."

"There must have been a good reason why the killer wanted Phillip to die on the island. Once the police work out the reason, they'll know who killed him."

"Unless he was killed because he came back to the island," Bessie suggested.

"You think Liam Kirk killed him?"

Bessie felt her jaw drop. "I never said that."

"But he's the only one who'd have a reason to kill Phillip for coming back to the island."

"You don't know that, unless you know why Phillip was killed."

"He must have been killed because he came back for Nicole," Maggie said thoughtfully. "She and Liam have been having difficulties. Liam even got himself a flat in Douglas to use when he and Nicole are arguing."

"Have you told the police all of this?"

"I haven't spoken to the police. They've no reason to question me. I barely knew the man."

"You seem to know a lot about him."

"As I said, I rang a few people."

"People with whom the police will be speaking, I hope."

Maggie shrugged. "I've no idea how a police investigation works. Will the police question Nicole and Liam's neighbours?"

"I don't know," Bessie replied. But I'm going to suggest that they do, she added to herself.

"The more I think about it, the more I'm convinced that Liam must have killed Phillip to keep him away from Nicole," Maggie said. "Phillip's relationship with Nicole was the only interesting thing that he'd ever done."

"He was very hard working."

"Yes, but with charities. None of his jobs would have paid very much. It isn't as if he was wealthy. Money must be the most common motive for murder, and love must come second, surely."

Bessie thought about the various cases she'd been involved with over the past two years. Maggie was probably right. "Maybe he's in line to inherit a fortune or some such thing," Bessie suggested.

"His parents would know about anything like that. What did they say when they visited you yesterday?"

"Nothing about money," Bessie replied, feeling annoyed that Maggie knew about Rebecca and Peter's visit. The woman didn't miss much.

"I'm sure they blamed Nicole. They're still angry with her, not that I blame them."

"Did your sources suggest anyone else who might have wanted Phillip dead?"

Maggie shook her head. "It must have been Liam. Phillip was good at fundraising, but all the lovely money that he raised went to good causes, not his own bank account. Oliver might have been annoyed that he was back, I suppose, after the way he left him so suddenly, but I can't see him killing Phillip over it, not after two years."

"Phillip left The Liliana Fund suddenly?"

"Don't you remember? It was right before their annual ball at the Seaview. Phillip had made all of the arrangements, but then he quit overnight and left the island. Poor Oliver had to scramble desperately to make everything happen. Dylan helped, of course, but he isn't the brightest bulb in the box."

Bessie frowned. Now that Maggie had mentioned it, she had a vague recollection of the incident. "I can't see Oliver killing Phillip over a fundraiser that happened two years ago."

"It was all good in the end, anyway. I believe they raised even more than their goal because people felt sorry for Oliver. Some people ended up buying tickets twice, because Phillip had the list and hadn't sent out all of the tickets, too. Oliver did his best to work out who'd paid, but I know at least a handful of couples paid twice."

"So it all ended well, which must have made Oliver happy."

"I suppose, but he may still have been angry with Phillip."

"Perhaps, but murder requires a good deal of anger," Bessie said, shuddering as she recalled the amount of blood she'd seen.

"I wonder how angry Harry was," Maggie said thoughtfully.

"Surely he should have been happy to have Phillip back on the island."

"Unless Phillip came back to see Nicole and didn't tell Harry he was coming. Maybe he found himself in trouble, hiding from Liam, let's say, and he rang Harry for help. That might have made Harry angry, don't you think?"

"I think we're wasting our time speculating. Let's leave the investigating to the police, shall we?"

"Oh, of course, but there's one other theory I wanted to ask you about."

"Really?"

"What if Callum Sharp killed Phillp?"

"I'm not sure what motive he would have had."

"He's been sleeping rough for weeks. Who knows how long he'd been making himself at home in my cottage? Maybe he broke in the other night and found that Phillip was already there. He'd have been furious."

"When were you last in the cottage?" Bessie asked.

"I thought I told you that we've been working on clearing it out, ready for demolition."

"So you'd have noticed if Callum was using it as a temporary home."

"Maybe, if he'd left any mess behind, but perhaps he was very careful not to disturb anything."

"I suppose that's possible, but it seems unlikely. You and Thomas know every inch of every cottage. You'd have noticed if someone was staying in one without your knowledge."

Maggie shrugged. "I hope you're right. We're having alarms fitted on all of them, although I'm sure they'll be a nightmare when we have guests. No doubt Thomas or I will be down here every night resetting alarms that guests have set off themselves because they've forgotten the codes."

"Will you change the codes after each guest, then?"

"Oh, heavens, I don't know. I suppose we'll have to, won't we, or there's no point in having the codes in the first place. Thomas and I need to think this through. Perhaps the alarms could only be used when the cottages are empty. Then we wouldn't need to change the codes, as Thomas and I would be the only ones who would know them." She sighed. "Maybe we should think about selling."

"I hope you don't," Bessie told her.

Maggie shrugged. "I wish I had time to stand and chat with you all day, but I've ever so much work to do, you know. Let me know if you hear anything about the murder. I'm sure the next thing that will happen will be Liam's arrest. Mark my words on that."

Bessie nodded as Maggie turned and walked away. After a sigh and a deep breath, Bessie set off at a rapid pace across the sand. She passed Thie yn Traie quickly and kept pushing onwards. Curtains were tightly drawn in all of the windows at the new houses. Bessie kept walking, not stopping until she reached the large sign that gave the details of yet another housing estate being developed on the beach.

"Only seven plots remaining," the sign said in big letters. Bessie counted and then smiled to herself. There were only eight plots in the development, so they'd sold a single plot thus far. Unless they were hugely overpriced, Bessie didn't doubt that they'd end up selling them all fairly quickly, though. House prices kept going up all over the island.

She stood next to the sign and stared at the beach that still stretched out in front of her. While she was tempted to keep walking, it was getting late and she had a busy day in front of her. With a small sigh, she turned back towards home.

Hugh was opening the dining room curtains at his house as Bessie strolled past. "Good morning," he called as he opened the sliding doors to the beach.

"Good morning. I hope you slept well," Bessie said as she walked over to join him on the small patio behind the house.

Hugh flushed. "I feel a bit guilty, sleeping well, because I know Grace is up and down with the baby all night, but she has her mother with her and they both told me to come home and get some extra rest before Grace and the baby get here."

"I haven't wanted to ask, but do you have a name for the baby?"

Hugh sighed. "We're struggling a bit with that, actually. We agreed on a name before the baby was born, but now Grace isn't sure that it suits her. We can't keep calling her the baby forever, but for now that's easier than arguing all the time."

Bessie grinned. "How long do you have before you have to register the birth?"

"I'm not sure, but a few weeks, anyway. It isn't me being difficult, though, it's Grace and her mother. They don't agree and neither is prepared to compromise."

"Oh, dear. I am sorry."

Hugh shrugged. "I'm going to work for a few hours this morning and then spend the afternoon with Grace and the baby. I'm going to tell Grace's mum to go home for a few hours and rest. Maybe Grace and I can agree on a name while she's gone."

"Good luck."

"We're going to need it. I believe they're keeping Grace for one more night, so I should be at the gathering tonight. John said he'd collect dinner from the new Indian restaurant that just opened across from the station. Doona will be bringing pudding."

"As much as I hope Grace gets home soon, I do hope you'll be there tonight."

Hugh nodded. "I'd hate to miss one of our discussions about a case, especially this case, since I found the body."

Bessie was tired when she got back to Treoghe Bwaane. She drank a glass of cold water and then switched the kettle on for tea. Maybe, if she hurried, she'd have time to transcribe another of Onnee's letters before her meeting at two o'clock, she thought. The phone interrupted her plans.

"Is there any chance you could do a lunch meeting?" Mark asked when Bessie answered. "Otherwise, we'll have to move the meeting to six o'clock tonight."

"I can do lunch," Bessie said. "I can't do this evening."

Mark sighed. "Sometimes organising this committee is more work than organising the entire event."

Bessie laughed. "Everyone is busy this time of year."

"Yes, I know. I don't suppose anyone would come if we did Christmas at the Castle in September, though."

"No, probably not."

"I'll collect you in half an hour, if that's okay."

"I can get a taxi."

"But you're practically on my way as I'm working in Ramsey today," he replied. "Or rather, I'm working in Ramsey this morning. I suspect I'll be at Castle Rushen all afternoon. You'll probably need to get a taxi home after our meeting."

"I'll see you in half an hour, then."

Bessie put the phone down and headed for the stairs. It only took her a few minutes to comb out a few windblown tangles from her hair. She added a touch of lipstick to her lips and decided that she was done. The other committee members all knew her well. She could be herself with them.

Mark was at her door a short while later. "I'm sorry about all of the changes in plans," he said as he drove south.

"I'm the one who couldn't make it yesterday," Bessie reminded him.

"It wasn't just you, though, and it was the first time you've ever had an issue. I wish I could say the same for the rest of the committee."

"You said Mary couldn't make it yesterday either?"

"One of her grandchildren had a bit of an accident. He's fine," Mark added quickly, "but she wanted to be at Noble's with her daughter-in-law while they were treating his bumps and bruises."

"It isn't like Mary to miss a meeting, either."

"No, she's a wonderful asset to our committee."

Bessie hid a smile. After everything that had happened last year, Mark had been very careful this year when selecting committee members. Carolyn Teare, who'd been nearly impossible to work with, had been left off the list. In her place, Mark had added another wealthy woman who made a habit of joining committees. Anabella Patterson turned out to be a very hard worker when she managed to actually be at the meetings. It was getting her to attend that was difficult. Her husband, Edgar, travelled a great deal, and Anabella often dropped everything to fly to wherever he was, just for a day or two. Bessie had lost track of how many meetings had been rescheduled because Anabella had suddenly been unavailable. As December had progressed, Mark had finally decided that the committee would simply meet without Anabella if necessary.

"I thought we were about done with committee meetings, actually," Bessie said. "We aren't that far away from opening night."

"We aren't, but we have something of a problem to deal with, which is why we're meeting today."

"Oh?"

Mark sighed. "I'd prefer to just wait and discuss it with the whole committee, if you don't mind."

"Of course not. Tell me about your plans for Christmas," Bessie suggested.

They chatted for the rest of the journey about Christmas dinner and the best way to roast a turkey. As Mark parked in the car park next to the castle, Bessie found herself smiling up at Castle Rushen. The huge medieval castle was still one of her favourite places on the island, even after having to spend so much time working there for the past month or so. The clock on the tower, a gift to the island from the first Queen Elizabeth, showed exactly midday as Mark escorted Bessie across the street and up the steps to the castle's entrance.

"Everyone else is already here," Don, one of Manx National Heritage's staff, told Mark.

Mark nodded and then led Bessie towards the staff rooms that were tucked up behind the spaces open to the public.

Bessie greeted Mary Quayle with a hug. "I hope your grandson is okay," she said.

"He's fine. He has a few bruises, and he may even be left with a scar on his forehead, but he's delighted with the idea and has already come up with a dozen different exciting stories to tell people about how it happened."

"How did it happen?"

"He tripped over his own feet and fell down a few stairs," Mary told her. "He hit his head on the banister on his way down."

"That sounds painful."

"He's young enough to not really mind."

"Can't you go anywhere without finding a body?" Anabella demanded as she greeted Bessie with elaborate air kisses.

"I didn't find the body," Bessie said, feeling as if she'd said that a dozen times already.

"Technically, maybe not, but you were there," Anabella said. "I told my darling Edgar that I was going to start following you everywhere. I've never found a body in my life and I think it would be quite exciting, just the once."

"It isn't at all exciting," Bessie said flatly.

Anabella shrugged. "I haven't time to follow you around anyway. Please don't find any bodies at Christmas at the Castle this year. We've all worked too hard to have to deal with all of that."

"Bessie, there you are," Marjorie Stevens interrupted. "How are you coming with Onnee's letters?"

"I've completed the first year, but it's hard going. Every time I think I'm getting accustomed to the woman's handwriting, she seems to change a few letters here and there. It's frustrating, but fascinating."

"I want to hear all about it after Christmas," Marjorie said. "There are another forty-eight years of letters for you, as well."

Bessie sighed. "I may need forty-eight years to get through them all."

"Bessie, dear, I was so sorry to hear that you'd found another body," Agnes Clucas said.

As she gave Agnes a hug, Bessie made a face. "I didn't actually find the body," she said again.

Agnes sighed. "Of course not. I hope young Hugh wasn't too upset. Imagine becoming a father for the first time just before finding a dead body. It was quite a day for the young man, wasn't it?"

Agnes was in her mid-sixties. She was a keen volunteer with Mannanan's Kids, a charity that did wonderful work across the island. Agnes had decorated a room in the first year of the event on behalf of the charity, and she'd been kind enough to agree to serve on the planning committee this year. The room she was decorating was one of the most ambitious that Bessie had seen and the last time she'd peeked in on it, everything was coming together beautifully.

"We should get started," Anabella said. "My flight leaves at two."

"I haven't been here since last week. How are the rooms coming?" Mark asked Agnes.

"Things are coming together nicely," she replied. "Except for the one problem, of course."

Bessie frowned. It was late in the day to have to deal with a problem.

"We'll get to that at the end," Mark said.

"Here we are," a voice said from the doorway. A man carried in a large tray that was covered in sandwiches. Another worker came in behind him, carrying a similar tray. They put the trays on the table. "We'll be right back," one of them said. When they returned, they added a tray full of fresh fruit and one of cheese and crackers to the table.

"Was there anything else?" the first man asked.

Mark shook his head. "Sorry for the short notice. Everything looks great."

Marjorie found paper plates and napkins and passed them around to everyone. A few minutes later a kettle boiled and Marjorie made tea for them as well. For several minutes everyone ate in silence.

"From which restaurant did you get this?" Agnes asked as she reached for a second helping of fruit. "This is exactly what I need for another committee meeting that I'll be attending soon."

Mark named a restaurant that had just opened in Castletown, not far from the castle. "They were incredibly accommodating, considering I rang them an hour ago."

Agnes made a note. "I'm impressed."

"As am I," Mary said. "I shall suggest them to Elizabeth for events down here."

Mary's daughter, Elizabeth, had recently started a party planning business. At first it sounded as if it would be a fun and easy job for the spoiled only daughter of wealthy parents, but Bessie had quickly discovered that party planning was hard work. Elizabeth had thrown herself into it with enthusiasm though, and thus far she'd impressed Bessie with her dedication and determination. Elizabeth had planned Grace's baby shower on Bessie and Mary's behalf and everyone had enjoyed that afternoon a great deal. Now Bessie was trying to find another event for Elizabeth to plan for her, although from what she'd been hearing, Elizabeth was quickly becoming quite busy without any help from Bessie.

When everyone had finished eating, Mark and Marjorie cleared the table.

"If I'm right, we have pudding," he said, taking the empty trays out of the room. He was back a moment later carrying a tray full of biscuits and other sweet treats.

"My goodness, how lovely," Mary said.

"It's much nicer than I was expecting," Mark told her. "I asked them for a tray of biscuits, with a few slices of cake or whatever they had lying around."

"If they had all of this lying around, I'm going to have to start dropping in there regularly," Agnes laughed.

Bessie took two bite-sized pieces of chocolate sponge with chocolate icing, a biscuit, and a tiny jam tart. As everyone else filled plates, she sipped her tea.

"Right, let's get on with things while we enjoy the puddings," Mark said. "Everything is going very smoothly, especially compared to last year." He glanced at Bessie.

"I hope that doesn't just mean that no one has been murdered yet," she replied.

"No one has been murdered, but we also haven't been saddled with a designer who wants to change everything at the last minute, either,"

Mark said. He flushed and then cleared his throat. "Obviously, Carolyn was simply doing what she thought was for the best, but it is much easier letting all of our charity partners simply design their own rooms without trying to find a unifying theme."

The designer, whom Carolyn had hired at her own expense, had ended up murdered and the entire event had nearly had to be cancelled. Bessie hadn't wanted the man to interfere with the decorating that each charity had done, so she was pleased that nothing similar had happened this year.

Mark quickly ran through a few minor issues, mostly to do with ticket sales and distribution. They briefly debated a few catering options for the auction evening on the last night, reaching a consensus with little difficulty.

"That just leaves our one little problem to discuss," he said eventually.

"We'll need to talk fast. I have a plane to catch," Anabella said.

"One of the charities has decided not to take part after all," Mark announced. He named the group. "Sadly, they've decided that they simply don't have the time to deal with the decorating and also with staffing the room while the event is happening. I'm certain we were very clear about our expectations when we invited people to apply for rooms. Apparently, they just lost several of their best volunteers. It was a family where the father, mother, and three teenaged children all worked with the charity. The mother unexpectedly got a new job across and they moved rather quickly. That left the charity with far fewer people to help with Christmas at the Castle and their own end-of-year fundraiser. After much debate, they decided that their own event had to take precedence, and they've pulled out of Christmas at the Castle."

"What a shame," Bessie said. "I really liked the young man who spoke to us during the application process."

"He was lovely," Agnes agreed.

"He was the oldest child of the family that left," Mark said.

"Oh, dear," Agnes sighed.

"That leaves us with an empty room," Mark continued. "It's very short notice to try to fill it, but all of our advertising talks about having ten decorated rooms this year."

"Can't we just decorate it?" Anabella asked.

"Manx National Heritage has already done a room," Mark reminded her. "We've also decorated all of the public spaces that will be used during the event. I don't think anyone at MNH has the time or the energy to do another room. Besides, one of the goals of Christmas at the Castle is to help other island charities. I'd really like to find someone else to fill the empty spot."

"Do you have a short list of candidates?" Mary asked. "Have you actually spoken to anyone about the space?"

"I haven't spoken to anyone, but I do have a short list," Mark replied. "I went back through the list of charities who applied and were turned down. There were three of them that I believed were nearly as good candidates as the ones we accepted." He named the three groups.

Bessie sat up a bit straighter when he mentioned The Liliana Fund.

"There were reasons why we turned all three of them down," Mary said. "The first group has an incredibly narrow focus, the second was on the periphery of that scandal in the UK recently, and The Liliana Fund sends nearly all of its money off-island."

Mark nodded. "You're right that the Cortlett Fund is entirely focussed on curing a very rare disease, which is why we didn't select them the first time. As for the scandal in the UK and the second group, there's been no suggestion that anyone from the island was involved in what was happening, and the local group is now moving towards separating itself from the international organisation and establishing itself independently."

"And The Liliana Fund?" Bessie asked.

"They do send most of their funding off-island," Mark admitted. "I did think that we might invite them to take part as long as they agreed to use the funds they get from the event here on the island."

"Do you think they'd agree?" Agnes wondered.

"I can't see why they wouldn't," Mark replied. "The island has plenty of people who could use their support, I'm sure."

"So what's the next step?" Anabella asked as she rose to her feet.

"We have to decide which charity we're going to invite to take the empty space. I'll contact them today, as they'll need as much time as possible to get the room done," Mark replied.

"I don't care whom you invite," Anabella said as she headed for the door. "I voted for every single charity to be included, and I still think it's a shame we had to turn so many down. See you soon." She opened the door and disappeared through it, leaving Mark frowning at her back.

"Let's take a vote," Agnes suggested.

A few minutes later, the meeting was over and everyone was heading for the door.

Mark grinned at Bessie, "I'll take you home after we're done, if you'll come with me to talk to Oliver at The Liliana Fund," he offered.

CHAPTER 5

"Of course," Bessie said quickly. A chance to talk to Oliver Preston was not something she wanted to miss.

Mark had to ring a few people before they left, so Bessie wandered around the castle, looking into each room and smiling at the beautiful decorations. It seemed unlikely that anyone would complain if they only had nine rooms to visit on their tour around Christmas at the Castle, she thought.

"Sorry about that," Mark said a short time later. "Let's go and see if Oliver is still interested in being a part of things."

The drive into Douglas didn't take long. The Liliana Fund had its offices on the ground floor of a small Victorian building not far from the centre of the town. Mark parked on the street and then he and Bessie climbed out of the car.

"Oliver said he'd be in all afternoon," Mark told Bessie as they walked.

There was a small reception area right inside the door. Bessie sat down on an overstuffed couch while Mark spoke to the receptionist.

"She's going to ring Oliver and let him know we're here," he told Bessie as he sat down beside her.

"Mr. Preston will see you now," the receptionist said a moment later.

Bessie followed Mark into a short corridor. He knocked on the last door along the hall.

"Ah, Mark, how good to see you," Oliver said, shaking hands with Mark and smiling brightly at Bessie. "Miss Cubbon, this is an unexpected pleasure."

"We were working at Castle Rushen together," Mark explained as Oliver shook Bessie's hand. He was a tall man with dark brown hair. His dark grey suit fit his athletic frame perfectly. He was wearing a light purple shirt with a darker purple tie that had the charity's logo woven into it. Bessie knew he was in his mid-forties, but he looked younger.

"Ah, yes, Christmas at the Castle. I'm still terribly disappointed that I didn't get a room to decorate," Oliver replied. "Come in and tell me what's on your minds today, then."

He ushered them into a small room that looked more like a sitting room than anyone's office. There was a long couch and several chairs centred around a low table. Bessie and Mark sat together on the couch.

"Can I get either of you a drink?" Oliver asked.

"I'm fine," Bessie told him.

"Thank you, but no," Mark said. "We don't want to take up too much of your valuable time."

Oliver nodded. "Let me get Dylan, then, and we can get started."

He opened a door in the corner of the room and disappeared from view. A few minutes later he was back. Dylan Collins was at his heels. Dylan was younger than Oliver, perhaps by as much as ten years. His medium-brown hair fell in a thick tangle almost to his shoulders. Bessie wasn't sure where he'd purchased his suit, but it certainly hadn't been tailored for him. The trousers were several inches too long, as were the sleeves on the jacket. He smiled at Bessie and Mark, but he looked almost nervous as he dropped into a chair across from them.

"Good afternoon," he said, nodding at Bessie and then looking at the ground.

"Good afternoon," she replied.

Oliver took the chair next to Bessie and rubbed his hands together. "So, what can we do for you?" he asked Mark.

"I'd like to start by offering my condolences," Bessie said before Mark could speak.

Oliver looked surprised and then frowned. "Thank you, Miss Cubbon. It's very kind of you to think to say that. Phillip was a very valuable member of our little team and we were all sorry to see him go. I understand you found the body. That must have been a horrific experience for you."

"I didn't find the body, actually," Bessie countered.

"I must have been misinformed," Oliver said smoothly. "On an island that thrives on skeet, that's hardly surprising."

Bessie smiled at the man's use of the Manx word. Oliver wasn't from the island originally, although she wasn't sure where he'd spent his childhood.

"It's really sad," Dylan muttered. "I didn't even know he was back on the island."

"But you didn't come to talk to us about Phillip," Oliver said. "Or rather, I hope you didn't. Not that I don't want to discuss him, but I spent hours with the police, telling them everything I could about him. I'm sure your friend, Inspector Rockwell, will tell you everything I said."

"Inspector Rockwell never tells me anything that he was told in interviews," Bessie replied.

"Oh, dear. Are you here to ask questions about Phillip, then?" Oliver asked.

"Not at all," Bessie said. "I simply wanted to offer my condolences."

Oliver nodded. "It is appreciated. Phillip's parents must be devastated. I was going to ring them later today, but I'm not certain they'd be interesting in speaking with me. Have you spoken to them?"

"Just briefly. As you say, they're heartbroken," Bessie replied.

"I simply can't imagine what Phillip was doing in an empty holiday cottage," Oliver said. "Do you know if he'd had a falling-out with his family?"

"I don't believe he had," Bessie said.

"He must have been avoiding someone," Dylan suggested. "Maybe that nasty ex of his."

Oliver sighed. "You know I don't want you saying negative things about people, even her," he told Dylan. "She and Phillip had problems, which is what led him to leave the island somewhat unexpectedly, but we only know Phillip's side of the story."

"She cheated on him," Dylan said.

"I didn't realise he'd left so quickly once he and Nicole ended their relationship," Bessie said. "That must have left you with difficulties."

Oliver nodded. "We were right in the middle of our biggest event of the year, so yes, it did cause us some difficulties. I understood, of course. Phillip needed to get away. The island was too small. He kept seeing Nicole or her friends everywhere that he went. I was angry for a short while, but as I said, I understood. I'd like to think that he knew that and would have rung me at some point to let me know he was visiting."

"Do you have any idea who might have wanted him dead?" Mark asked.

When Bessie looked at him in surprise, he flushed "I was just curious," he said.

Oliver smiled. "Of course you are. We all are. I've never been involved in a murder investigation before. I've seen them on telly, but this seems very different to what I've seen. In answer to your question, I've no idea why poor Phillip was murdered. I hadn't spoken to him in two years or more. Goodness only knows what he was involved with in the UK."

"You think someone from across followed him here and killed him?" Bessie asked.

"Or came to the island with him and then killed him," Oliver replied. "Maybe he brought a girlfriend with him and they had a disagreement about staying in that holiday cottage. That's one possibility, anyway."

"I'm not certain that Phillip had recovered from losing Nicole yet," Bessie said.

"Perhaps it was something completely random, then," Oliver said. "I'm sure I heard that some homeless man was standing over the body when it was discovered. Maybe he was staying in the cottage and got upset when he came back and found Phillip in his bed or something."

"I know the man in question. He wouldn't hurt a fly," Bessie said with more confidence about Callum than she actually felt.

"Could have been anyone," Dylan muttered. "He was probably just in the wrong place at the wrong time."

That seemed obvious under the circumstances, but Bessie refrained from saying as much. After a slightly awkward pause, Mark cleared his throat.

"Right, well, the reason that Bessie and I are here today is to put a proposition to you," he said. "We've had a charity withdraw from Christmas at the Castle, and we were wondering if you'd be interested in stepping into their place."

Oliver and Dylan exchanged glances. "You aren't giving us much time to do the decorating," Oliver complained.

"I only found out a short while ago that the other group was no longer going to be able to take part," Mark replied.

"I don't know," Oliver said. "I can't remember what the original application said, but there was something about someone having to be at the event every afternoon and evening, wasn't there?"

"Yes, that's right," Mark replied. "A member of the charity's staff needs to be available in the room during opening hours. Members of the public often have questions about the charity, the decorations, or both."

"Dylan and I are rather busy at the moment," Oliver said. "We were going to take someone on part-time if we'd been allocated a room, but when we weren't, we decided not to bother. Between the two of us, we can just about handle the workload without costing the charity too much money for salaries. It's too late in the day now to hire someone and get them sufficiently trained before opening night."

"There's another caveat, too," Mark said. "The event should bring in a good deal of money for The Liliana Fund. We'd like you to agree to spend the money raised on the island for people on the island who need your services."

Oliver frowned. "I don't like the idea of having restrictions imposed upon us. I've been running this fund for ten years and I've always done it my way."

"I appreciate that, but the focus for Christmas at the Castle is on funding local charities to benefit local residents. We don't want to restrict what you do, but I'm sure you must have plenty of funding requests from men and women on the island," Mark replied.

"We do, of course, but I have my own methods for choosing whom to assist. I've spent years developing them and I'm not interested in changing them in any way."

"In that case, perhaps it would best if we offered the empty room to someone else," Mark said.

Oliver frowned. "There must be a compromise position here," he said. "I'd hate to miss out on the chance to take part in one of the island's biggest fundraising events."

"It's important to us that the money raised stays on the island," Mark said.

"We don't have time to decorate, anyway," Dylan said softly.

Oliver glanced at him and then sighed deeply. "Dylan may be correct, although I'd be prepared to try. Not if you're going to insist on imposing restrictions on the money, though."

"Perhaps in future years, as the event grows larger, we'll be able to invite a greater number of charities to take part, even those who send most of their funds across or further afield," Mark said. "For now, however, we really do want to keep the event as island-focussed as possible."

"Let me show you something," Oliver said. He got to his feet and left the room. A moment later he was back, carrying a large envelope. He handed the envelope to Mark.

"These are the sorts of letters we get every day," he said. "Look through them. See what you think."

Mark opened the envelope and pulled out several sheets of paper.

He read the top one and then passed it to Bessie. It was a touching letter from a young girl whose mother was undergoing cancer treatment. She asked the fund to consider sending her mother enough money for a wig so that her mother could feel pretty again.

Bessie turned the sheet of paper over and found a note on the back. "Sent money for wig, matching mother and daughter dresses, and for dinner at the fanciest restaurant in the area," it read.

Half an hour later, Bessie put the final sheet of paper down. "It's clear that you do a lot of good," she said. The letters had been broadly similar, each one a request for money for some of the smaller things that most charities probably didn't support. A few books here, a wig or a new dress there. None of the grants were for large amounts, but they all added up, of course.

"Those are the letters for which we provided some support," Oliver replied. "I have a file folder with ten times that many requests which we had to refuse. As I said earlier, I have my own methods for choosing where the money goes. I've never let anyone else influence my decision-making process. As much as I'd love to be a part of Christmas at the Castle, I can't do it on your terms."

Mark nodded. "As much as we'd like you to take part, as I said earlier, we want the focus to be on the island. Hopefully, as the event grows, we'll be able to include The Liliana Fund one day."

"That would be great," Oliver said. "Dylan and I are planning to attend, anyway. I missed it last year. You sold out of tickets before I managed to get one. Having heard so many good things about the event, I didn't make that same mistake this year."

"I'll be there, whenever you come through," Mark told him. "Make sure you ask for me at the ticket window and I'll escort you around myself."

"I'd appreciate that," Oliver said with a smile. "I'm sorry we couldn't reach an agreement, but there's always next year."

Oliver stood up and held out his hand. Mark rose and shook hands with him. Bessie got to her feet more slowly. After a moment, Oliver shook her hand as well. Dylan remained slouched in his chair, staring at the ground.

"I'll just walk you out," Oliver said. "Dylan, when I get back, we need to go over the numbers for the Christmas party."

Dylan nodded. "I have them all ready."

"Christmas party?" Bessie asked as Oliver escorted them back through the house.

"We have a small gathering for some of our best donors," Oliver explained. "We share some of the requests that we've received and the thank-you letters we've been sent after we've provided funding to people. It's just mulled wine and mince pies and an hour of celebrating the people we've been able to help over the past year."

"It sounds just right for this time of year," Bessie said.

"It is exactly that," Oliver laughed. "I understand you and Mary Quayle are friends. She and her husband come to the party every year."

"I didn't realise they donate to The Liliana Fund," Bessie replied.

"Mary has been a donor for many years, since she and George moved to the island, really."

"Mary is very kind and generous," Bessie said.

"Yes, we're hoping she might be even more generous going forward. We'd really like to expand what we do, if we can find the funding to do so," Oliver told her.

Bessie wondered if that sort of thing happened to Mary everywhere she went. It was very different from what Bessie typically experienced. As far as Bessie could tell, everyone on the island knew her and her life story, and also knew that she lived frugally, in order to stay within her means. All those years of living so carefully had left her quite well off by most people's standards, but it seemed as if Bessie and her advocate, Doncan Quayle, were the only two people who knew that fact.

Bessie was rarely asked to donate to charities, and if she was asked, it was usually for her time as a volunteer rather than for a cash donation. Of course, everyone on the island knew Mary and her husband, George. George was friendly and gregarious and made no secret of the fact that he was very wealthy. Mary's generosity was also well known throughout the island. It must be frustrating to be asked for money from nearly everyone, Bessie thought as she followed Mark back out to his car.

"On to the next name on the list," he said cheerfully as he started the engine. "Do you want me to take you home first?"

"Aren't their offices just down the street?"

"They are, yes, but I did promise to take you home if you came with me to see Oliver. You've no obligation to stay with me through this next meeting."

"I don't mind. I just need to be home by half five."

Mark glanced at his watch. "We have plenty of time, then."

He drove a short distance and parked again. "I did worry that Oliver would say no. I believe we'll have a better chance here, unless they don't feel as if they have enough time to decorate."

Half an hour later they were back at the car, having secured a new participant in their event.

"I think they're going to be a good solid addition," Mark said as he pulled away from the kerb.

"They were incredibly excited to be given the opportunity, anyway. I was shocked to hear how much support they've lost because someone in the UK branch of the charity was dishonest."

"I think their plan to separate completely from the UK charity is wise. Hopefully they'll be able to get that message out at Christmas at the Castle."

"I think they have some good ideas for decorations, as well. If they can put together what they're planning, their room will be unique and interesting. I just hope they have enough time to make it happen."

"I'm down at Castle Rushen full-time now until opening night. I'll give them a hand whenever I can spare a few minutes. I'm also going to ring the office and see if we can get an extra member of staff down to the castle to help out. It's in everyone's best interests to have their room done right, after all. A lot of MNH staff only work limited hours during the winter months. No doubt we can find at least one person who would like a few extra hours of pay just before the holidays."

"If I can find the time, I'd love to come down and help, too," Bessie said. "It would be easier if I weren't tangled up in another murder investigation."

"I'm just glad this case doesn't involve Christmas at the Castle. That made things much more difficult last year. I did wonder if some of our ticket sales were to morbid curiosity seekers last year, but as nearly every night of this year's event is already sold out, it seems not."

"Last year's event was a huge success, in spite of the murder investigation. I can't tell you how many people have been asking me about tickets for this year based on things they were told about last year. We should discuss adding more days next year, I think."

"I don't know if I have enough energy to do even more," Mark laughed. "There are only a limited number of days in December, as well. I can't imagine anyone would want to come to Christmas at the Castle in November."

"They might, if those were the only tickets they could get. We can discuss it in the new year."

"Yes, let's get through this year first," Mark said with a sigh.

"You sound fed up."

"Just a bit. I feel as if we've been working hard on this for half the year already and we've still over a week to go before it opens. I'm ready for it to be over so I can get back to all my other projects."

"It will be over before you know it," Bessie said soothingly. "What exciting things are you planning for next year?"

Mark told her about a few special events that MNH were going to be hosting around the island in the early months of the new year. By the time he was finished, they were at Bessie's cottage.

"Will I see you again before the next committee meeting?" he asked Bessie as he walked her to her door.

"Do I need to let you know if I'm coming down?"

"Not at all. You're welcome any time."

"I may simply turn up one day, then. I'm sure there will be lots I can do to help if I'm there. Otherwise, I'll see you at the committee meeting on Tuesday."

"Two o'clock, although I'm tempted to move it to midday just so I can get lunch from the same place again. It was delicious."

"It was very good. I may come down early on Tuesday and have lunch there before the meeting."

"If you decide to do that, let me know. I'll probably want to join you."

Bessie let herself into the cottage and dropped her handbag on the kitchen counter. She had an hour before her friends were due. Onnee's letters called to her, but she was also tempted to take another walk. As she tried to make up her mind, she glanced at the answering machine. The message light was flashing.

"Bessie, it's Rebecca, um, Rebecca Tyler. Can you ring me back, please?" The woman said her number so quickly that Bessie had to listen to the message three times before she was fairly certain she'd written it down correctly.

The man who answered the phone sounded angry. "What?"

"This is Elizabeth Cubbon. Rebecca left a message on my answering machine, asking me to ring her."

"Really?" the man snapped. It sounded to Bessie as if he dropped the telephone's receiver onto the table from a great height. She winced at the noise it made in her ear. After two full minutes ticked past, she began to think about putting the phone down.

"Bessie?" Rebecca's voice came down the line. "Sorry to keep you waiting, but I was lying down."

"Oh, dear, I am sorry."

"No, no, it's fine. I'm not sleeping at night, so I thought I'd try sleeping in the day, but I was wide awake, staring at the ceiling, when you rang."

"I was simply ringing you back."

"Yes, of course. I'm sorry. I'm tired and I'm not functioning very well. I keep forgetting things and," Rebecca sighed. "But you didn't ring to hear all of that. Sorry."

"It's fine. You've undergone a huge loss."

"Yes, it's, well, more difficult than I'd ever imagined, not that I'd ever imagined anything like this, of course."

"Of course not."

71

"I'm babbling. Sorry. I rang you earlier to ask you for a favour, but now I'm having second thoughts."

"Ask anyway. I can always refuse."

"Madison wants to talk to you. She has it in her head that you can solve Phillip's murder. There's been so much in the local paper about you in the past few years, you see, that she believes you can do things the police can't."

"On the contrary, the police are the ones who will solve Phillip's murder. I'll do anything I can to help, but the job is theirs."

"Yes, of course, but she thinks that if she tells you everything she knows about Phillip, that you'll be able to solve the case."

"I hope she's already told the police everything she knows."

"She has. She talked to them for three hours, but she felt as if the constable who questioned her was bored and uninterested. Apparently, he asked her out, as well. She wasn't pleased."

"I suspect he could get into a good deal of trouble for that, if she reported him."

"Maybe, but she's much more interested in finding Phillip's killer than anything else. She wants to come and see you, maybe with a few of Phillip's friends."

"She's more than welcome here, of course, but all I can do is offer tea and sympathy, really."

"Which may be exactly what she needs," Rebecca sighed. "She wants to feel as if she's doing something, you see. If she drags a few of Phillip's friends to see you, she'll feel as if she's involved in the case and working towards the solution."

They agreed to two o'clock the next day before Bessie put the phone down. A quick look in her cupboards showed that she was running low on biscuits. Friday was her usual day for grocery shopping, but she'd had to rearrange her schedule to work around committee meetings and now a murder investigation. With Hugh expected shortly, there was no way she had enough biscuits for tonight and tomorrow. A further search revealed that she didn't have enough flour to bake anything. She needed a trip to the shop at the top of the hill.

"You wanted another walk," she reminded herself as she put on her shoes. It was cold and grey outside, but dry. She marched determinedly up the hill, pumping her arms and feeling grateful for her warm coat. As she walked into the shop, she glanced behind the counter. Another unfamiliar face stared back at her. Lately it seemed as if the shop's owner couldn't keep staff for very long at all. Many of the young people who'd served Bessie in the past year had been rude and impatient with her. One girl had even tried stealing money from Bessie by giving her change for a ten-pound note rather than the twenty that Bessie had given her. After smiling at the new shop assistant, Bessie turned and headed for the small selection of biscuits on the back wall.

"Good afternoon," the girl said loudly. "If you need anything, just shout."

"Thank you," Bessie replied, feeling hopeful that the new hire might be an improvement over the people she'd replaced.

"Those are my favourites," the shop assistant said a moment later. She'd come up behind Bessie, and now she pointed to a packet of biscuits. "I could eat the entire packet myself, which wouldn't be good for me, I know."

"No, it wouldn't, but it is tempting," Bessie replied. She put the biscuits under discussion into her shopping basket.

"These are nice, too," she suggested, pointing to another packet.

"Are they? I've not tried them."

"Oh, they're really nice, actually." Bessie grinned as the girl launched into a detailed description of them. When she was done, Bessie added them to her basket, too.

"Any other recommendations?" she asked.

The shop assistant flushed. "I hope you don't think I'm odd," she said softly. "It's just rather lonely in here on my own all day. We have a bit of a rush around five when people are heading home from work, but otherwise it's usually just me, hanging around, tidying the shelves, and watching the clock tick."

"Most of the other people who work here seem to spend their time on their phones."

"I don't really know anyone on the island, at least not yet."

"You've come over recently?"

"Yes, just a few weeks ago, actually. My father works for one of the banks in Douglas. He was transferred here from London. I wasn't sure if I should stay there or come with him, but Mum really wanted me to come, so here I am."

"Welcome, then."

"Oh, thank you. So far I think the island is nice. I worked in a retail shop in London with rude customers and a dreadful boss. This is better, at least so far, even if it is a little lonely."

"You could read a book," Bessie suggested.

"I would, but my books are still in boxes waiting to be unpacked. Mum and Dad are still looking for a house, so everything is in storage until they find one. House prices are a bit crazy, really."

"They are, yes."

"Anyway, I'll get my books back eventually and then I'll read while I wait for customers."

"I can lend you some books," Bessie offered.

"Oh, no, that's quite all right. I didn't mean to suggest, that is, I never thought..."

Bessie held up a hand. "You didn't suggest anything. I'm offering because I have a house full of books, most of which I'll never read again. The next time I'm coming up, I'll bring you a few."

"That's very kind of you, but I'd worry about them getting damaged, especially here. Things get spilled and broken all the time."

"I won't lend you anything that you'll need to worry about. What sort of books do you enjoy?"

The girl blushed. "Mostly romance," she said in a low voice.

"I don't have many romance titles, but I'll see what I can find," Bessie said. "I mostly read mysteries, myself."

"Oh, those would be a close second."

Bessie found a few more things she hadn't known she needed and then carried everything to the till. It only took the shop assistant a moment to ring everything up and she took the money and got Bessie her change very efficiently.

"I'll be back one day soon," Bessie promised as she headed for the door.

"Thank you so much."

Feeling as if things had just improved in her world, Bessie walked back down the hill smiling. Back at Treoghe Bwaane, she put the biscuit packets and other things away and then sat down with a book while she waited for her friends.

CHAPTER 6

"*J*'m early," Doona said as she hugged Bessie. "I hope you don't mind. I did bring pudding."

Bessie laughed. "You know you're always more than welcome, with or without pudding." She took the bakery box and set it on the counter, only just resisting the temptation to look inside. Doona had taken a seat at the kitchen table. "How are you?" Bessie asked.

"I'm okay, I suppose," Doona replied with a sigh.

"What's wrong?"

"Nothing, really." Doona sighed again as Bessie sat down next to her. Anyone who didn't know the pair might think they were unlikely friends. Doona was twice divorced and in her forties. She and Bessie had met when Doona had signed up for the beginner's class in the Manx language, hoping to meet some unattached men. Instead, Doona had been the youngest in the class by a considerable margin. She and Bessie had bonded over the difficult Celtic tongue while Bessie helped Doona get through the difficult end of her second marriage.

In the years since, the pair had supported one another through numerous murder investigations, including that of Doona's second husband. Now Bessie was trying to limit her involvement in Doona's personal life as the woman seemed to be getting closer and closer to John Rockwell.

"I think I'm going to quit my job," Doona blurted out after a moment.

"You aren't happy at the station?" Bessie asked.

Doona had moved to Laxey from elsewhere on the island, to take a job with the island's constabulary as civilian front desk staff at the Laxey police station.

"I wouldn't say that exactly, but, well, I don't know. I'm spending a lot of time with the children and it would be easier if I weren't working. They don't need me around all the time, obviously, but Amy needed a ride somewhere yesterday and John and I were both working. I felt terrible telling her that I couldn't take her to her game."

"There are buses and taxis," Bessie pointed out.

Doona flushed and nodded. "And I'm sure most of her friends arrived by bus, but I feel responsible for her and Thomas, especially as Sue isn't around."

Sue, John's ex-wife, was honeymooning in Africa with her second husband, Harvey. She and Harvey had been a couple years before Sue had met John. They'd ended things, at least partly because Harvey hadn't wanted children. Some years after Sue had married John, while she was pregnant with their first child, she'd admitted to him that she was still in love with Harvey. John and Sue had tried hard to make their relationship work anyway, even having a second child together, but when circumstances reunited Sue and Harvey, the marriage had crumbled. Harvey was an oncologist who'd always dreamt of travelling to a developing country where he could help people in need. Now he and Sue were following his dream, leaving the children, who were in their teens, with John. They'd left in July with plans to return in September, but it was nearly Christmas and from what Bessie had heard, they still hadn't arranged return flights.

"John doesn't know when she'll be back yet?" Bessie asked.

"No, she hasn't rung in over a week, which is worrying in its own way. At first she rang twice a week, then it dropped to once a week, but at least she still rang every Wednesday. When she rang last week she only talked to John for a minute, and spoke with the children for not much more than that, really. She and Harvey were heading into a more remote area, but she promised that she'd find a way to ring this week, no matter what."

"Is John worried?"

"A little bit. I think he's also frustrated. The kids are upset and worried, and there's nothing John can do to make things better. I just keep thinking that, as I don't need to work, I could quit and help out more."

Doona had been shocked to discover that her second husband had left his entire estate to her, even though they'd been separated when he'd died. Once she'd been cleared of his murder, she'd received a small settlement, but the rest of the estate was currently caught up in a messy battle with the man's former business partner and several solicitors. The business partner had been found guilty of a number of crimes, so the courts were busy trying to work out how much, if any, of Doona's former husband's estate had been amassed through criminal activity. A short while ago, though, her solicitor in the UK had sent her a cheque for a large amount of money from a life insurance policy he'd discovered. Doona could quit work at any time and live off of her unexpected inheritance.

"At least you're around to help some of the time," Bessie said.

"Yes, but that's starting to cause tensions, too."

"Oh?"

"John and I need to talk. I'm happy to help with the kids, as his friend and because they're great kids, but they seem to think that John and I are, well, a couple. Amy has even been asking me about wedding dresses and whether she and Thomas can be in the wedding party. John has to talk to them and make them understand that he and I are just friends."

"But are you?" Bessie asked.

Doona blinked hard. "I wish I knew what John was thinking," she said softly. "He's become far too important to me, him and the kids. I don't want to get my heart broken, but it may be too late for that."

Bessie patted her arm. "As you say, you need to talk to him."

"Yes, but we never seem to find the time to talk. Obviously, we can't talk at work, but when we're together, the kids are always there. Thomas stays up later than John most nights, so it isn't as if we can tuck them up in bed and then have a serious conversation. There simply isn't any time."

"You should have had him drive you tonight."

"He's coming straight from the station. I had the afternoon off."

"Maybe it's time for Amy and Thomas to spend a night here," Bessie suggested. "I'd love to have them, and then you and John could have that conversation."

"Maybe you should suggest it to John. Not the part about him and me talking, but the part about having the kids, anyway."

"I'll do that tonight. As I said, I'd love to have them."

"I'm sure they'd enjoy staying here as well. Even in winter, the beach is beautiful."

"Is seeing John every day at work difficult?" Bessie asked.

"It's just frustrating. I have so many things I want to say to him and I can't. I took a message in to him in his office this morning, and I very nearly grabbed him and kissed him. He just looked so gorgeous, sitting at his desk with his jacket off and his shirt partly unbuttoned. He would have fired me, no doubt."

"He might have because it wasn't appropriate behaviour for work, but maybe not because of the kiss."

Doona smiled "I'd love to believe that you're right about that."

"Let's see what I can do about having the children for a night," Bessie said. "Maybe, instead of having a long talk with the man, you could simply kiss him."

Doona blushed again. "I'm not sure I'm that brave."

Another knock on the door had Bessie getting back on her feet. Hugh rushed in and gave Bessie a big hug.

"They're coming home tomorrow," he said loudly. "Grace and the baby are coming home tomorrow."

"That's good news," Bessie said.

Hugh looked at her with a wild expression in his eyes. "I'm not sure about that. I don't know anything about looking after babies. I know Grace's mum will be there for a few days, but she might want to sleep some time, and I know Grace will have to sleep, too. What if they leave me in charge of the baby?"

Bessie and Doona exchanged glances and then they both began to laugh.

"You'll be fine," Bessie said, patting Hugh's back. "No one knows what to do with a baby when they first have one. You'll work it all out eventually."

"But she's so tiny," he said in a low voice.

John knocked before Bessie could reply. Hugh sat down next to Doona as Bessie opened the door. John came in carrying a large box full of takeaway containers.

"It smells good," Bessie said as John began to unpack the box.

"I hope it is good. I've not heard very good things about this place," John replied. "I would have gone elsewhere if I'd had time."

"How bad can it be?" Bessie asked.

She passed out plates and everyone filled them from the various containers. Doona got drinks for them all and then they sat down together to eat.

"This one isn't bad," Bessie said after a while, gesturing towards one of the items on her plate.

"Yeah, I liked that one," Hugh agreed. "That was about the only one, though."

"Some of it is barely edible," Doona said.

"I am sorry," John replied.

"It isn't your fault," Bessie said stoutly. "Where is this new restaurant?"

"It's right across from the station," John said. "In that space that no one stays in for more than a few weeks."

"That's the good news, then," Doona laughed. "They'll be gone soon."

"I certainly hope so," Bessie said, pushing her plate away. She'd only eaten a few bites, but she didn't want any more. Even Hugh, who was always hungry and would eat anything, struggled to clear his plate.

"I'm glad I brought extra fairy cakes," Doona said as Hugh cleared the table. "I thought John could take the leftovers home for the children, but we can eat them all to fill ourselves up instead."

Bessie took a chocolate and a vanilla fairy cake. They were delicious and helped fill the void that dinner should have sorted. When she was finished, she made tea and served everyone.

"Are we ready to talk about Phillip Tyler, then?" John asked.

"I'd really rather not," Hugh said. "Finding the body myself makes the case feel too close to home."

"And it did happen just down the beach from your house," John said. "I hope that isn't worrying you?"

"No, not really. Grace's mum said a few things, but I think I was able to reassure her. The holiday cottages were all sitting empty, whereas we have neighbours in residence on both sides. We also have much better locks on our doors and we're not far away from the main road. The whole incident has reminded everyone that we did have a murder in our house once, but the new baby has everyone pretty well distracted."

"Babies have a way of doing that," John replied.

"So, where should we start?" Bessie asked.

"Means, motive, opportunity," Hugh rattled off the list.

"The local paper already printed the fact that the knife used in the murder was one from the cottage itself," John said. "Maggie Shimmin was happy to share that fact with Dan Ross after she identified the knife for us."

Bessie made a face. "So the means were at hand once someone had broken into the cottage."

"Yes, and breaking in wasn't much of a challenge," John said. "Someone simply forced the front door open. He or she damaged it so badly that it wouldn't close properly afterwards. I suspect that the killer held the door shut with something while he or she was in the cottage, but then simply left the door ajar on the way out. There was a large mixing bowl on the floor in the kitchen that would have been suitable for that purpose."

"Did Callum find the door open when he arrived, then?" Bessie asked.

John made a face. "Believe it or not, he climbed in through a window. He broke the small window on the side of the cottage and then climbed inside. Did you see his interview in the paper today?"

Bessie frowned. "I forgot to get the paper when I was at the shop earlier."

Doona cleared away the plates from the fairy cakes while Bessie got up and filled a plate with biscuits. It was a good thing she'd bought more. She was still hungry, so no doubt Hugh was starving.

"Callum sold his story to Dan Ross," John sighed. "It's pretty graphic, all about climbing into the completely dark cottage not knowing that death lurked in the shadows."

"There aren't any shadows when it's completely dark," Doona said.

"Yes, well, tell that to Dan Ross. That isn't the only thing he got wrong in the article, but I can't talk about the rest," John replied.

"So Callum climbed in a window?" Bessie repeated.

"Yes, although Dan glossed over that part and didn't bother to mention that Callum was in the cottage illegally," John said.

"I'm surprised Callum didn't try the front door first," Bessie said. "That seems as if it would have been easier."

"Easier, but more exposed. The front door faces the road, and even though it's a short road that doesn't go anywhere other than past the cottages, he was probably worried that he might be seen. Only someone walking on the beach in the middle of the night could have seen him climbing in through that side window."

"And no one walks on the beach in the middle of the night in December," Bessie said.

"Except for us," Hugh added with a wink.

Bessie took a biscuit and nibbled on it while she thought. "You're sure Callum had nothing to do with the murder?" she asked John.

"As sure as I can be under the circumstances. He has a solid alibi for the time of death, and if he had been involved, I can't imagine why he would have gone back to the cottage hours later. I believe he simply broke in, looking for a place to stay for the night. I doubt he'll do anything like that ever again."

"Where is he staying now?" Bessie wondered.

"With a friend," was all that John could or would tell her.

"So if Callum is off the list of suspects, who is on that list?" Doona asked.

"Pretty much everyone on the island who can't provide an alibi," John replied. "While I was busy interviewing Phillip's family and friends, Dan Ross tracked down his ferry crossing. Phillip arrived on the ferry at six o'clock the evening he died. He hired a car at the Sea Terminal. We found the car on the main road near the cottages. The mileage suggests that he drove straight there from Douglas."

"So he must have arranged to meet someone at the cottage," Doona suggested.

"Or told someone he was going to stay there for the night," John said. "What we don't know is why he'd select that holiday cottage for a meeting or to stay in overnight."

"Maybe he didn't choose it. Maybe the killer did," Hugh said. "The killer must be someone on the island, so it would make sense for Phillip to let him or her make the plans."

"So whom would he have journeyed back to the island to meet in secret?" Doona asked.

"Nicole Carr," Bessie said. "She was his ex-girlfriend. She cheated on him, which is why he'd left the island in the first place."

"If he left the island to avoid her, surely he wouldn't arrange to meet with her now," Hugh argued.

"Maybe she rang him and told him that her husband was abusing her, or that she'd realised she'd made a terrible mistake and begged for a second chance," Doona suggested. "If he'd stayed off the island for two years just to avoid accidentally bumping into her, he may well have still had feelings for her."

"I'm fairly sure that he did," Bessie said. "We should also think about her husband."

"Liam Kirk," John supplied. "They have a house together, but he also has a flat of his own."

"That suggests they're having difficulties," Hugh said.

"From what Phillip's mother said, Phillip wouldn't have taken Nicole back under any circumstances," Bessie said.

"Maybe Liam didn't know that," Doona said.

"I don't suppose Liam has an alibi?" Bessie asked John.

"While everyone has given me some sort of alibi, I don't believe any of them are completely solid. For the sake of this discussion, let's assume that any of the susp, er, witnesses could have been at the cottage when Phillip arrived," John said.

"So Nicole killed him because he wouldn't take her back or Liam killed him because he was going to take Nicole back," Hugh said. "Those are both strong motives, in my opinion."

"They're certainly strong enough to keep both parties on my short list," John replied.

"What about Phillip's family?" Doona asked.

"His mother, Rebecca, was heartbroken. I won't even consider her as a suspect in her son's death," Bessie said.

"I'm inclined to agree with you," John said.

"She and her husband, Peter, both seemed shocked that Phillip was even on the island. He was angry, while she was hurt, but I can't believe that either of them were aware of his visit," Bessie added.

"He has a sister, Madison," Hugh interjected.

"She's coming to visit me tomorrow," Bessie said. "Rebecca rang earlier and asked if she could. Apparently, Madison seems to think that I can solve her brother's murder by speaking with her and some of Phillip's friends."

John frowned. "You know I don't like you spending time with witnesses during investigations."

"I couldn't say no. The poor girl is devastated and wants to feel as if she's doing something to move the investigation forward. I can meet with her somewhere else if you don't think the cottage is safe."

"I may just have to pop over tomorrow," John muttered.

"I'll come," Doona offered. "I have the afternoon off and the kids both have activities after school, so they won't need rides anywhere until after five."

John frowned. "I'm not sure I feel any better about you being here than Bessie," he said. "You're both important to me."

Doona blushed bright red and looked down at the table.

"Doona could hide in the dining room and just observe," Hugh suggested. "Then, if anything goes wrong, she could ring 999."

"Let's worry about that later," Bessie suggested. "For now, having not seen Madison in a great many years, I'm reserving judgment as to whether or not she's the killer. From what her parents have told me, she seems incredibly unlikely, but they wouldn't be the first parents to be blind to their children's faults."

"You said she was going to bring some of Phillip's friends with her?" John asked.

"That was what Rebecca said, but she didn't give me any names," Bessie replied.

"His closest friend was Harry Holt," John said.

"As I understand it, Phillip and Harry had a massive falling-out when Phillip decided to move away. Peter, Phillip's father, didn't know if they'd even spoken since Phillip left," Bessie said.

"He probably isn't going to be much help, then," Hugh said. "Unless he was the one person whom Phillip told about his return visit. Maybe Harry convinced Phillip that it would be fun to surprise everyone else, and then lured him up here and killed him."

"That seems a bit extreme," Doona said. "I understand that he was angry that Phillip had left, but murdering him when he came back feels over the top."

"Not speaking to the man for two years seems over the top to me," Bessie said thoughtfully. "I understand being upset that he was leaving, but I would have thought that supporting your friend, especially as he was going through a difficult time, would have mattered more than anything else. With email and texting and everything else available today, they could have easily stayed in touch, even at a distance."

"I hope he does accompany Madison tomorrow," John said. "I'll be interested in hearing your opinion of him."

Bessie wanted to ask a million questions, but she knew better than to bother. "I talked to Oliver Preston today," she said instead.

"How did that happen?" John asked.

"Remember how I told you that he wasn't given a room at Christmas at the Castle? We had someone drop out, so Mark and I went to see Oliver and offer him the space."

"Does that mean he'll be taking part?" was John's next question.

"No, he turned us down."

"Why?" Doona demanded. "I thought all of the charities involved made quite a lot of money last year."

"They did, but the focus is on the island, and Mark wanted Oliver to agree to use the money raised from Christmas at the Castle to help people in need on the island, rather than elsewhere. Oliver didn't want to agree to any restrictions."

"What do they do, exactly?" John asked.

"They fund things that people might struggle to afford during cancer treatment. Things that aren't necessities but still matter, like wigs or books or maybe even a weekend away," Bessie told him, remembering the letters she'd read in Oliver's office.

"Surely there are plenty of cancer patients on the island who could benefit from that sort of assistance," Doona said.

"There are, but Oliver has his own way of selecting whom to help, and where people live isn't part of his criteria, or so I believe."

"What did you think of Oliver?" John asked.

"I'd met him once or twice before," Bessie replied. "There's something about him that suggests used-car salesman, but he's always very nice, really."

"He reminds me of George Quayle," Doona said.

Bessie nodded. "George is far more obvious, but there are similarities. Of course, Oliver is raising money for a good cause where George was always all about making money for himself, but they have similar personalities."

"I didn't realise you knew Mr. Preston," John said to Doona.

She shrugged. "I knew him years ago, but I haven't seen him in five years or more. We, um, we went out a few times, but it wasn't anything serious."

"No?" John asked.

Doona looked at him, her cheeks turning pink as she shook her head. "We had dinner together twice, I believe. It may have been three times, but after that he began to pressure me to have him back for coffee." She used her fingers to put quotation marks around the last two words. "It wasn't long after my first marriage had ended. In fact, it was my ex-husband who introduced us. I wasn't ready to get involved with anyone at that point, not seriously, so I ended things."

"On good terms?" John asked.

"I believe so. It wasn't acrimonious or anything. The next time he rang me, I simply said I didn't think things were working, and he never rang me again. That's how I remember it anyway. He may tell a different story, if he even remembers me. I suspect he's had a fair few women in his life since then."

"What about Dylan Collins?" John asked.

"I never went out with him," Doona said firmly. Everyone laughed.

"He seemed a bit dim," Bessie said. "I don't believe that I'd ever met him before, and I was surprised that he'd taken over for Phillip. Being Oliver's assistant is a big job and he didn't seem up to the challenge. At least that was the impression I got from the short time I spent with him."

John nodded and made a note. "He was working for The Liliana Fund when Phillip was there, though. He did know Phillip."

"Maybe he was worried that Phillip was going to want his old job back," Hugh said.

"That's a possibility," Bessie mused. "As I understand it, Dylan only worked part-time before Phillip left, so his leaving was good for Dylan."

"Do you think that Oliver would have taken Phillip back?" Doona asked.

"There were definitely some hard feelings there," Bessie told her. "Apparently Phillip left just before an important event, which made things difficult for Oliver and probably for Dylan, too."

"Would they have held a grudge over that for two years?" Hugh asked.

"As motives go, it's pretty weak," Doona said. "It's enough to keep them on the list, though, isn't it?" she asked John.

He nodded. "I'm not crossing anyone off the list just yet."

"Who else haven't we discussed?" Bessie asked.

"Rebecca gave me a list of Phillip's friends," John replied. "I'm working my way through it, but thus far I haven't found anyone who was more than just a casual acquaintance, really. None of them seem to have heard from Phillip since he'd left, and none have admitted to contacting him, either."

"It's always possible that it was something random," Hugh said. "Maybe he walked into the cottage and found someone already there."

"Surely he would have just apologised and left," Bessie said. "I'm not even sure why he was in Laxey at that cottage. If he didn't want anyone to know he was on the island, he could have arranged to stay at any number of hotels around the place. Nearly everyone has vacancies this time of year."

John nodded. "If we knew why he was in Laxey, we'd probably be closer to identifying the killer. My instincts say that he was here for an arranged meeting. That's what makes the most sense to me, anyway."

"And he was probably meeting one of the suspects we've discussed," Hugh added.

"Witnesses," John corrected him.

"Yes, of course," Hugh laughed.

"I'm going to spend tomorrow chasing down the last of Phillip's friends," John said. "Hugh, I believe you're going to be using the first day of your paternity leave, aren't you?"

Hugh shrugged. "I can work for a few hours in the morning and only take half a day, if that's okay with you."

"You know I won't complain if you want to work," John told him. "Make sure you have Suzannah track your hours."

Doona made a face. "I can do it for you," she said to Hugh.

"It's Suzannah's responsibility now," John said. "She's had the necessary training. It isn't meant to be your problem any longer."

"I don't mind doing it," Doona replied. "At least then I know it's been done correctly."

"Suzannah will do it correctly," John said. "If she makes any mistakes, we'll sort them," he added.

Doona chuckled. "You don't seem all that confident in her doing it right the first time."

"She has to learn the process. It may take her a short while to master it," John replied.

"As she hasn't mastered answering the phones yet, I'm not optimistic," Doona said quietly.

John sighed. "She's getting better, or at least she's trying to get better. It isn't as if we had dozens of qualified applicants for the position."

"If she spent less time flirting with the constables and more time paying attention to her job, I wouldn't mind so much," Doona said.

"Has she been flirting with the constables?" John asked.

"She's been flirting with you, too," Doona said. "I can't believe you haven't noticed."

"She's just friendly," John waved a hand. "She's far too young for me."

"She is a flirt," Hugh interjected. "She even flirts with me, even though I'm married."

"I'll have a word with her," John sighed.

"Leave your office door open when you do," Doona advised.

John looked surprised and then nodded slowly. "Maybe I'll have a word with all of the reception staff at the same time."

Doona laughed. "I'm pretty sure Mary hasn't been flirting with anyone," she said.

"Mary?" Bessie asked.

"She's a retired woman who used to work at the Douglas station. She's helping out up here since we're so short-handed," Doona told her. "She's sixty-eight and has never been married."

"Surname?"

"Corlett."

Bessie nodded. "I know her, not well, but I know her. She was something of a flirt when she was a teenager, actually, but I can't imagine her behaving in that way now."

"Suzannah is a problem, though," Doona said. "One that may take some sensitive handling."

John nodded. "I'll talk to her tomorrow. I wasn't aware of the situation. You really should tell me about these things, you know."

"I don't like to complain about coworkers," Doona replied.

"Especially since everyone will think you're getting special treatment because you and John are, well, friends," Hugh said.

Doona and John both flushed. "I don't give anyone special treatment," John said tightly.

"No, of course not," Hugh replied quickly. "It's just that Doona spends a lot of time with your kids and, well, some of the staff have commented on it, that's all."

John nodded. "Maybe it's time I stopped relying on Doona so much."

Bessie frowned at the sad expression that passed over Doona's face. "I could quit my job," Doona said quietly.

"No one wants that to happen," John replied. "All of the young constables love you."

"Because I buy biscuits and let them tell me about their problems with women," Doona said. "I'd be easy enough to replace, though, and I don't need to work, not for a while, anyway."

"You wouldn't be at all easy to replace," John replied. "Look at the trouble we're having now. Mary won't do any more hours than she's already doing and Suzannah still has a lot to learn. Please don't quit, not until Suzannah is ready to take your place, anyway."

"Only ten years to go," Doona muttered.

Bessie laughed. "I'm sure it won't be that bad," she said, "but all of this has reminded me that I wanted to invite the children to stay with me one night," she told John. "Maybe one night next week? I thought we could bake American Christmas cookies and have a late-night stroll on the beach."

"They'd probably both love that," John replied.

"Maybe you and Doona could go and do some Christmas shopping together," Bessie suggested. "I'm sure she has some ideas about what the children would like from Father Christmas."

Doona laughed. "Their lists are far too sophisticated for Father Christmas. I don't think the elves can manage fancy electronics or trendy clothing."

"And I don't have a single thing bought for them yet," John sighed. "I'd really appreciate your help with some shopping."

"See if they want to stay here for a night," Bessie urged him. "Do it when Douglas is having a late-night opening so you and Doona can get a lot done."

John nodded. "I'll let you know. I can't promise anything because of the murder investigation, but if we get that wrapped up, I'd love to take you up on the offer."

Bessie grinned at Doona. She'd done her best to get her friend a night alone with John. If they managed it, it would be up to Doona to make good use of the time.

CHAPTER 7

$\mathcal{B}$essie slept late the next morning, not waking up until six-fifteen. She frowned at the clock and then decided that she was entitled to the extra minutes after everything that had happened lately. After breakfast, she headed out for her walk, taking her time to enjoy the empty beach. Time seemed to pass much more quickly these days than it had in her youth. She knew it wouldn't be long before the beach was once again crowded with holidaymakers. The police tape around the last cottage seemed to be flapping gently in the wind. Bessie kept going, to the stairs to Thie yn Traie, and then turned for home.

"Ah, Bessie, there you are," Maggie Shimmin said as she marched down the beach towards Bessie. "You're late today."

"Am I?" Bessie replied.

"Yes, by at least fifteen minutes. You're never late. Are you feeling okay?"

"I'm fine. There's been rather a lot going on lately, though."

Maggie nodded. "For all of us, of course. Thomas and I have been trying to work out what to do next with that last cottage. If we can't get permission to tear it down and build a larger cottage, we may just tear it down and leave the space empty, at least for now. We were also discussing selling that plot of land, but I'm not sure we could get permission to do that, either."

"I've no idea."

"Anyway, my back has been bothering me terribly, so I went and saw the doctor yesterday. He's given me three separate prescriptions to try to help things. I'm nearly losing my mind trying to keep track of which tablet to take when, but the pain is a bit better today, anyway. Thomas is nearly back to normal, but still very weak, so he isn't any help with anything at the moment. I've been thinking about starting the winter refresh by myself, as it needs doing and the sooner we get started, the better."

"You need to paint all of the cottages, don't you?" Bessie asked.

"Yes, all of them. I don't quite know what people do in the cottages on their holidays, but every single one of them needs a fresh coat of paint. We need to replace the flooring in one of the cottages, too, as it was allowed to get completely soaked by one of the last sets of guests who stayed there. I suppose I should be grateful they didn't stay in the first weeks of spring, otherwise we might have had to shut the cottage and turn people away while we were having the floors redone."

"The cottages are a lot of work, aren't they?"

"Far more than I expected when Thomas suggested that we have them built," Maggie said with a hint of bitterness in her tone. "On the other hand, what do you think of this?" she asked, holding out her wrist.

Bessie looked at the gold watch that appeared to be studded with diamonds. "My goodness, it's lovely," she lied politely.

"I won't tell you what it cost, but it's real gold and those are genuine diamonds," Maggie said with a giggle. "Thomas said I could have a little treat since we had such a good summer season this year. Last year I got the car, of course, so this year I chose jewellery."

Expensive and gaudy jewellery, Bessie thought. "So the cottages are doing well for you," she said.

"Oh, yes, they're very nearly worth the hard work. Of course, we could probably get a good deal of money for the land if we decided to sell up and retire. I'm not sure I could stand having Thomas at home all day, every day, though. He's been difficult enough while he's been ill. Perhaps we need to keep the cottages so that he's kept busy."

"Well, I wish you good luck with planning permission on the last cottage, anyway."

"I don't suppose you know when Inspector Rockwell is going to be finished with it."

"I have no idea."

"That's a shame. I'd really like to get back to clearing it out, but the police don't seem to be in any hurry to take down their tape and let us back inside."

"I'm sure they're working as hard as they can to find the killer."

"They aren't going to make us wait until they've arrested someone to get back into the cottage, are they? That could take ages."

"As I said, I know they're working hard. If I speak to John later today, I'll ask him about the cottage on your behalf."

"I'd appreciate that. Now I really must dash. I've so many things to do, especially if we're going to be getting back into that cottage later today."

"I didn't say that," Bessie protested as Maggie rushed back up the beach. Although Bessie was certain that Maggie had heard her, the other woman didn't acknowledge Bessie's comment.

Sighing, Bessie turned and headed for home. John could deal with Maggie, she decided, planning to ring him the moment she got back to Treoghe Bwaane. The phone was ringing as she stepped inside the door.

"John asked me to ring to let you know that I'll be coming over around half one," Doona told her when she answered. "He wants me there when Madison visits. It's up to you whether I hide in another room or simply join in the conversation."

"I'm not comfortable with you hiding somewhere," Bessie said. "That doesn't seem fair to Madison or anyone else who comes with her. We'll simply tell them that you came by for a chat. If they don't want to talk in front of you, we'll have to make other arrangements for another time."

"Sounds good," Doona replied.

"I saw Maggie Shimmin this morning," Bessie told her. "She wants to know when John is going to be done with the last cottage. She and Thomas are trying to clear it out while they wait for planning permission to tear it down."

"I can ask him about it when he comes in," Doona replied. "I suspect he'll say something along the lines of being done when he's done and not before."

Bessie chuckled. "That sounds about right."

"Are you asking him to hurry on Maggie's behalf? If you're asking him for a favour, I'm sure he'd speed up as much as he can."

"Oh, goodness, no. I told Maggie I would ask, but I never offered to try to expedite things. As far as I'm concerned, John should take his time and be absolutely certain that he's finished before he turns the cottage back over to Maggie and Thomas. Once they start clearing it out, any missed evidence will be lost forever."

"I'll talk to him when he comes in. He's not starting until ten today because he has a morning meeting with the chief constable."

"Is everything okay?" Bessie always worried when the chief constable was involved.

"As far as I know, everything is fine. He often meets with the chief constable during murder investigations."

"So I'll see you later," Bessie wound up the conversation.

"As I said, I should be there around half one."

Bessie put the phone down and checked the clock. She had a few hours to fill before she needed to get lunch. Onnee's letters called her name loudly and clearly.

"Dearest Mother," the next one began. Bessie started her transcription on a clean sheet of paper, eager to find out what happened next to the young woman. When she was finished with the sheet, she had tears in her eyes.

Onnee had written to confirm that she was indeed pregnant again. The letter was full of her excitement as she talked about feeling the baby move for the first time. The rest of the letter was full of sadness, though, as Faith had ended her relationship and was now spending even more time with Clarence. Onnee was certain that they were sleeping together and she hinted to her mother that she might not be the only one pregnant with Clarence's child. It was heartbreaking to read, even though it had all happened fifty years ago.

Bessie put the letter down and headed for the kitchen. She'd spent longer than she should have with Onnee. Lunch would have to be something quick. As she put her sandwich together, she couldn't get Onnee out of her mind. *Would my own life in America have followed a similar path?* she wondered. Her sister had had ten children during the course of her marriage. If Bessie had married Matthew, she might have ended up as mother to her own large brood.

While she'd been born on the island, soon after Bessie's parents had made the choice to emigrate to the US. She'd only been two years old when they'd made the sea crossing. Fifteen years later, when they decided to return to the island, she'd wanted to remain behind. Her sister, two years older, had been allowed to marry the man she'd been involved with for years. Katherine had remained behind in the US to raise her family there. Bessie had begged her parents to be permitted to do the same. She and Matthew Saunders had only known one another for a few months, but she was certain they'd be happy together. After much debate and many tears on Bessie's part, her parents had insisted that she return to the island with them, leaving Matthew behind.

The sea journey had been long and difficult and the family had struggled with how much the island had changed during their years away. Bessie had been elated when Matthew wrote that he was coming to the island. He told her that he couldn't live without her. As she had just turned eighteen, there was nothing to stop them marrying and returning to the US, whatever her parents thought. Matthew fell ill on the voyage, however, and passed away not long before the boat he was travelling on docked in Liverpool. Bessie had been devastated, blaming her parents for the loss of the man she'd loved.

When she received word that Matthew had written his will just before he'd sailed and that he'd left all of his worldly goods to her, Bessie had taken her small inheritance and bought herself her tiny cottage on the beach. It already had the name Treoghe Bwaane, which means widow's cottage in Manx. That felt appropriate to Bessie as she'd mourned her loss. Now, so many years later, Bessie often wondered how life with Matthew might have been. She still felt sad about Matthew's untimely death, but she had no regrets about staying on the island and living out her life in her little cottage on the beach. Matthew was very much on her mind when Doona knocked a short time later.

"Hello," Doona said, greeting Bessie with a hug,

"How are you?" Bessie asked.

"I'm doing better, I think. John is eager to have that evening of Christmas shopping you suggested, anyway. I don't think he's realised that it will also give us an evening alone together."

"You need it."

"We do. Harvey rang last night."

"Harvey rang? What's wrong?"

"He was a bit vague, but I gather, from what John and the kids said after the call, that Sue has fallen ill. Harvey insisted that it's nothing serious, but that Sue didn't want to worry them, so she had him ring instead."

"Which is instantly more worrying."

"Exactly," Doona sighed. "For a highly intelligent and well-educated man, Harvey can be incredibly stupid sometimes. From what John said, he didn't seem to understand why the children didn't really want to speak to him. Apparently, Sue was sleeping but she'd asked Harvey to ring before she went to bed for the night."

"How very odd."

"John keeps insisting that everything is fine, but I'm sure that's for the children's benefit."

"Can he ring Sue directly?"

"She and Harvey are sharing a mobile phone while they are away. That was deemed the most cost-effective option, apparently. John really doesn't want to talk to Harvey again. He said it was quite awkward last night."

"I'm sure it was."

"Anyway, we're both carrying on as if everything is fine, for the sake of the children."

"Did John ask Harvey when they might be coming back to the UK?"

"Harvey gave him a vague answer about the new year, which isn't any help at all, really. I think the kids handled it all better than John did, really. We're doing our best to make sure they feel loved and secure here."

A knock on the door interrupted the conversation. Bessie shrugged as she glanced at the clock. It was quarter to two.

"I'm so sorry. We're very early. I couldn't wait any longer," the girl at the door said.

Bessie nodded. "You're more than welcome, although I have a friend here at the moment. She can move into another room if you want privacy."

"I couldn't care less," the girl replied before she burst into tears.

The man behind her in the doorway put his arm around her. "It's okay," he said softly.

She shook her head. "It's never going to be okay again."

Bessie stepped back. "Come in, please," she invited. As the trio made their way into the kitchen, Bessie studied them.

The girl had to be Madison Tyler. She was probably quite pretty when she wasn't crying. Her brown hair had been pulled back into a ponytail, but strands were coming out in every direction. Her eyes were brown, but they were red-rimmed and swollen. She was slender and wearing a black dress that seemed too old for her.

The man rubbing her back looked to be a few years older than Madison, maybe approaching thirty. A slightly crooked nose kept him from being classically handsome, but gave his face character. Both he and the other man were wearing jeans and sweatshirts advertising different brands of athletic shoes.

As Doona moved an extra chair into the room, Bessie looked at the other man, whom she assumed was Harry Holt. His brown hair was thinning on the top, and his eyes were hidden behind thick glasses. He too looked as if he'd been crying, although he seemed to be doing everything he could to keep back the tears as he looked around Bessie's kitchen.

"I'm Doona Moore," Doona introduced herself. "As Bessie said, I'm happy to wait elsewhere while you talk."

"You can stay," Madison said dully after she'd introduced herself. "I'm sure the whole island is discussing my brother's death. None of us are going to say anything here that hasn't already been said in the local paper or on the local radio news."

"I'm sorry for your loss," Bessie told Madison.

She nodded and then wiped her eyes and blew her nose with a tissue that Bessie provided. "It's been unbelievably difficult," she said in a low voice. "I'd be lost without these two." She glanced at the men and then flushed. "Sorry, this is Luke, my, well, my boyfriend, and Harry Holt."

Bessie offered her hand to each man in turn.

Luke smiled at her. "It's nice to meet you," he said. "I've heard a lot about you in the short time I've been on the island."

"How long have you been here?" Bessie asked.

"Just about three months, just long enough for me to realise that I don't ever want to leave," he replied.

"From where did you come over?" was Bessie's next question.

"Dad was in the army and Mum was American, so I've been all over the world, really. The island is the first place that feels as if it's home, which is odd but wonderful. Maybe some of that is because of the people I've met, though." He rubbed Madison's back and then rested his head on hers for a moment. Madison managed a weak smile.

"I was Phillip's closest friend," Harry told Bessie. "I let him down because I was too proud to admit that I'd behaved like an idiot. I'm afraid his death was my fault."

"How could it have been your fault?" Bessie asked as Madison made a derisory sound.

"If we'd still been friends, he might have told me that he was coming back to the island for a visit. I might even have met his ferry and given him a ride wherever he was going. He would have been safe with me."

"It's no use speculating about such things," Madison said emphatically. "I was his sister and he didn't tell me he was coming for a visit. He probably wouldn't have told you, either. Anyway, if the killer wanted him dead, it wouldn't have mattered."

"Let's sit down," Bessie suggested. "Tea?"

"Tea would be wonderful," Madison replied. "Nothing helps, but at least tea gives me something to do with my hands."

Doona made the tea and put biscuits on a plate while Bessie sat down with the others.

"As I said, I'm sorry for your loss. I'm not sure why you wanted to talk to me, but I'm glad I've been given an chance to offer my condolences," Bessie told Madison.

"This is the first time I've ever been involved in a murder investigation, but you do this all the time," Madison replied. "I know you've helped the police find the killer on more than one occasion, too. I want your help working out what happened to Phillip."

"I have been involved in several murder investigations, but never intentionally," Bessie told her, "and I do my best to let the police handle the cases."

"I thought maybe, if we just told you everything we could think of about Phillip, you could put it all together and come up with a motive," Madison told her. "I can't think of a single reason why anyone would want to hurt Phillip. It simply doesn't make sense."

"I'm happy to listen to anything you want to tell me," Bessie replied.

"Phillip was older than me by five years," Madison began. "In my eyes, when I was smaller, he was almost another parent to me. It wasn't until I was older, maybe six or seven, that we began to bond as siblings. He was already old enough to have lots more freedom than I did, and I used to beg to be allowed to go with him when he went outside to play or over to visit friends. I'm sure it drove him crazy, but he never once complained when I tagged along with him."

"Harry, you didn't know Phillip in those days, did you?" Bessie asked.

Harry shook his head. "We met on our way to uni. Neither of us knew anyone else going to the school we'd chosen, so we quickly became good friends, united by a sort of shared history of growing up on the same small island."

"Phillip was the perfect older brother and I was inconsolable when he went away to uni," Madison continued. "I used to count down the days until he'd be home on breaks and I actually counted down the entire three years until he'd graduate, as well."

Luke patted her arm. "I was thrilled when my sister went away to school," he said. "She and her friends used to fill up the entire house all weekend long, laughing and talking about things that I didn't understand. I'm eight years younger, and the gap meant that we never really became friends, although I love her dearly now."

Madison nodded. "I was thrilled when Phillip finished school and came back to the island, although I was disappointed that he decided to get his own flat rather than move back into the family home. Of course, I headed off to uni myself not long after that. I used to ring Phillip every Sunday evening just to chat. I'd ring Mum and have a long talk with her about classes and exams and all the boring things, and then ring Phillip and tell him the really interesting things that were happening. He heard about the boys and the late-night parties." Madison laughed. "At the time I thought I was doing outrageous things, but now when I think back, all of it was pretty tame, at least compared to some people."

Luke shrugged. "She's saying that based on a few stories I've told her about my days at uni," he admitted. "I did two years in the US and two years here. The US years were by far the wildest. I joined a fraternity, and we did a lot of drinking and partying. My marks were so bad that my parents made me transfer to a university in the UK where they could keep an eye on me. I'd learned my lesson, anyway, and once I got there, I knuckled down and worked hard."

"And after school you moved back to the island?" Bessie asked Madison.

"I did. I rented a flat in the same building where Phillip was living, and we used to spend a lot of time together."

"So much so that I got jealous," Harry admitted. He shrugged. "I barely knew Madison when she first moved back, and then once I got to know her, well, I sort of had a thing for her for a while. Phillip told me that he didn't want me going out with his sister, which made me angry."

Madison flushed. "I never knew that," she said. "I once asked Phillip if you were available and he told me that he didn't think we were right for one another. I never thought about it after that."

Harry sighed. "We could have had a great romance," he said lightly.

Madison looked at Luke. "If things don't work out, I have options," she teased.

"Things are going to work out," he replied seriously, sliding his arm around her. "I'm not losing the best thing that's ever happened to me."

Harry frowned and then looked down at his teacup. Bessie wondered if Harry was still carrying a torch for his friend's younger sister.

"Anyway, I came home and got a job and life was good," Madison said. "Then Phillip met Nicole."

"Cue the villainous music," Harry said.

Madison nodded. "I never liked her, although she seemed nice enough at first. I never thought she was genuine, though. There was just something about her, something unpleasant or untrustworthy."

Bessie reached for a biscuit as Madison drew a deep breath.

"I'm not being fair. That's hindsight talking. When Phillip first brought her home, she seemed lovely. In the first few months they were together, Nicole and I became friends. We used to go shopping together on a Saturday afternoon once in a while. Eventually, after she'd moved in with Phillip, that stopped, but it wasn't for any specific reason. We were just busy with other things, or at least, that's how it seemed. I didn't realise that she was busy sleeping with other men."

Luke took her hand as Harry growled. "I wish I'd known what she was doing. When it all came out later, she'd been cheating for over a year. Phillip wouldn't have been as upset if he'd found out in the early days."

"He might have been," Madison said. "He was already crazy about her, even from the first few months."

Harry nodded. "I barely saw him once he'd met her, actually. We went from spending every Saturday together to seeing each other once or twice a year, almost overnight. I didn't like Nicole for that reason, but I never imagined that she was cheating, not until much later."

"So what happened?" Doona wondered.

Bessie got up and topped up everyone's tea and refilled the biscuit plate. As Madison had said, the refreshments were giving everyone something to do with their hands, if nothing else.

"Phillip was talking about proposing," Madison replied after a moment. "He wanted to get married and start a family. It was when he started dropping hints to Nicole that their problems started."

"He mentioned marriage and she told him that she didn't think she was ready," Harry interjected. "Then she told him that she had to go away for work for a few days. That wasn't unusual. She travelled a lot for work, mostly for training. This time, though, after she'd left, Phillip realised that she'd forgotten her passport."

"Where was she meant to be going?" Bessie asked.

"She'd told Phillip she was going to Paris. When he rang her mobile, she claimed she was in Paris having a boring time at meetings. When he asked about her passport, she told him some elaborate story about not needing it because she was with a group from the same hospital or some such thing. After Phillip put the phone down, he rang Noble's and found out that no one else was away."

"He moved his things into my flat before she got back," Harry said. "He couldn't stand the thought of seeing her again, but he couldn't bring himself to throw her out, either. That was at the same time as the charity in the UK started trying to recruit him."

"It was the perfect job for him, really," Madison said sadly. "One that he knew he'd love and that would make good use of his talents and training. The charity was smart enough to realise that as well. He was hired based on a phone interview, before they'd even met him."

"So he moved across," Bessie said.

"It wasn't quite that simple," Harry interjected. "Nicole came to see him at my flat. She tried to insist that it wasn't what it seemed. She told him that she'd simply needed to get away, so she'd gone to the UK to visit a friend. Phillip almost believed her, too, but by that time I'd tracked down the man with whom she was cheating."

"Liam Kirk," Madison spat out the name as if it were poison.

"When Phillip said his name, Nicole burst into tears. She told him a dozen different lies about how long she'd known him and when they'd met and all sorts, but I'd done my detective work and I'd already told Phillip the whole story. Nicole eventually left in tears, still swearing that she'd done nothing wrong."

"Phillip left a week later and less than a month after that Nicole married Liam," Madison said. The way she said "Liam" almost sounded like a curse.

"I hear they aren't happy together," Harry said, sounding grimly satisfied. "He has a flat in Douglas now, even though they still have a house together in Foxdale."

"They live in Foxdale?" Bessie asked. She knew someone who lived in Foxdale, and it was a small community. No doubt Joney would know Liam and Nicole and would have something to say about their relationship.

"That's where Nicole grew up, I believe," Harry said. "Liam is from across, but he has family on the island. He moved over to work for his uncle who has a gym in Douglas."

Bessie nodded and made a mental note to ring Joney. "I understand that Phillip told everyone he was never coming back," she said.

Harry flushed. "He did say that. That was what we fought about."

Madison leaned across the table to pat his hand. "You were angry. You both said things you shouldn't have said. You would have made up eventually."

"I don't know about that," Harry sighed. "I was being stubborn and stupid. Phillip rang me twice after he left, but I never rang him back. I was too angry that he'd gone to try to understand why he'd needed to leave."

"Did he ring you recently?" Bessie asked.

"No, not recently. He rang about three months after he'd moved and left a long message about his new life. He told me that he was finding it difficult settling into a new place and finding new friends, but that he was sure he'd made the right choice. He rang again about six months later. This time he just left a short message to say that he missed me and that he'd like to hear from me. I..." he stopped and cleared his throat, swiping at his eyes with his hand. "I ignored both messages," he said finally.

"He was adamant about not coming back," Madison said. "I went over to see him three times and he always refused to discuss coming home even for a short stay, let alone moving back. I was seriously considering moving there for a while, not just because I missed Phillip but also for the job opportunities, but then, well, things changed and I decided to stay here."

Luke smiled and then winked at Madison.

"Did he ever mention having any problems over there?" Bessie asked. "Problems with work or in his personal life?"

"He didn't have much of a personal life," Madison said sadly. "That's one of the reasons why I was thinking of moving there, actually. Phillip was friendly with the people where he worked, but they never did things together outside of the office. He refused to consider getting involved with another woman, too. I'd hoped if I were closer to him that I could drag him out once in a while."

Bessie nodded. "When did you speak to him last?" she asked.

Madison blinked and then shook her head. "I'm not sure I can talk about that, not yet."

"Did Phillip ever say anything about problems with any of his jobs on the island?" Doona changed the subject.

Madison frowned and looked down at her teacup. "I need some fresh air," she said. "Can we take a walk on the beach and talk?" she asked Bessie.

"Of course," Bessie agreed.

"You two can wait here," Madison told the men. "We won't be long."

Luke objected, but Madison just shook her head and then walked with Bessie to the door.

CHAPTER 8

*B*essie and the girl walked to the water's edge and then turned and began a slow stroll along the sand. Madison didn't speak for several minutes. When they reached the first holiday cottage, she stopped.

"I'm not sure I want to see the cottage where, well..." she trailed off and then swallowed hard. "Maybe we could walk in the other direction."

"The tide is coming in. There isn't anywhere to walk in the other direction," Bessie replied. "Let's just go and sit on the rock behind my cottage. We can talk there."

Madison nodded and fell silent again. It wasn't until the pair were both settled on the large rock that she spoke.

"I don't know Harry well enough to say some things in front of him," she told Bessie. "He and Phillip were incredibly close, but they only met after Phillip had left home. I never really got to know Harry, not well. I'm sure it would be fine, but I'd rather talk to you privately about some things."

"What things?"

"Phillip didn't talk about work much. He was good at what he did, raising money for good causes, but he didn't really tell me much about his job. He could talk for hours about whatever charity he was working with at any given time, but he never complained about going to meetings all day or having a difficult boss, or anything like that. Am I making any sense at all?"

"I think so," Bessie replied, patting Madison's arm. "He would talk about the causes, but not his day-to-day routine."

"Yes, that's right. I never really gave it much thought, but when the police inspector interviewed me after, well, you know, he asked me about Phillip's bosses and coworkers over the years and I had to admit that I didn't know very much about any of them."

"Was Phillip friendly with his coworkers?"

"Friendly but distant might be the best answer. He had this thing about keeping his work life and his personal life separate. Fundraising is difficult work and it can be stressful, especially when it involves big charity events and that sort of thing. Phillip wanted to leave work at the office so that he could relax when he was at home."

"That makes sense."

"As I said, I'm sure he was friendly with his work colleagues, but I don't believe that he saw them outside of work. That may have changed when he moved across. I'm not sure."

"So you don't know anything about anyone at work with whom he may have had problems?"

"Not really, although I know there were some issues with Oliver Preston."

"Were there, now?" Bessie asked.

"I know Oliver. We, um, went out a few times back when Phillip was working with him. Phillip introduced us at one of the fundraisers they held not long after Phillip had started working there."

"Was it a great romance?"

Madison laughed. "Not even close. We kept it really casual for the first few months. It was slightly awkward, Oliver working with Phillip, I mean. Things got a little bit serious later, and then, well, then we stopped seeing one another."

"I don't want to be nosy, but I'd like to hear the whole story."

"There isn't much of a story to tell. As I said, it wasn't much of anything at first, and then after a few months, Oliver suggested that we stop seeing other people. I hadn't been seeing anyone else, so I didn't object."

"Why hadn't you been seeing anyone else if you and Oliver were just casual?"

"I just hadn't," Madison shrugged. "I know some people seem to have men in and out of their lives all the time, but I've always seemed to have trouble finding good men and then keeping them around. Things are going really well with Luke so far. I'm keeping my fingers crossed."

"What happened with Oliver, then?"

"I'm not really sure. We were spending more and more time together, and I was starting to take a real interest in the work that The Liliana Fund does, until one day he cancelled our plans on short notice. I was a little angry. We were meant to be having a romantic dinner at my favourite restaurant for my birthday and he rang me half an hour before our booking to tell me he couldn't make it. He never rang me again."

"Had you had an argument when he cancelled?"

"No, that's the weird part. I was disappointed, but he told me that something had come up at work, and I tried to be understanding during the phone call. I planned to shout at him a bit the next time I saw him, but I never got the chance."

"That seems odd."

"It does, now that I'm talking about it. At the time, I was hurt and confused, but when I think back it was odd behaviour."

"Did Phillip get angry with Oliver for upsetting you?"

"He wasn't happy, but I made him promise not to treat Oliver any differently, regardless."

"But you said that he and Oliver had problems."

"They did, but later. I'm trying to make sure that you know everything that might be relevant. I can't imagine why my short-lived relationship with Oliver matters, but I suppose it may have coloured Phillip's feelings towards Oliver to some extent."

"You were Phillip's baby sister. I'm sure he was angry with Oliver for treating you badly."

"He didn't treat me badly, not really. He should have taken the time to end our relationship in person, or at least rung me again to tell me it was over, but I can't complain about how he treated me when we were together. Anyway, that was all at least a year before anything else happened."

"What happened next, then?"

"As I said, Phillip didn't talk about work much, but one day we met for a drink after work and he seemed really upset. When I asked him about it, he said that there'd been an issue with one of the grants they'd awarded. The man who was meant to be getting the money had never received the cheque or something. Oliver was tracking it down and I'm sure it was all sorted in the end, but it upset Phillip at the time."

Bessie nodded slowly, trying to think. Was it possible that Oliver was doing something illegal or immoral with his funds?

"That was about the same time that Oliver hired Dylan Collins. Dylan and Phillip had never liked one another, so that made things difficult."

"When you say never, do you mean that they knew each other before Oliver hired Dylan?"

"Yes, Dylan's grandmother had a house near ours. He used to visit on weekends and sometimes he would join in games with Phillip and the other boys on the street. Phillip didn't like him and the feeling was mutual."

"Did Oliver know that they had a shared history?"

"Yes, Phillip told Oliver at least some of the background when they interviewed Dylan for the job, but Oliver still hired him, in spite of Phillip's feelings."

"That must have made things awkward for Phillip."

"It did, but he loved his job, so he stayed even after Dylan was hired. He managed to make it work for almost a year, too. Then things blew up with Nicole and, well, you know the rest."

"Was Oliver upset when Phillip left?"

"I only ever heard anything secondhand, but I believe he was pretty angry. Phillip left just before their biggest fundraiser of the year. I know my brother would have done his best to make the transition as smooth as possible, but I also know that he was heartbroken and not necessarily performing as well as he should have been."

"Did Phillip tell you anything about his job in the UK?"

"Not really. I did meet one or two of his colleagues on one of my visits, when I met him at his office one evening, but only briefly. They both seemed pleasant enough, but we didn't really speak. Phillip didn't tell me anything about them, other than what they did at the charity, really."

"So if his death had something to do with work, Oliver or Dylan seem to be the most likely suspects," Bessie concluded.

Madison stared at her. "I can't get my head around that," she sighed. "I can't imagine anyone I know killing Phillip, or anyone else for that matter. Murder is something that happens in books or on telly, not in real life."

"I wish that were true."

"I know you've been through this a number of times. Do you ever get used to the idea that people are capable of killing other people?"

"I suppose I find it easier to believe now that I've seen so many examples of it," Bessie admitted. "Often the motives are the most shocking part. People kill other people for the oddest reasons."

"I know Dylan never liked Phillip, but murder? I don't know."

"Let's try looking at it from a different angle," Bessie suggested. "Whom would Phillip have come back to the island to see?"

Madison nodded slowly. "That's an excellent question." She shivered and then sighed. "Let's go back in the house and ask the others that question. Harry might have a better answer than I do."

"No one," Harry said emphatically as Bessie put her question to the group.

Doona had made a pot of coffee while Bessie and Madison had been outside. Bessie took a long drink of the lovely hot liquid before she replied.

"But he did come back," she pointed out.

"Maybe he was brought here against his will," Harry suggested.

"That's the only thing that makes sense."

"I believe the newspaper has tracked his arrival at the Sea Terminal," Bessie replied. "From what I've been told, Phillip was alone when he disembarked and hired a car."

"Maybe he thought someone he loved was in danger," Doona suggested.

"Nicole," Harry said loudly. "If she rang and said she was in danger, he'd have come back to help her. He was still crazy about her."

Madison shook her head. "You hadn't spoken to him in two years," she reminded him. "I know he was still badly hurt, but I think anger had replaced love in his feelings for Nicole. If she'd rung him to say she thought she was in danger, I think he would have told her to ring the police."

"But the sneaking around and meeting in an empty cottage might have been to avoid Liam," Harry suggested. "He wouldn't have wanted to start a fight with that man."

"Liam is a kick-boxer," Madison told Bessie. "He's nationally ranked, I understand, or he used to be, anyway."

"Phillip would have come back if he thought you or your mother or father needed him," Luke told her, squeezing her hand.

"But who would have told him that we needed him?" Madison demanded. "If he was worried about any of us, he would have rung to speak to us directly. I can't imagine someone ringing to say we needed help and Phillip just rushing to the ferry without giving the matter any thought. He wasn't like that."

"No, he'd have rung you straight away," Harry agreed. "If someone rang and told him that you had all been injured in a car accident or something, he'd have rung me or one of his other friends to confirm before he'd rush to catch a ferry back here."

"What if one of his former work colleagues needed something?" Bessie asked.

Madison opened her mouth and then shut it again. After a moment, she nodded slowly. "I can almost believe that he'd come back here to help Oliver. I can't imagine why he'd feel as if he had to keep the visit a secret, though."

"Maybe he was planning to surprise you all," Luke said.

"That wouldn't have been like him either," Madison replied. "Phillip didn't like surprises, not giving or getting."

They talked for a while longer about Phillip's childhood friends, neighbours, and former girlfriends. Eventually, Madison looked at the clock and sighed.

"It's getting late. We should go. I wish I felt as if we'd accomplished something."

"You've given me a number of things to think about," Bessie told her. "I'll be discussing everything with John Rockwell later today or tomorrow. Maybe, just maybe, he'll spot something that will help him solve the case."

"I was hoping you'd work it out while we were here," Madison admitted.

Bessie swallowed a laugh. "It isn't that easy, I'm afraid. I'll talk to John. What I'd really like to do now is meet Nicole Carr and Liam Kirk. I don't suppose any of you know where they work?"

"Nicole works at Noble's. She's a nurse, which was one of the things that Phillip loved about her. He thought she was kind and caring and special," Madison said scornfully. "Liam is part owner of the gym in Douglas, the one that specialises in kick-boxing and other martial arts."

"I can't imagine finding a reason to go there," Bessie murmured.

"Maybe I could be interested in joining," Doona suggested. "I'm sure after a single class I'd have a reason to visit Noble's as well."

Everyone laughed.

"Nicole may be at the memorial service," Madison said.

"When and where is the service?" Bessie asked.

"It's tomorrow," Madison replied, naming the small church in Port Erin as the location. "We're going to have a reception in the church hall after the service. You're more than welcome to attend."

"I may," Bessie replied. "Do you really think that Nicole will come?"

"She'd better not," Harry said darkly. "I blame her for Phillip's death, no matter who actually killed him."

"Let's reserve judgment on that until the police work out exactly what happened to Phillip," Madison said. "In answer to your question," she told Bessie, "yes, I can see Nicole turning up. I don't think she ever truly appreciated the seriousness of what she did to Phillip, and I believe she's just stupid enough to think that she'd be welcome as someone mourning his loss."

"What about Liam?"

"I can't see him coming," Madison said. "He'd hardly be able to claim that he was mourning Phillip in any way."

"Did Phillip and Liam know each other at all before Phillip found out that Nicole was seeing him behind his back?"

"I don't believe so. Phillip wasn't the type to try kick-boxing and Liam isn't the type to do much else," Madison replied.

"How well do you know him?" Doona asked.

Madison shook her head. "I've never even met him."

"I have," Luke offered.

Madison stiffened. "You have?"

"When I first moved to the island, I wanted to join a gym," Luke replied. "I went around three different ones in Douglas. Liam gave me the tour and sales pitch at his gym."

"What did you think of him?" Bessie wondered.

"At the time, I simply thought that he was much the same as the men who gave me tours at the other two gyms. He wasn't terribly bright, but he knew a lot about fitness and exercise. The facilities were okay, but not the newest or nicest that I saw. That wouldn't have put me off, but it was clear that the emphasis was on the various martial arts and that wasn't what I wanted."

"Did he mention his wife at all?" Bessie had to ask.

Luke frowned. "Give me a minute. All three places are sort of jumbled up in my head at the moment."

While he was thinking, Bessie turned to Harry. "Have you ever met Liam?"

"Once, when he came with Nicole to collect her things from Phillip's flat. Saying that I met him is an overstatement, though. I was there when they came over and I stood and stared daggers at the pair of them as Nicole grabbed the box that Phillip had packed and left."

"He did mention his wife," Luke said. "We were talking about the benefits of joining a gym and he said something about it being a good place to meet women. He said he'd met his wife at his gym and then he said something about her being attracted to him because he was the owner, or some such thing. I didn't pay that much attention, sorry."

"You couldn't possibly have known it would matter," Madison said, patting his arm.

He beamed at her and then covered her hand with his.

"Is there anything else any of you want to discuss?" Bessie asked.

The trio exchanged glances with one another. After a moment, Madison shrugged. "Maybe you'll learn more at the memorial service tomorrow."

"I certainly hope so," Bessie replied. "Don't be surprised if Inspector Rockwell rings any or all of you with questions based on what you've told me. He often notices little things that turn out to be significant."

"It's peaceful here," Madison said, looking around the kitchen. "I feel better here than I have since I heard about Phillip."

"You're welcome to come and stay for a few days," Bessie told her, feeling a rush of sympathy for Madison. "I have a spare room, one that used to be occupied on a fairly regular basis by guests who wanted to escape from something."

Madison nodded. "I've met a fair few people who grew up in Laxey. They all talk about running away to Aunt Bessie's to get away from their parents and their problems. I may take you up on that offer one of these days. I'll ring first."

"You could always stay with me for a few days," Luke suggested.

"Maybe," Madison replied, flushing and looking at the ground.

"I have a spare room at the moment, too," Harry said. "Although I wouldn't blame you if you didn't want to stay with me, not after the way I treated Phillip."

"I don't blame you for being angry with Phillip. We were all upset with him for leaving the way he did, really. I was quite annoyed that he wouldn't come back, as well. I hated having to deal with Mum and Dad on my own." Madison sighed and then slowly got to her feet. "We'll get out of your way," she told Bessie.

"You're always more than welcome," Bessie replied.

"But your friend must be tired of listening to our troubles," Luke said, nodding at Doona.

"Your troubles make mine seem small indeed," Doona replied.

Bessie walked the trio to the door and then let them out. Doona joined her in the doorway, and they watched them walk to the car that was in the small parking area next to the cottage. Luke helped Madison into the passenger seat as Harry climbed into the back. Once Luke was behind the wheel and had started the car, Bessie shut her door.

"You need to ring John," Doona said as Bessie began gathering up plates and cups.

"I may ring Joney first," Bessie replied. "She knows everyone in Foxdale, after all."

Doona nodded. "I thought of her when Harry first mentioned Foxdale. Wasn't she a teacher?"

"She was, so she may well know a great deal about Nicole, anyway."

Doona started the washing-up while Bessie dialled Joney's number.

"Hello?"

"Joney? It's Bessie Cubbon."

A loud laugh greeted her words. After a moment, Joney cleared her throat. "I was just saying it wouldn't be long before Aunt Bessie rang me," she said. "I reckon you want to know all about Nicole Carr, don't you?"

"I do indeed."

Joney chuckled again. "I should make you buy me tea and a cake somewhere nice in exchange for that information, but I'm too busy right now for such things."

"I'd be happy to buy you tea and cake anytime."

116

"It'll have to wait at least a fortnight," Joney told her. "My William is taking me on holiday tomorrow. We're going to Greece, him and me and his girlfriend. He said I deserve a treat for all the years I spent looking after him. I reckon it's his girlfriend who's putting ideas in his head, but I'm not complaining, am I?"

"I should hope not."

"She's lovely, anyway, and she lost her own mother a few years back, so she appreciates me in a way that William doesn't."

"I'm glad things are going well for you," Bessie said sincerely. She liked Joney and her sister, Bahey. The sisters were more than a decade younger than Bessie, but they had grown up in Laxey and knew many of the same people. Bahey had never married, although she did have a man in her life now. Joney was a widow who'd taught school both before her marriage and after her husband's death. William was her only child.

"Better for me than for young Nicole, I reckon," Joney said. "I never did like her, and I can say that now that I'm retired."

"You did teach her, then?"

"I tried to teach her, but she wasn't much interested in learning. As I said, I didn't care for her, but she was just one of hundreds of children who didn't like school and made no effort to hide that fact. Her parents had a house about four doors from mine, though, which means I got to know her rather better than most."

"Did you get on with her parents?"

"They were okay. Again, not much for book learning, but her father worked hard at the local garage and her mother kept the house clean and tidy. They were pleased when she took up nursing and from what I've heard she did okay with her studies at that, anyway."

"What else can you tell me about Nicole?"

"She was ever so pleased with herself when she started seeing Phillip Tyler," Joney said. "He'd been to uni and everything. She seemed to settle down, too, not that she'd been all that wild, to be fair. I was surprised when it came out that she'd been cheating on him. I'd spoken to her once or twice about Phillip and she always seemed to be crazy about him."

"What about Liam Kirk?"

"That man should have a warning label tattooed on his forehead," Joney replied.

"Why?"

"He's some sort of boxer, but that hasn't hurt his handsome face. He's superficially charming, but it wouldn't surprise me to hear that he smacks Nicole around now and then. Not that anyone has suggested that he does. I just think he's the type that would. You may have guessed that I don't like him."

"Do they live near you?"

"Thankfully, no. They're almost as far away from me as anyone can be and still be in Foxdale. Nicole's parents moved away a while back, so I don't really see Nicole or Liam very often. I've heard stories, though."

"That's why I rang you," Bessie laughed.

Joney chuckled. "I have a friend who lives across the road from them. She told me that they fight nearly all the time. Not just little disagreements, either, but huge screaming rows where one of them ends up slamming out of the house and driving away with tyres squealing."

"Oh, dear."

"Exactly."

"I don't suppose your friend knows what the fights are usually about?"

"Well, last year a lot of them seemed to be about whether or not they should have children, or at least that's what my friend told me. She said Nicole wants kids but Liam doesn't. He likes being able to do whatever he wants whenever he wants and he reckons kids might get in the way."

"He's probably right about that."

"Unless he simply ignored them and let Nicole handle it all on her own, which is likely."

"You said that was last year. Have the fights changed, then?"

"Just in the last few months my friend said they've been fighting more about other things. She said it's almost always something different every time they argue. One night they fought about the brand of toothpaste that Nicole bought at the shops and another night Liam stormed out because Nicole hadn't ironed the shirt he wanted for the next day."

"My goodness. It sounds as if they'll argue about anything and everything."

"Apparently they do just that. Lately, as in the past week or two, my friend reported hearing Nicole say that she was sorry she'd ever met Liam and that she should have stayed with Phillip, who'd treated her much better than Liam does."

"And what did Liam have to say to that?"

"My friend said that he told her to get on the ferry and go find Phillip if that was how she felt. He said he'd happily file for divorce once she'd gone."

"She should have gone."

"I agree. Liam already has a flat in Douglas that he uses several nights a week. It wouldn't surprise me to learn that he has at least one girlfriend who is staying over at the flat when he's there."

"I'll never understand women who sleep with married men."

"As I said, he's superficially charming. I'm sure Nicole thought he was wonderful before she married him."

"Enough so that she was willing to cheat on Phillip."

"Yes, exactly that."

"Has your friend ever seen any evidence that Liam is physically abusive?" Bessie asked.

"No, she hasn't. I keep expecting it, really, but so far the abuse has all been verbal."

"And Nicole just lets him yell at her?"

"Oh, no, she gives as good as she gets. The abuse goes both ways in that relationship."

Bessie sighed. "Why don't they just divorce and move on with their lives?"

"I didn't think you'd approve of divorce."

"I don't, usually. Many times I think couples see it as an easy answer, far easier than working together to make their marriage work, but when either or both parties are abusive, for whatever reason, divorce seems justified."

"Yes, well, as I said, this is all secondhand information, but from what my friend says, the relationship is pretty grim."

"Can you tell me anything else about them?"

"Just that things have been very quiet at the house since Phillip's murder. My friend thinks Liam has been staying in Douglas, and she hasn't seen Nicole except from a distance. She's been trying to think of an excuse to go over and try to talk to her, but she hasn't come up with one yet."

"I suggest she stay away from both Nicole and Liam until Phillip's killer is behind bars."

"Yes, I suppose that's good advice. I can't see Nicole killing anyone, but Liam might. Phillip wasn't killed with some weird martial arts technique that doesn't leave a mark, was he?"

"No, he wasn't."

"What a shame. I suppose if he had been, Inspector Rockwell would have already had the case all wrapped up, though. I'll ring you back if I think of anything else or if my friend rings again before I go. Otherwise, you owe me a cuppa when I get back from Greece."

"That sounds good. I'll look forward to hearing all about Greece."

Bessie put the phone down and then told Doona what Joney had said. "And now I must ring John and tell him all of that again," she sighed when she was done.

When she reached him, John offered to come to Bessie's cottage. "It will probably be easier to speak to you in person, rather than over the phone," he said.

Bessie put the kettle on while they waited for John to arrive. When he did turn up, she did her best to repeat everything that Madison and the others had said before telling him about her talk with Joney. John took extensive notes.

"What did Harry and Luke have to say while Bessie and Madison were outside?" John asked Doona when Bessie was done.

"Nothing much," Doona replied. "Mostly they talked about football. I made coffee and kept quiet."

"That isn't like you," John teased.

Doona chuckled. "It wasn't easy, but I was hoping one of them would say something relevant to the murder investigation."

"But they didn't?" John checked.

"Not unless the defensive line in the England squad has something to do with the murder," Doona sighed.

"A few new things to consider, anyway," John said as he shut his notebook. "The memorial service tomorrow may be interesting. Take Doona with you," he told Bessie. "I'll be there as well, officially."

"So we'll see you tomorrow around two," Bessie said as John got to his feet.

Doona stood up and followed John to the door. "I should go and get some dinner," she said.

"You're welcome to come home with me," John invited. "Amy is making shepherd's pie again. Last time it was only barely edible. If there are more of us, we can make it look as if more was eaten this time."

Doona laughed. "What a tempting invitation."

"Is that a no?"

"It's a yes. I'd love to have dinner with you and the kids," Doona told him.

Bessie studied the pair as they walked back to their cars. Doona said something that made John laugh and left Bessie thinking that they were good together. Hopefully they'd both reach the same conclusion soon.

She made herself some dinner while she went back over everything that she'd learned that day. An idea had occurred to her while she'd been talking to Madison, but she wasn't certain it was a good one. The more she turned it over in her head, the more it sounded as if it were worth pursuing. That meant talking to one of her least favourite people in the world, though.

It was too late to worry about anything for that evening, so Bessie curled up with a book for a few hours. Unless she could think of an alternative, she'd make a final decision in the morning.

CHAPTER 9

*B*essie woke up with a sick feeling in the pit of her stomach. Her subconscious had been unable to come up with a better plan, which meant she was going to have to seek out someone she generally tried to avoid. She made a face at herself in the mirror as she combed her hair.

"It doesn't matter what you wear," she told herself as she stood in front of her wardrobe. She was aware that she'd pulled out a slightly nicer jumper than what she might normally have chosen. After a quick breakfast, she headed out for her walk.

Having reaching Thie yn Traie in what felt like only a few steps, she continued onwards at a rapid pace. It was only when the new houses came into view that she slowed down and had stern words with herself.

"It's no use trying to walk away from the idea," she scolded herself in a low voice. "If the idea has merit, you'll simply have to grit your teeth and get through it. Otherwise, just drop the whole thing." The more Bessie thought about, the more she felt that the idea was a good one. After briefly considering discussing it with John, she decided it would be better not to mention it to him. He'd probably feel as if Bessie was meddling in the investigation, even though she was simply trying to find out more about something that was bothering her.

She'd walked past the new houses by the time she'd reluctantly decided it was time to return to Treoghe Bwaane. She turned around and retraced her steps, smiling as Grace's mother slipped out of Hugh and Grace's home through the sliding door at the back. She was carrying the baby, and Bessie picked up her pace to join the woman as she dropped into a chair on the small patio.

"Good morning," Bessie said softly. The baby was wrapped up warmly against the cold December air, which meant Bessie couldn't see if she was awake or asleep.

"Good morning. No need to whisper. Baby Watterson doesn't seem to need very much sleep," Grace's mother replied with a sigh. "You're welcome to join us," she added, nodding towards the other chairs.

Bessie sat down and gave her a sympathetic smile. "I take it you're not getting much sleep?"

"I went to bed around nine and got a few good hours of sleep while Hugh and Grace were still up. Grace was then up and down with the baby every two hours or so until I finally took her away at four. When my children were small, we fed them on a schedule, which meant mums could get a few hours of sleep between feeds. I appreciate that feeding on demand is kinder to the baby, but sometimes I think babies just cry when bored or windy, not hungry. Grace is making herself crazy trying to feed the baby every time she whimpers."

"I can't imagine," Bessie murmured.

"Anyway, Grace fed her at four and then I took her into my room. She just woke up a short while ago, and we've come outside for some fresh air so that she can't wake her mother until she's properly hungry."

Bessie looked at the baby, who was staring out at the world with unfocused eyes. "She's beautiful," Bessie said.

"Here." The other woman handed the tiny bundle to Bessie, who was too surprised to refuse.

"Well, hello there," Bessie said.

The little girl looked up at her and then stared, seemingly trying to recognise Bessie.

Grace's mother sat back and sighed. "If we can keep her quiet for another hour, Grace and Hugh might get enough sleep to function for at least part of the day."

"I don't know how people do it. What do they do if they don't have family on the island?"

"I've no idea. My mother moved in with me when I had my first. She stayed for six months until the baby was sleeping through the night most nights. I don't intend to stay here that long, but I'm happy to help while I can."

"I know Grace and Hugh are grateful to you."

"I hope so. I'm sure they think I'm pushy and that I have old-fashioned ideas about taking care of babies, but I don't think I did my children any harm."

"Your children are lovely. I'm sure ideas change all the time when it comes to baby care, but I doubt many of the new ideas make much difference."

"Putting the baby on her back to sleep is just about the only one that seems to really matter. We used to put babies on their tummies, but apparently putting them on their backs is much safer for them. Baby Watterson doesn't seem to care how she's put down. She naps for a few minutes or maybe an hour and then wakes up and cries."

"I don't believe it," Bessie said as the baby lay peacefully in her arms. "She's not making any fuss now."

The words were barely out of Bessie's mouth when the baby suddenly began to squirm as her tiny face scrunched. Noises emerged from inside the blanket and then, as the baby began to cry, an unpleasant odor hit Bessie's nose.

"I think she needs a new nappy," Bessie said.

Grace's mother laughed. "When she isn't eating, she's filling nappies. I'd forgotten that about babies." She stood up and took the baby from Bessie. "It was nice talking to another adult," she said. "Even if all we talked about was babies."

"She's a very special baby."

"Yes, she is at that," the woman agreed. She turned and headed back into the house with the sobbing infant while Bessie got back to her feet. The chat had been a nice interlude, but she still had the very unpleasant task ahead. She marched home, keeping her eyes focussed on the sea so that she wouldn't notice the police tape around the last cottage. When she was back at Treoghe Bwaane, she rang her car service.

"I need to go into Douglas," she told the dispatcher who'd answered the phone.

The car arrived only a short while later, although Bessie would have been happy to wait a good deal longer. She told Dave, her favourite driver, where she was headed.

He raised an eyebrow. "I've never taken you there before."

"And I hope you'll never take me there again," Bessie replied.

Dave smiled at Bessie and then changed the subject. They chatted about the weather and Dave's wife on the drive into Douglas.

"Do you want collecting later?" he asked as he pulled into the building's car park.

"I'll ring or grab a taxi from the nearest taxi rank," Bessie told him. "I've no idea how long I may be here."

Dave looked as if he had questions for Bessie, but he simply nodded and then got out of the car to help her out of the passenger seat. "I hope things go well," he said as Bessie began to walk away.

"Thanks," Bessie replied. As she approached the door, she began to think that she probably should have rung and booked an appointment. It was too late for that now, though. The large glass door was heavy, and Bessie frowned as she pulled it open. It was almost as if they didn't want visitors, she thought.

"Welcome to the *Isle of Man Times*," the very perky young girl behind the reception desk said. "How can I help you?"

"I'd like to speak to Dan Ross," Bessie said, feeling as if she were choking on the words.

The woman beamed at her. "Is he expecting you?"

"No, not at all."

She frowned. "I'll have to ring upstairs and see if he's available," she said. "May I ask your name?"

"It's Elizabeth Cubbon."

The girl wrote her name very carefully on the sheet of paper in front of her and then picked up the phone at her elbow. "Ah, yes, Mr. Ross. There's an Elizabeth Cubbon here to see you."

After a moment she looked up at Bessie. "She's certainly not young," she said tentatively. Bessie hid a grin as the girl swiveled in her chair. "I don't know, maybe sixty or seventy," she said in a loud whisper. When she turned back around, her face was scarlet. She put the phone down and then cleared her throat. "Mr. Ross will be down shortly," she said. "You're welcome to have a seat."

There were two long couches against the wall. Bessie sat on one of them, frowning, as they were far less comfortable than they appeared. She didn't have long to wait, though, as Dan Ross rushed out of one of the lifts only a moment later.

"Miss Cubbon? This is a completely unexpected surprise. I do hope you're here to finally give me an in-depth interview about all of the bodies you've been finding over the past two years," he said.

Bessie shook her head. "I was speaking to someone about something and I had an idea for a story, that's all. You're the only reporter that I know here, but you may well want to give the idea to someone else." Maybe someone less obnoxious, she added to herself.

"I'm intrigued," the man said. "You could have simply rung and told anyone your idea. That you sought me out suggests there's something more going on here. Come up to my office and let's talk."

Feeling that Dan was rather too clever for her to feel comfortable, Bessie followed him into the lift. It only took a moment to carry them to the third floor. Dan's office was a tiny room, with the smallest window Bessie had ever seen on one wall.

Dan waved her into a chair that was not any more comfortable than the couch in the lobby. He sat down behind the scarred wooden desk and grinned at her. "Be it ever so humble," he said. "Believe it or not, this office is a big step up from where I started. I used to just have a desk in the middle of a dozen other desks. It was only once I'd landed a few big stories that I was promoted into an office of my own."

"Congratulations," Bessie said dryly.

He grinned. "I know you don't like me or what I do, but I feel as if I perform a valuable public service. Anyway, you must agree on some level, because here you are, ready to give me a hot story."

"I'm afraid I'm going to do nothing of the kind. As I said, I have a story idea for you, but it isn't anything exciting."

"I'll be the judge of that."

"I'm sure you know that I'm involved with Christmas at the Castle."

"Yes, of course. I did wonder how ticket sales were going this year. You received quite a bit of publicity last year when your designer got murdered just before the event."

Bessie bit her tongue. There were several inaccuracies in his statement, but there was no use arguing with him. After an awkward pause, she shrugged. "I believe most nights have already sold out. It's a wonderful evening, suitable for the entire family."

"Yes, yes, of course. We have a department that deals with charity events. They'll be giving it some coverage, but it's nothing to do with me."

"Perhaps I need to speak with someone from that department, then."

"Oh?"

Bessie took a deep breath. "I had a long talk with Oliver Preston the other day. His charity, The Liliana Fund, does a lot of good, both on the island and elsewhere. I thought it might be interesting to read an article about the charity in the local paper, that's all. It would be even better if different charities were featured each day for the next few weeks in the lead-up to Christmas. Perhaps some extra money could be raised for good causes before the holidays."

Dan tilted his head and stared at Bessie. "The Liliana Fund," he said thoughtfully.

"Yes, them, but I can give you, or rather someone from the correct department, a long list of charities that could be featured."

127

"I'm sure you could," Dan muttered. His forehead creased and he seemed to be thinking hard. "I need coffee," he announced a moment later. "I'll be right back."

He disappeared out of the room before Bessie could protest. She thought seriously about simply leaving. She'd made the suggestion she'd wanted to make. It was up to Dan to decide what to do with her idea. She was getting to her feet when Dan rushed back into the office.

"Coffee," he announced, handing Bessie a cup. He put his own mug on the desk and then returned to his chair.

Bessie didn't really want coffee, but as she was holding the cup, she took a sip. "This is very good," she exclaimed.

"Our home and garden reporter makes great coffee," Dan told her. "I pay her a small fortune to share it with me."

"Oh, dear. I didn't mean for you to buy me coffee," Bessie said, appalled.

He waved a hand. "Happy to do it. I needed to give your suggestion a bit of thought, you see. You want me to investigate The Liliana Fund, which means you think there might be something illegal going on there."

"Not at all," Bessie protested weakly. She wasn't sure what she thought, actually. A few of the things that Madison had said were worrying, that was all.

Dan nodded. "It can't be coincidental that young Phillip Tyler used to work for The Liliana Fund. His turning up dead, brutally murdered at that, has to be connected, doesn't it?"

"I've no idea."

"Do you suspect Oliver Preston or Dylan Collins?" Dan asked.

"I don't suspect either of them of anything," Bessie replied.

"Dylan was only working for the fund on a part-time basis before Phillip left. I wonder if he found out that Phillip was back on the island and was concerned that he might lose his job. That wouldn't make sense if it were an ordinary fundraising job, of course. If Dylan killed Phillip over his job, it must be because he's doing something dodgy."

Bessie took a sip of her coffee, determined not to speak. After a moment, Dan chuckled and then continued.

"Of course, The Liliana Fund has been Oliver Preston's baby since he founded it after his mother's death. I would find it difficult to believe that Dylan could be doing anything without Oliver's knowledge. That suggests that, if Dylan is doing something wrong, Oliver is just as involved, maybe more so. Phillip hadn't worked with the fund for what, two years, though. Why would he be a threat to either man, even if they were doing something wrong?"

Because Phillip was trying to track down grant recipients, Bessie thought as the idea flashed through her head. Phillip's parents had told her that, hadn't they? She wasn't about to feed that bit of information to Dan Ross, though.

"The next obvious question is why you've come to me," Dan continued. "I'm sure Inspector Rockwell would love to hear about your suspicions, so either you've already told him and he discounted them, which seems unlikely given your track record, or that your suspicions are so ephemeral that you don't want to bother the man with them. Perhaps, if circumstances were different, you'd mention them to Hugh, but of course young Hugh is on paternity leave, isn't he?"

"He is, yes," Bessie said, grateful for a question she was willing to answer.

Dan grinned. "Have you seen the baby yet? Does she look just the same as every other baby ever born?"

"She's lovely."

"Of course she is," Dan laughed. "I decided a long time ago that I didn't want children and I've never had reason to regret my decision."

I think it was a wise one, Bessie said silently. The last thing the world needed was the offspring of Dan Ross.

"Right, so you're suspicious of Oliver and Dylan, but not so concerned as to mention your thoughts to Inspector Rockwell. Instead, you decided to drop it in my lap under the guise of trying to help support a good cause in the lead-up to Christmas. Am I right so far?"

Bessie sighed. "I'm sorry to have bothered you," she said as she got to her feet.

"Oh, don't go. I wasn't really expecting you to agree with me. You're welcome to maintain whatever fiction suits you. Of course, what I really want to know is, what's in it for me?"

"I'm not sure what you mean."

"I investigate The Liliana Fund for you, find out what Oliver and Dylan are really doing with the money they're raising, and in return you give me an exclusive interview about how it feels to find a dead body."

Bessie gasped. "I will do nothing of the kind."

"Okay, how about an interview into how it feels to listen to someone confess to murder? I know you've heard more than your fair share of confessions."

"Thank you for the coffee," Bessie said stiffly. She turned towards the door.

"If you leave, you'll never find out what's really happening at The Liliana Fund," Dan warned.

"Threats are wasted on me, Mr. Ross," Bessie said tartly.

"Please, Miss Cubbon, let's not argue. We can find a middle ground, I'm certain. You want a favour from me. It's only logical that I'd expect one in return."

"Maybe logical to you, but not to me. I came to give you what I thought was a good idea for a story. I actually believed that I was doing you a favour, not the other way around. Perhaps I'll find the person who writes the stories about good causes and see if he or she is interested in pursuing my story idea instead."

"Her name is Jane Stoddard. Her office is just down the corridor from here. Tell her I sent you," he replied in a bored tone.

Bessie nodded and then left the room. She found Ms. Stoddard's office without difficulty. The door was shut and the room was dark. Frowning, Bessie returned to the ground floor.

"May I leave a note for Jane Stoddard?" she asked the girl behind the desk.

"Of course," she said brightly. "What do you want to say?" She held her pen, ready to write.

"I thought maybe I could write something and you could give it to her," Bessie explained.

"Oh, sure, I mean, that would work." She handed Bessie a sheet of paper and a pen.

Sitting back down on the hard couch, Bessie wrote quickly. She was well aware that the receptionist was going to read the note, but it didn't much matter.

Ms. Stoddard,

Dan Ross suggested that you would be the appropriate person to reach out to with a story idea. As Christmas approaches, I thought it might be nice for the local paper to highlight some of the good work that is done by many of the island's charities. My work with Christmas at the Castle has allowed me to meet several incredibly hard-working and dedicated men and women who work for such good causes.

Not wanting to make her interest in The Liliana Fund too obvious, Bessie put it in the middle of a list of half a dozen different charities that she thought might benefit from a bit of extra publicity before ending the note.

I'd be more than happy to discuss any of this with you at your convenience. All the best,

Miss Elizabeth Cubbon

Treoghe Bwaane, Laxey

She folded the paper in half and then in half again before writing "Jane Stoddard" across it. Then she handed it to the receptionist.

"Thank you so much," she said as she returned the pen.

"You're very welcome. Happy holidays," the girl replied.

Bessie turned for the door. As she pulled on the handle, she glanced back to see the receptionist reading through the note she'd just written. Sighing, Bessie left the building and made her way down the steps.

Douglas town centre was only a short walk away, and she'd have better luck getting a taxi there than she would in front of the newspaper building. Bessie headed for the promenade, pulling her winter coat more tightly around her as she went. The wind was cold and almost icy as it blew against her.

"It's a lazy wind," a man walking the other direction told her. "Wants to go right through you."

Bessie nodded and picked up her pace. When she reached the outskirts of town, she walked into the first shop she found, anxious to get out of the cold. It was a card shop and Bessie amused herself by looking through the many cards she couldn't ever imagine actually sending. "From our dog to yours," she read in a bemused voice. "On the occasion of your divorce," she said in surprise. "In sympathy on the loss of your hamster," she muttered before shaking her head and leaving the shop.

Obviously, losing a hamster would be sad, and for some people divorce was a very good thing, but it still seemed odd to her that people actually sent one another cards on such occasions. Cards from dogs to dogs made no sense to her at all.

After wandering around a few more shops, Bessie concluded that there was nothing she needed from Douglas. As she headed for the nearest taxi rank, she stopped to purchase a box of chocolate truffles that she didn't need but that she wanted very much. The ride back to Laxey felt long, as the taxi driver, a stranger to Bessie and new to the island, had very strong opinions on just about everything. Moreover, his opinions were very different to Bessie's, causing her to bite her tongue more than once.

She had a firm rule about not arguing with anyone who was driving her anywhere, no matter what he or she said. The last ten minutes of the journey were spent with Bessie giving very careful directions to him, most of which were ignored until he was hopelessly lost. When she finally got out of the car at Treoghe Bwaane, having paid more than she should have for the unnecessarily extended journey, Bessie found herself hoping that the man would get just as lost on his way back to Douglas. She couldn't resist a small chuckle as she noted that he pulled out of the parking area for her cottage and immediately turned in the wrong direction. He'd have a pleasant enough drive past the holiday cottages and on past

Thie yn Traie, but unless he spotted the turning for the narrow road that led back to the main road, he'd probably end up having to turn around and drive back down to Bessie's to find his way out of Laxey.

After she switched the kettle on, she stood near a window with views of the road behind the house. Sure enough, just a few minutes later the taxi roared past at a dangerous speed. When she heard the siren a moment later, she wondered if it were connected to her taxi driver. After she'd eaten her lunch, she got her answer.

"I'm here," Doona said when Bessie opened the door to her knock. "I had planned to be here not long after midday. I thought we could chat before the memorial service, but it didn't work out that way."

"What happened?" Bessie asked.

"John was following me down here. He wanted another chance to warn you about being careful today."

"I'll have to be careful. You're going to be with me, after all," Bessie pointed out.

"Yes, I know, but John was just being John. Anyway, he was right behind me, waiting to turn down the hill, when a taxi suddenly shot out from the road and nearly hit me. The taxi driver was driving far too quickly, and then he actually honked at me as if I were at fault."

"Was the driver around sixty with grey hair and a grey moustache?"

"Yes."

"He drove me home from Douglas. I hope John gave him a dozen tickets."

Doona laughed. "I don't think it was a dozen, but it was more than one, that's for sure. He was speeding. He hadn't indicated. He had a broken headlamp. He wasn't wearing his seatbelt. There might have been more as well."

"He's also misogynistic, small-minded, and rude."

"I noticed that, actually. When John stopped him, he tried to blame everything on me, saying that I was blocking the road and that he'd had to speed up to avoid hitting me. John very nearly laughed at him, but of course he's too professional to do that."

"I paid him a good deal more than he deserved for getting me home, so I suppose it's my money the police will be getting, not his."

"Speeding tickets are costly," Doona replied. Bessie gasped when Doona told her how much the fine would be.

"I was hoping he would get lost on his way back to Douglas, but even I wasn't wishing that much misfortune on him. Perhaps he'll give up and go back across. Everything was much better there, anyway."

"Yes, he said as much to John when he tried to convince John to take a hundred pounds and forget he'd seen anything wrong. Apparently, that used to work for him back where he'd been in the UK."

"Let's hope he goes back, then, and quickly."

"Anyway, I stayed to give John a witness statement in case he needs one. The man did seem the type to argue about the tickets."

"I hope no one questions your relationship with John if it comes to a court battle."

"John took statements from three other witnesses, actually. He didn't need mine, except mine was the car that was nearly struck. If the taxi driver is smart, he'll pay the fines and then stay out of Laxey."

"I won't get into a car with him again, anyway."

"What were you doing in Douglas?" Doona asked.

Bessie sighed. "I had this idea that someone should investigate The Liliana Fund, but only unofficially. I went to see Dan Ross to suggest it to him."

"You went to see Dan Ross voluntarily?"

"It was miserable, and I won't make that mistake again."

"What did he say about your idea?"

"That he'd conduct an investigation if I gave him an interview about finding murder victims or hearing people confess to murder."

"He's not a nice man."

"No, he's not. He did give me the name of the woman who covers good causes, though. She wasn't in her office, but I left her a note. Maybe she can do an article about The Liliana Fund."

"You don't really think they're doing anything illegal, do you?"

"I'm not sure what I think. I'm probably adding two and two and getting five. Phillip's parents said something about Phillip trying to track down grant recipients when he went across, but they said that he'd actually found one, too. Madison said a few things about Oliver that seemed off, but that may just have been my impression. Considering he'd ended things with her rather badly, her comments are suspect anyway."

Doona nodded. "But you have good instincts for these things. You should tell John."

"I've told him everything that I know. If I am reaching untenable conclusions, well, I'd rather not share them with him."

"I still think you should tell him, but we'll argue about that later. We have a memorial service to attend now."

Bessie glanced at the clock. It was getting late and they still had to drive to Port Erin. "I'll be as quick as I can," she said as she headed for the stairs.

She changed into a black skirt and a dark grey jumper. No other colours would do for a memorial service, at least in her mind. Sliding into black flats, she glanced in the mirror. A bit of lipstick and some powder on her nose were as much effort as she ever made. With her hair neatly combed, she went back down to the kitchen.

"Ready when you are," she told Doona.

"John's going to be there," Doona said as Bessie locked the door to Treoghe Bwaane.

"That's good, although people might be less likely to speak to me if he's with us."

They climbed into the car and Doona headed out of Laxey.

"He's going to stay in the back of the room and just observe. He wants you to have every opportunity to speak to everyone," she said once they were underway.

Bessie grinned. "As long as I'm careful."

"Well, yes. No sneaking away with one of the suspects to chat together in the graveyard or the basement. Why do people insist on doing that in murder mysteries?"

"I don't know. I suppose I can understand it in the first in a series. We weren't terribly smart the first time we were caught up in a murder investigation, after all."

Doona shuddered. "I try not to think about that."

"I do as well, but the important thing is that we learned from our mistake. I know better now than to meet suspects in dark alleys or in empty holiday cottages. The protagonists in some series books never seem to learn from their mistakes."

"Too bad Phillip didn't know better than to meet someone in an empty holiday cottage."

Bessie frowned. "Yes, truly. I have to wonder whom he would have trusted."

"I believe just about everyone who falls into that category will be at the service."

"Yes, and I want to speak with each and every one of them."

CHAPTER 10

*T*he church car park was already nearly full when Doona turned into it a short time later.

"Quite the turnout," she remarked as she pulled into a parking space.

"I wonder how many people came just because Phillip was murdered," Bessie said softly.

"I hope not many. The family members don't deserve to have to deal with curiosity seekers today."

"Speaking of curiosity seekers," Bessie said, nodding towards the man who was climbing out of a car on the other side of the car park.

"Dan Ross," Doona sighed. "I still can't quite believe you went to see him voluntarily."

"I must have taken leave of my senses."

Doona shrugged. "Maybe he'll learn something interesting if he does investigate."

"He won't investigate though, not since I refused to do an interview with him. I'll talk to John about my thoughts, though. I'm sure John will investigate at some point, but he's awfully busy at the moment."

The pair got out of the car and walked into the small church. It was nearly full to capacity, with some people already standing along the walls at the side. Doona frowned and then pushed her way through the people at the back to find somewhere for Bessie to sit. About halfway up the aisle there was a pew with some room near the centre. Bessie and Doona stopped at the end of the pew. An older woman who was a stranger to Bessie glanced at her and then sighed deeply before sliding over a few inches to give Bessie a tiny bit of space.

"Would you rather we climb over you?" Bessie asked. She didn't mind sitting in the centre if the woman preferred to be on the aisle.

"I believe the people on the other side are holding those seats for someone," she was told.

"Well, that's too bad," Doona said. "We'll climb over."

She began to do just that, when Bessie heard her name.

"Miss Cubbon? Come and sit with us," a soft voice said.

Bessie smiled at Madison Tyler. "I'm not family."

"No, but you're a genuine mourner, not like most of these people, who didn't even know Phillip," Madison replied.

The woman in the pew harrumphed under her breath.

"There's room for you and your friend in the pew behind mine," Madison continued. "Please."

"If you're certain," Bessie said. She didn't feel right sitting with the family, but she didn't fancy climbing over the difficult woman in the pew, either.

Madison led Bessie and Doona to the front of the church. They slid into seats, nodding greetings at Rebecca and Peter. Madison sat back down next to her parents, with Luke on her other side. As they waited for the service to start, Bessie identified everyone for Doona.

"The man at the very end of this pew is Harry Holt, Phillip's closest friend," she whispered.

"The one who stopped speaking to him when he moved across?"

"Yes. Oliver Preston is next, and then Dylan Collins."

"The Liliana Fund people."

"Exactly. I'm not sure who the man next to me is," Bessie concluded.

He chuckled. "I'm Paul Harris. Phillip and I were friends in primary school. We hadn't seen one another for ten years or more, but I still felt as if I had to come and honour his memory. He used to share his biscuits with me every day. His mum used to give him loads, and my mother rarely gave me anything but fruit for pudding."

Rebecca obviously overheard. She turned around in her seat. "Phillip asked me to give him extra every day so that he could share with his friends. I always wondered whether he really did share or simply ate the extras himself."

"He shared generously. It wasn't just me who benefited," Paul told her. "There were three or four of us who used to fight over who got to sit next to Phillip in the lunchroom. Some days, Phillip would end up giving away all of his biscuits, rather than eating any himself. I asked him about it once, and he said that he didn't mind because he knew he'd have more tomorrow."

Rebecca blinked hard. "Thank you for sharing that memory."

A moment later the vicar appeared and cleared his throat. When everyone was quiet, he began the service. It was a simple service and a fairly short one. Peter got up and said a few words about Phillip and then invited others to do the same.

"Phillip was my older brother. He was always a part of my life, from the day I was born, and I can't imagine how I'm going to live without him," Madison said. She looked as if she wanted to say more, but after a moment she dissolved into tears and returned to her seat where Luke pulled her close.

"I met Phillip on the ferry," Harry said. "We were both heading to uni for the first time. I was terrified, travelling on my own, which I'd never done before. Phillip was sitting there reading a book, completely at ease while I kept going through my notes, wondering how I was going to find my way into a taxi, and worrying about, well, everything. I was sure, before I spoke to him, that he was several years older than me. We became close friends before the ferry docked and I have many wonderful memories of our university years. I deeply regret that I argued with him when he decided to leave the island. If I could turn back the clock, I wouldn't make that mistake again." He stopped and then wiped angrily at his eyes. After a few deep breaths, he shook his head and walked back to his seat.

"Phillip was a dedicated, hard-working man who did a lot of very good things for The Liliana Fund during the years he was employed there," Oliver said. "I'm grateful that I was able to work with him and for all that he did for my cause."

A few other people spoke, including Paul, who repeated what he'd told Rebecca about the biscuits at primary school. When everyone was finished, the vicar spoke again.

"The family would like to invite everyone who knew Phillip to join them for tea and biscuits in the church hall," he said.

Bessie exchanged glances with Doona. The invitation had been carefully worded, presumably designed to discourage the simply nosy from the genuine mourners.

"I wonder if they'll have someone at the door asking everyone how they knew Phillip," Doona whispered as people began to get to their feet.

"I wouldn't blame them if they did," Bessie replied.

When they walked into the church hall a moment later, Bessie grinned. The family had put a book of condolences right inside the door. The vicar and another man were standing next to it, encouraging everyone to write something before they went any further. Madison was a few steps away, watching everyone as they entered.

"Such a tragic loss," the vicar said to Bessie a moment later. "How did you know young Phillip?"

"Bessie's okay," Madison said. She winked at Bessie. "Having the vicar at the door seems to have discouraged a few people, anyway."

After Bessie had signed the book, she glanced around the room. Madison was right. The vicar did seem to be keeping the crowds away. There were only a dozen or so people in the hall, and Bessie was fairly certain she knew all of them.

"I feel as if I shouldn't be here," Doona muttered as she and Bessie made their way across the room.

"At least you aren't just here to be nosy," Bessie countered, nodding towards Dan Ross, who was filling a plate with biscuits.

"It looks as if he's just here to get fed," Doona replied.

Bessie crossed to Peter and Rebecca, who were standing together in one corner. "I'm so sorry for your loss," she said when she reached them.

"It doesn't feel real," Rebecca told her. "I keep thinking that I'm going to wake up and this will all have been just a bad dream. Sometimes I tell myself that Phillip is just across, busy working, and that he'll ring soon. Sometimes I almost believe it, because that's less painful than believing anything else."

"Whatever helps you cope," Bessie replied.

"I think we'll both feel better when whoever did this to Phillip is behind bars," Peter said gruffly. "How are the police getting on with that, then?"

Bessie opened her mouth to reply, but John Rockwell, who'd come up behind her unseen, interrupted her.

"I can assure you that we're working on the case as hard as we can," he said. "I want Phillip's killer caught as much as you do."

Peter made a face that suggested that he didn't believe John's words. Rebecca shook her head.

"We're getting desperate," she said with tears in her eyes. "We need to know what happened to Phillip, why he was killed, why he was on the island, even."

John nodded. He opened his mouth to reply, but Madison's voice cut him off.

"Get out," the girl said angrily.

Bessie spun around and stared at the woman Madison had addressed. She was tall and thin, with blonde hair and blue eyes. She'd obviously been crying, but her makeup had been expertly applied and hadn't smudged or run in spite of the tears.

"Madison, it's been a while," the woman said. "I was sorry we didn't stay in touch after, well, after."

"I wasn't," Madison said tightly. "You aren't welcome here. Please leave."

"Ah, but I wanted to pay my respects," the blonde replied. "No, that isn't right. I needed to pay my respects. Phillip was the only man I ever truly loved. I lost him due to my own foolishness, but I never stopped believing that we'd be reunited one day."

"That wasn't going to happen. Phillip wouldn't even come back to the island to visit his family because he didn't want to see you. There was no way he'd have ever given you another chance," Madison said bitterly.

"If I'd asked him, begged him, he'd have forgiven me," the other woman said confidently.

Bessie glanced at Rebecca. Her face was pale and she was leaning heavily on Peter's arm. When her eyes met Bessie's she whispered, "Nicole."

"You're married," Madison said.

"A technicality," Nicole replied with a wave of her hand. "One that I would have cleared away in a heartbeat at Phillip's request."

"That's good to know," another voice cut through the room. The man who emerged from the corner was scowling. He looked to be of a similar age to Nicole, with dark hair and eyes.

"Liam," Nicole said, putting her hand to her chest. "I didn't know you were here."

"Clearly," he retorted.

"You told me you had work today," Nicole replied.

"I was at work, and then I started to wonder how the service was going to go. Poor old Phillip was such a dull and ordinary man. I still can't imagine how he managed to get himself murdered. I decided to come down and see for myself how many people could be bothered to turn up to pay their respects."

"The church was full," Nicole told him. "I arrived too late to get a seat and had to stand at the back. As it appears I'm not welcome, perhaps that was for the best."

"Did you really think you'd be welcome?" Rebecca demanded. "You broke Phillip's heart and drove him away from his home and the people who loved him. Because of you, he had to start all over again in a strange place. He was alone and friendless and it was all your fault."

"I never meant to hurt him," Nicole protested. "We never said we weren't going to see other people. I would have agreed, if he'd asked, though, because I loved him."

"No one here is going to believe any of your lies," Peter said. "As far as I'm concerned, you're as responsible for Phillip's death as whoever wielded the knife. That's assuming it wasn't you holding the knife, of course."

"I would never have done anything to hurt Phillip," Nicole protested.

"Except sleep with other men," Liam taunted.

Nicole glared at him. "It wasn't other men, it was just you, and that was back when you were charming and doing everything you could to convince me that life with you would be exciting and fun all the time."

"Life with me has been a lot more fun than it would have been with Phillip," Liam replied. "All you ever did when you were with me was complain about how boring he was, in and out of bed."

It felt to Bessie as if everyone in the room inhaled sharply at Liam's words.

"I think that's quite enough," John Rockwell said. He took a few steps towards Nicole.

"I don't think it's nearly enough," Liam said loudly. "Everyone here is talking about how much they're going to miss Phillip and what a wonderful man he was, but considering he sneaked back onto the island and was hiding out in an empty cottage, he clearly had something to hide."

"Maybe he'd arranged to meet Nicole," someone suggested. "Maybe you found out about it and went in her place."

"What are you implying?" Liam demanded.

"I believe he's implying that you killed Phillip," Madison said tartly.

Liam took a deep breath and then curled his hands into fists. He moved his feet into something like a fighting stance and then glanced around the room. "Anyone here man enough to say that to my face?" he asked.

"I think it's time for you to leave," John said to Liam. He crossed to his side and said a few words in a low voice.

Liam shook his head. "I'm not leaving without Nicole," he said.

"I'm not leaving until I feel as if I've mourned properly," Nicole shot back. "I have so many things that I want to say. Phillip was the most special man I ever met."

"Stop it!" Madison shouted. "You have no right to talk about him, not after what you did to him. Dad was right. His death was your fault."

Nicole stared at her for a minute and then laughed. "You can't possibly blame me for Phillip's death. I didn't even know he was on the island."

"No one seems to have known," Madison said. "Except someone did. Someone who wanted Phillip dead. Maybe you did know, and maybe you didn't tell Liam. Maybe, instead, you met Phillip at that empty house. I can almost picture it, you trying to persuade Phillip to forgive you, him refusing. You must have been incredibly angry."

"Now you're suggesting that I killed Phillip, which is simply impossible," Nicole protested.

"Someone killed him. If it wasn't you, maybe it was Liam," Madison replied.

"Come over here and say that," Liam snarled.

Madison looked defiantly at him. "You would have killed him, if Nicole told you she was going back to him, wouldn't you? Your fragile ego wouldn't have survived if your wife left you for a man you'd deemed boring."

"Nicole wasn't going back to Phillip," Liam laughed. "I'm much better at meeting her needs, all of her needs."

"But you've been having problems," Peter said. "You've even moved out of the marital home."

Liam stared at him for a moment. "The marital home? Who says that? Anyway, I haven't moved out of anywhere. I've simply taken a flat in Douglas so that when the gym is open late I can crash there instead of having to drive all the way to Foxdale. Nicole even stays with me in the flat once in a while."

"I've stayed there once," Nicole said flatly. "I don't have a key, either."

"I can get you a key, if you want one," Liam said.

"He brings other women back there," Nicole told Madison. "That's why he wanted the flat, so that he'd have somewhere to take his girl-friends."

"Why would you put up with that?" Madison asked.

Nicole shrugged. "I'm thinking about getting a divorce. I probably would have already filed if I'd been able to reach Phillip. If he'd have agreed to give me another chance, I was going to leave Liam and move across to be with him."

"You were trying to contact Phillip?" John asked, reaching into a pocket for his notebook.

"I was," Nicole replied. "He'd changed his mobile number, and the person who has that number now claimed he'd never heard of Phillip. I rang Harry, but he never rang me back. I rang Oliver, too. We even met for dinner to talk about Phillip, but after dinner he refused to give me Phillip's new number."

"I told you that I'd let Phillip know that you wanted to speak to him," Oliver said.

"Yes, but it would have been much easier if you'd simply given me the number. I really wanted to talk to him myself," Nicole said with a sigh.

"Did you pass along Ms. Carr's message, then?" John asked Oliver.

He hesitated and then shook his head. "I didn't speak to Phillip very often. He used to ring once in a while, just to see how we were doing, but that had tapered off a lot in the past few months. I think the last time I spoke to him was in October."

"You were really considering going back to that man?" Liam asked, his tone incredulous. "After all the things you'd told me about him?"

"He was kind and caring and he never would have cheated on me," Nicole replied. "We'd have been happy together."

"He would never have forgiven you," Madison said. "He never would have trusted you again."

"I could have changed his mind," Nicole laughed. "I can be very persuasive when I want to be."

"This is pointless," Liam said. "Nicole, let's go."

"I'm not leaving with you," she snapped.

"Well, I'm leaving," he replied. He turned and headed for the door as people scrambled to get out of his way. When he reached the exit, he turned back to Nicole. "I'll just go back to the house and pack my things. By the time you get home, I should be long gone. If you want to discuss anything with me, you can contact me through my advocate."

Nicole stared at him for a minute. "Don't be silly," she said eventually. "I don't want you to go anywhere."

"What, now that Phillip is gone you want to try to make our marriage work?" Liam asked. "I think it's probably too late for that."

"I'm prepared to try, if you're willing to give up your other women."

"You know there aren't any other women. The flat in Douglas is for convenience, not so that I can cheat on you."

"I don't believe you."

Liam shrugged. "You know what? Divorce is sounding better and better." He spun back around and walked out of the building. The room was completely silent as the door swung shut behind him.

"He doesn't mean that," Nicole said, her voice shaky. "He's just angry because he knows how much Phillip meant to me." Tears began to stream down her face as she spoke.

"No one here cares in the slightest whether Liam meant what he said or not," Madison told her. "None of us care if he's cheating on you or if you cry buckets. We all hate you."

Nicole looked as if she'd been slapped. "You were like a sister to me," she said after a moment.

"I don't think you truly appreciate what you did to Phillip," Madison replied. "You seem to think that he would have forgiven you and you don't seem to understand how upset we all are."

"I know I behaved badly," Nicole said, wiping away her tears with the back of her hand.

"Phillip was getting ready to ask you to marry him," Madison said as tears began to slide down her cheeks. "He loved you more than he loved me or our parents. You were his entire world. He wanted nothing more than to marry you and have children with you. He

146

saved up for over a year to buy you the perfect ring. I went shopping with him to help him pick out something that I was certain you'd love. The next step was finding just the right time and place to propose."

Nicole shook her head. "Phillip didn't want to get married. He told me that several times. He wasn't ready yet."

"He told you that so that the proposal would be a complete surprise. You know that trip you two were planning? The one to Paris? He was going to propose at the top of the Eiffel Tower. He hated heights, he was terrified of them, really, but he was determined to take you up there for a romantic proposal."

"I don't believe you," Nicole snapped.

"I wish I were lying," Madison replied. "When he found out that you were cheating, he was completely broken. I wish more than anything that he hadn't really cared so much. He cancelled the trip to Paris and he gave me the ring, then he packed up all of his things and moved to a strange place where he didn't know a soul, all so that he could avoid seeing anything that reminded him of you."

"Liam was just a casual fling. It didn't mean anything," Nicole said.

"You married him less than a month after Phillip left," Madison replied.

"I didn't know what else to do. I felt as if my heart was broken, too, you know. I truly did love Phillip, and he'd left me. I know it was my fault, but he could have given me another chance. Most men would have given me another chance."

"Phillip wasn't most men. He was someone very special," Madison replied sadly.

Nicole nodded. "I really did love him, you know," she said softly.

"I still hate you," Madison shot back. "You broke his heart and turned him into someone different. He became someone who wouldn't visit his own mother, just because he was afraid he might be reminded of you. You ruined his life two years before he was murdered."

Nicole wiped her tears away again and then inhaled slowly. She opened her mouth and then shut it again. Without saying a word, she turned and headed for the door. The vicar was still standing nearby.

He pulled the door open and held it for Nicole. As it swung shut behind her, Bessie blew out a long breath.

"That was horrible," Rebecca said. "I must see to Madison." She crossed to her daughter, who was sobbing in Luke's arms.

"She did very well, Madison, I mean," Peter said. "She said a lot of the things I've been wanting to say to Nicole for two years, and she managed to stay reasonably calm while doing so. I'm proud of her."

"Nicole shouldn't have come," Harry interjected.

"No, she should have known she wouldn't be welcome," Peter agreed.

"Liam shouldn't have come, either," Harry added.

"He just wanted to catch Nicole saying things she shouldn't have been saying," Peter replied.

"And he did just that," Harry sighed. "Those two deserve each other, really."

"They certainly don't seem very happy together," Bessie remarked.

"I wonder if Liam really is cheating on her," Harry said.

"Probably," Peter shrugged. "She's probably cheating on him, too."

"What did Phillip ever see in her?" Harry asked.

"She was lovely when they first met," Madison said as she joined them. "I really liked her, and I was thrilled when Phillip said he was going to propose. She had us all fooled."

"Is it possible that she asked someone else to contact Phillip on her behalf?" Bessie asked.

Several people exchanged glances. "Anything is possible," Madison said eventually, "but Phillip was pretty careful not to give his contact information to very many people once he'd moved across."

"And he didn't mention Nicole at all the last time you spoke to him?" Bessie wondered.

Madison blinked back tears. "He rang when I was getting ready to go out. Luke was taking me out for a nice meal and I didn't want to be late for our booking, so I barely said three words to Phillip. I'll never forgive myself for not taking the time to talk to him properly."

"You weren't to know," Bessie said, "and Phillip would have wanted you to go out and enjoy yourself. I'm sure he would have liked Luke."

Madison nodded. "He said he'd only rung to say hello, that it wasn't for anything important. I'm sure he would have said something if he'd heard from Nicole."

"He didn't mention her the last time I spoke to him," Rebecca interjected. "He rang me just a few days ago, on Thursday. We talked about a dozen different things. He was working hard and looking forward to the holidays." She stopped and took a deep breath.

Peter put his arm around her. "It's okay," he said softly.

"It isn't, though. We argued. I wanted him to come home for Christmas, but he refused. I said things I shouldn't have said, tried to make him feel guilty. I'd do anything to take back the things I said to him that day."

"You made up before the end of the call," Peter said.

Rebecca nodded. "I didn't mean to argue with him. I hated arguing with him. I was so upset about Christmas, though. I couldn't imagine celebrating with him so far away. Now I won't celebrate at all."

"Yes, you will," Peter told her. "We won't do much, but we'll still do something to mark the day."

Rebecca clearly wanted to argue, but she simply shook her head. Madison crossed to her and put an arm around her. "We won't do anything you don't want to do," she told her mother.

"You said you hadn't talked to Phillip since October?" John asked Oliver.

He shrugged. "I don't remember when I spoke to him last, actually. I feel as if it was some time ago, but I could be remembering incorrectly. As I said, he used to ring me occasionally, but I rarely rang him."

"Mr. Collins, did you ever speak to Phillip?" John asked Dylan.

Dylan stared at him for a minute and then shook his head. "When we worked together, sure, but after he left, I don't think I spoke to him again. Maybe, once in a while, if he rang the office and I answered, I'd chat with him a bit, but usually I just transferred him to Oliver. We didn't really get on, Phillip and me."

"Why not?" Madison demanded.

Dylan looked shocked. "Why not? I mean, I don't know. He was a good guy, but we just have very different personalities, I suppose. I was only working part-time before he left, so we didn't see much of each other. Maybe we'd have been friends if we'd had a chance to get to know one another."

The room fell silent and Bessie felt as if everyone was waiting for someone else to speak. After a minute, Luke cleared his throat. "You need some tea," he said to Madison.

She hugged her mother and then followed Luke to the table with the refreshments. As Luke poured her a cup of tea, she nibbled listlessly on a biscuit. A moment later, Rebecca joined them. Peter followed as whispered conversations began all around the room.

"That was awful," Doona said to Bessie.

"It was pretty horrible. I can't believe that Nicole actually came here."

"She doesn't seem to realise how badly she hurt Phillip," John said.

"Maybe because she's too shallow to have actually cared about him herself," Doona suggested.

"I'm surprised that Liam came," Bessie said. "He had to know he wouldn't be welcome, surely."

"Obviously he doesn't trust Nicole," Doona replied.

"Doesn't trust her in what way?" Bessie asked. "What could she have done at a memorial service? Did he think she was going to try to chat up one of the other mourners?"

"I suppose he just wanted to hear her declare her undying love for Phillip, which he did," Doona said.

Bessie sighed. "I think I've had enough of all of this for today."

"Yes, I think it's time to head home," Doona agreed.

John gave them each a hug. "I'm going to stay until the end," he said. "I don't expect any more fireworks, but I don't want to risk missing out on anything that might happen."

Bessie found Rebecca in the small crowd. "I'm so very sorry about Phillip," she said, hugging her tightly.

"Thank you," Rebecca replied. "Thank you for coming. It's greatly appreciated."

"I wish I could do more."

"Help the police find the killer," Rebecca told her. "That's all I want now."

"I'll do everything I can," Bessie promised. She and Doona headed for the door. John stopped her just before they left.

"I'd like to talk to you later about everything that happened here today," he told her. "If I bring pizza, can we meet around six?"

"Of course. Doona and I will make something for pudding when we get back to my cottage."

"I'll invite Hugh, as well, but he may be too busy with the baby to come."

"As much as I'd like him to be there, I do understand that the baby should come first," Bessie said.

She and Doona drove back across the island. They discussed pudding as they went, agreeing in the end on American-style chocolate chip cookies. Bessie knew she had the necessary ingredients in her kitchen and she'd made them enough times to know that they were reasonably quick and easy. After the day she'd had, she didn't feel up to making anything complicated.

CHAPTER 11

*D*oona helped mix up the cookie dough and she and Bessie took it in turns getting trays in and out of the oven. When they were finished, there was just time for a short walk on the beach before John was due to arrive.

"I love it down here," Doona sighed. "I wish I could just buy one of the holiday cottages."

"Maggie and Thomas might be willing to sell you the last one," Bessie suggested.

"Any cottage but that one. Two people have been murdered in that cottage. I know someone was murdered in Hugh and Grace's house and they've managed to turn it into a lovely home, but I think too many bad things have happened in that cottage."

"I don't believe in curses or anything like that, but I don't think I'd want to stay in that cottage, myself. I'm not sure I'd want to live in Hugh and Grace's house, either, but they were able to get much more home for their money than they would have otherwise. It was a wise choice for them, and I'm more than happy to visit them there."

"The baby will soon chase away any ghosts," Doona laughed. "I'm sure she's keeping everyone in the house, living or dead, awake at all hours."

They turned around at Thie yn Traie, heading back towards Bessie's as the tide came in. When they reached the cottage, they sat together on the large rock rather than going inside.

"John wants to do some Christmas shopping one night later this week," Doona said after a few minutes. "Apparently all the shops in Douglas are having late-night opening every night from now until Christmas."

"You know I'm happy to have the children whenever John wants to go."

"Yes, but I think he'd prefer to wrap up the murder investigation before he takes a night off. He works all hours when it's murder."

"That could cause difficulties in any relationship."

"I know. In some ways I can see why Sue got frustrated. I'm sure it was very difficult when the children were small, especially. I understand what John does better than she probably did, and I still find myself getting angry when he has to cancel plans at the last minute or simply can't make any because he's too busy."

"You should give that a lot of thought before you have your chat with him."

"I've been giving it a lot of thought. Ultimately, whatever difficulties there will be, I still care about him a great deal. He's everything I've ever wanted in a man, aside from not being a multi-millionaire."

Bessie laughed. "Money can't buy happiness."

"No, I know, especially now that I have more than I ever wanted and all it's doing is making me miserable."

Bessie opened her mouth to reply, but Doona held up a hand.

"That isn't right. I'm not miserable, exactly. I just find the money worrying in ways I never imagined I would. I want to use it wisely, but I'm not sure how to do that, so I just keep leaving it where it is, earning a bit of interest, while I sit, frozen, worrying."

"I'm sure Doncan will have many different ideas for you."

"That's just it. He has dozens of ideas, but I can't seem to bring myself to choose one. He's been brilliant, he really has, but the money is mine and he can't bring himself to come right out and tell me what he thinks I should do."

"He was the same with me, or rather, his father was, all those years ago when I first inherited Matthew's estate. He made several suggestions and then left it up to me to decide."

"How did you choose?"

Bessie shrugged. "My first priority was getting away from my parents. I blamed them for Matthew's death, and I was still living with them, which had become unbearable. I told Doncan to find me a house, any house. He found three in what he considered my budget. I very nearly bought a cottage in Port St. Mary, you know. It was lovely, much larger than Treoghe Bwaane was, at least in those days before I added the extensions."

"Why didn't you buy that cottage, then?"

"It was in the centre of a row of other cottages on a long road with houses all around. I loved the cottage, but not having so many neighbours. There were sea views, but only at a distance from one or two of the rooms, as well. Even so, I was ready to make an offer, but Doncan brought me to Treoghe Bwaane last and as soon as I saw it, I knew it was meant to be mine."

"It suits you."

"I believe it does. The name felt just right after what I'd been through, and being right on the beach was a huge bonus. The nearest neighbour was about where the third or fourth holiday cottage is now, which was quite close enough for me."

"I can't imagine you living anywhere else."

"No, I can't either. I do wonder, as I get older, if I'll need to move one day into other accommodations. I hope not."

"I'll do whatever I can to help you stay at Treoghe Bwaane."

"Thank you. I don't want to be silly about it, but it's home and I don't want to leave if I can avoid doing so. I was thinking that I might turn the dining room into a bedroom at some point if the stairs get to be too much, but that's for many years in the future."

"Here's Hugh," Doona said, nodding at the parking area behind them.

Bessie got down off the rock and followed Doona across the sand. Hugh had climbed out of the car and walked around to the passenger door. He helped Grace out and then opened the rear door. Bessie grinned as Grace pulled a car seat out of the back.

"You brought Grace and the baby," she said happily when she and Doona reached Hugh.

"I did. Grace needed to get out of the house for an hour or two and we didn't want to leave the baby behind."

"You know you're all welcome, any time," Bessie told him.

She let everyone into the cottage. Grace looked tired, but happy as she sat down and began unhooking the baby from the seat.

"That looks complicated," Doona remarked.

"It isn't that bad," Grace told her. "I'm starting to get the hang of it, anyway. I haven't taken the baby very many places yet, so I haven't had many chances to practise."

She lifted the baby out and then pulled her close. "We're at Aunt Bessie's house," she said. "She lives just down the beach from us and she and Daddy have known each other for all of Daddy's life. She helped turn Daddy into the man he is today and we love Aunt Bessie because she did such a good job."

Bessie flushed. She would have replied if John hadn't knocked on the door just then. As she opened it, she could smell pizza and garlic bread.

"Hello, everyone," he greeted them. "I didn't know Grace and the baby were coming along."

"I hope it's okay," Hugh said quickly. "They can sit in the other room when we talk about the case, only Grace was desperate to get out of the house."

"The early days are difficult," John said. "I remember Sue telling me that she'd spent twenty minutes talking to the neighbours' window cleaner one day, just so she could talk to another adult."

Grace laughed. "It's not quite that bad yet, as my mum is still staying with us, but Mum needed a break from the baby and I needed a break from Mum. If we're in the way here, I can always walk home with the baby while you have your meeting."

"It's only an informal meeting," John said. "You're more than

155

welcome to stay and join in the conversation. I won't be sharing any confidential information."

Grace grinned. "I'll have to get that from Hugh later."

John raised an eyebrow at Hugh, who blushed. "I don't share confidential information with her," he muttered.

"I was only teasing," Grace said quickly as her cheeks turned pink. "He never tells me anything about his cases. Most of the time I don't even know which cases are his. I only know about this one because he found the body and that was in the papers."

"Let's eat," Bessie suggested.

"Yes, let's," Hugh said eagerly.

John brought an extra chair in from the dining room and they all filled plates with pizza and garlic bread. Doona got everyone cold drinks and then they settled in around the table. Grace held the baby on her lap, balancing her on her knees while she ate.

"Have you decided on a name yet?" Doona asked.

Grace sighed. "I know what I want, but some people don't agree with my choice."

"It's our baby. It should be our decision," Hugh said.

"But Mum could be right," Grace argued. "We don't want her initials to be EEW, do we?"

Doona and John both chuckled. "Perhaps you should choose something else for her middle name," Doona suggested.

Grace shook her head. "We can't. Her middle name is going to be Elizabeth. We're decided on that. I hope that's okay with you," she said to Bessie. "We wanted to honour you, and the part you played in Hugh's upbringing."

Bessie flushed. "What a huge honour. I don't blame your mother for not liking the idea."

"Oh, Mum is okay with Elizabeth for a middle name," Grace said. "She knows how important you are to Hugh and also how important you've become to me. It's the first name that we can't agree upon."

"Well, thank you," Bessie replied. "I'm deeply honoured and a bit overwhelmed."

"There must be hundreds of girls named in your honour," Hugh said. "After everything you've done for the children of Laxey over the years, every girl for generations should be Elizabeth."

"I think you're giving me too much credit," Bessie protested, "But what name are you considering for her first name, then?"

"I want to call her Ealish," Grace said. "It's the Manx form of Alice. *Alice in Wonderland* was one of my favourite books when I was a child and I always said I was going to name my first daughter Alice. Hugh and I both agreed that we prefer the Manx form, though."

"It's a lovely name," Doona said.

"Yes, but the initials are a problem. We don't want her to be teased at school," Hugh explained.

"You could always spell Ealish with two a's," Bessie suggested.

"E-a-a-l-i-s-h?" Hugh asked.

"No, A-a-l-i-s-h," Bessie corrected him.

"Can you do that?" Grace asked.

"Of course you can. I've seen it both ways in old records. Anyway, she's your baby. You can spell her name however you'd prefer," Bessie replied.

"What do you think?" Grace asked Hugh.

"I think it will take me ages to learn to spell it correctly, but I like it," he replied. "She shouldn't have any trouble with AEW as her initials, should she?"

"No more so than any other child," Grace sighed. She looked down at the baby who was fast asleep in her lap. "What do you think? Should we call you Aalish?"

The baby squirmed slightly and something like a smile flitted across her lips. Grace smiled. "I'm sure that's a yes," she said happily.

"I'm sure that's wind," Hugh replied. "The doctor said she wouldn't begin smiling properly for six weeks or more."

"What does he know?" Grace retorted. "She smiled when I said her name. I'm sure of it."

"I thought it was a smile," Doona said.

"Definitely," Bessie agreed.

Grace beamed. As she reached for her drink, the baby shifted again and then began to scream loudly.

"I think she's hungry," Grace said over the sudden uproar. "I'll just take her in the sitting room and feed her."

"She's lovely, but she's very loud," Doona said as Grace disappeared into the sitting room.

"That was nothing," Hugh said proudly. "You should hear her when she really gets going."

"I think I'd rather not," Doona laughed.

They finished their pizza and drinks and then waited for Grace to return before Bessie got out the cookies. She piled several dozen onto a plate while Grace handed the sleeping baby to Hugh. As everyone else helped themselves to cookies, Grace quickly cleared her dinner plate.

"So what happened at the memorial service?" Hugh asked around a bite of cookie.

"Hugh, don't speak with food in your mouth. You'll teach Aalish bad habits," Grace admonished.

"Aalish is fast asleep," Hugh countered.

"Babies are like sponges. They're always learning," Grace told him.

Hugh took a sip of his drink and then turned to John. "What happened at the memorial service?" he asked again.

John chuckled and then told him what he'd missed. Hugh made a few surprised noises during some of the more interesting parts, but he didn't interrupt.

"It doesn't sound as if anything happened after Doona and I left, anyway," Bessie said when John was done.

"Nothing as dramatic as the things that happened while you were there," John replied. "Oliver left right after you two did. Dylan stayed long enough to try to pull one of the girls who worked for another charity that had once employed Phillip. He was a bit too persistent, and I had to threaten to arrest him in order to get him to leave her alone."

"My goodness, how awful," Grace said.

John nodded. "I've given her my number in case he gives her any more trouble. I also gave him a stern lecture about such behaviour. I hope he listened."

"He didn't seem very bright," Doona interjected.

"That's no excuse," Bessie snapped.

"I wasn't making excuses for him," Doona told her. "I just doubt anything John said to him made any impression at all."

"I'm going to follow up with him tomorrow," John replied. "I have some more questions for both him and Oliver. I'll combine that with another little chat about boundaries and respect for women."

"What do you need to talk to them about?" Bessie asked.

"It's mostly just a general follow-up, but I'd also like to pin down exactly when they each last spoke to Phillip. They were both vague at the service, which was fine under the circumstances, but they were also vague when I interviewed them the first time. Now I want to push them a little bit."

"Do you think Oliver did tell Phillip about Nicole wanting to speak to him?" Bessie asked.

"That's one possibility," John said. "Something brought Phillip back to the island. His mother admitted to begging him to return, and according to her, he refused. Whatever brought him back had to be something serious."

"Everyone insists that he was still angry with Nicole. Why would he come back for her?" Grace asked.

"Maybe she said she was in trouble," Hugh replied. "If he'd never stopped loving her, in spite of everything, maybe she managed to convince him that she needed his help."

"That's a possibility, for sure," John said. "Sue and I are divorced and I'd still drop everything if she needed me. Part of that has to do with the children, of course. Whatever else happens, she'll always be the mother of my children."

Bessie glanced at Doona, who looked sad. As far as Bessie knew, Doona had never wanted children of her own, although she seemed to be adapting very well to helping with John's. Hearing that John still cared about Sue had to hurt, though.

"I can't imagine Grace and me not being together," Hugh said. "If she found someone else, I'd probably do the same as Phillip and run away. Except I couldn't leave Aalish behind, so I suppose I'd have to stay and simply be miserable for the rest of my life."

Grace shook her head. "I'm not going anywhere."

"Anyway, if Grace had refused to marry me, I might well have left the island," Hugh continued. "The memories would have been very painful."

"Would you have come back if your mother begged you to visit?" Doona asked.

Hugh shrugged. "Mum and I have had our difficulties over the years. I'm not sure how I'd feel about that."

"What if Bessie begged you to visit?" John asked.

"I'd come back for Bessie," Hugh said firmly. "If she needed me, I'd be here, no matter what else I was feeling."

Bessie patted his hand. "Have another cookie," she suggested.

Hugh grinned and took a cookie from the plate. He took a big bite and then frowned as a bit dropped onto the baby's head. When he tried to pick up the crumbs, he seemed to smash them into Aalish's very fine baby hair.

"Oh, goodness, you're making a mess of that," Grace laughed. She leaned over and took the baby from Hugh just as Aalish began to wake up, her tiny face seemingly scrunched in confusion.

"Would you like a comb?" Bessie asked as Grace tried to pick crumbs and melted chocolate out of the baby's hair.

"I'm not sure it would help," Grace sighed. "I think we may have to give her a bath."

"Oh, no," Hugh said.

"I thought babies loved baths," Doona said.

"They usually do when they're older," John told her. "When they're old enough to splash in the water and maybe have a few bath toys in the tub with them. When they're very small, like Aalish, they often hate the whole experience, though. It's probably rather scary for them, having all their clothes removed and then being dunked into a big tub of water. I don't blame them for crying, really."

"I don't blame her for crying, but when she does I feel awfully guilty," Hugh said, "and this is all my fault for dropping crumbs on her, too."

Bessie went into the bathroom and found a flannel. She wet it with warm water and brought it out to Grace. "Try this," she suggested. "It won't be perfect, but it should help."

It only took Grace a few seconds to clean away the worst of the mess. Aalish made faces as Grace worked, waiting until she was finished to begin crying loudly.

"I'm done," Grace told her. "You've nothing to cry about now."

"She probably wanted to eat the cookie," Doona suggested.

Grace laughed. "Maybe she takes after her father," she said, grinning at Hugh, who was reaching for another treat.

"Does anyone have any ideas about the murder based on the conversations from today's memorial service?" John asked after the baby was soothed.

"I didn't care for Liam," Doona said. "The fact that he came to the service just to spy on Nicole shows that he doesn't trust her. I don't know if he'd kill for her, though."

John shrugged. "I'm going to be talking to him and Nicole again tomorrow. At this point, I'm going to be going back through all of the witnesses, actually."

"I went to see Dan Ross this morning," Bessie said, somewhat sheepishly.

"Why?" John asked, looking surprised.

"Some of the things that Madison said about Oliver bothered me. I thought maybe Dan could do some looking into The Liliana Fund. I tried to persuade him that he should write a series of articles about the island's charities, but he was smart enough to realise that it was Oliver and The Liliana Fund that were my concern."

"Do you think Oliver is doing something illegal?" John asked.

Bessie shrugged. "I'm probably seeing things that aren't there, but Phillip's parents said something about Phillip trying to track down some of the grant recipients that The Liliana Fund had helped over the years. What if he couldn't find some of them?"

"Are you suggesting that they don't exist?" Hugh wondered.

"I don't know what I'm suggesting," Bessie replied. "It was just something that caught my attention. I'm not even certain why, but it feels as if it might have some bearing on what happened to Phillip. No one seems to know why he came back to the island. What if he'd discovered that some of the people who've been given grants by the fund didn't actually need them or weren't what they claimed to be? Maybe he came back to talk to Oliver about his concerns."

"And Oliver killed him because he's been pocketing the money from the fund," Doona concluded.

"It's a possibility," John said. "For what it's worth, The Liliana Fund has a spotless reputation on the island. I couldn't find any hint of any complaints or issues with the fund since it was established. Having Dan poke around a bit is probably a good idea. Without any complaints, I've no reason to begin a formal investigation into the charity, and my informal efforts have turned up nothing thus far."

"Dan would only agree to investigate if I'd agree to give him an interview. I refused, of course, which means it's highly unlikely he'll be doing anything. He did give me the name of the woman who covers good causes for the paper. I left her a note. I don't know if she'll follow up on it or not."

"Perhaps I should ring Dan and make a suggestion of my own," John said. "I'm going to give the idea some thought, anyway."

A loud buzzing noise startled everyone. Aalish, who'd been fast asleep, jumped in her mother's arms and then began to scream. Grace frowned and then dug her mobile out of her handbag.

"It's my mother," she said, sounding annoyed. "Hello?"

"Yes, you can hear the baby crying, actually. That's because she was fast asleep until the phone went off and woke her." Hugh took the baby as Grace frowned at her phone.

"We'll be home when we're done here. I didn't realise I had a curfew tonight."

"Aalish will be up all night because she's a baby who sleeps whenever she wants and gets up whenever she wants, not because we've kept her out too late."

"We've decided on Aalish, but we're spelling it with two a's."

"Can we have this conversation later? We're here on police business, after all."

Grace listened for a moment and then pushed a button on her phone and dropped it back into her handbag.

"Are we in trouble with your mother?" Hugh asked.

Grace rolled her eyes. "I love her dearly, but Aalish is our baby and our responsibility. I really appreciate everything Mum's done to help, but maybe it's time for her to go home."

"Already?" Hugh asked, looking concerned.

"Not tonight, but maybe before too much longer. We have to learn to look after Aalish by ourselves at some point. Maybe it will be easier if we have to start now, rather than later."

Hugh looked doubtful, but he nodded anyway. "Whatever you want is fine with me," he said.

Doona chuckled. "More marriages would succeed if all men felt that way."

Everyone laughed.

"He doesn't always give in to me," Grace said. "In this instance, though, I'm the one who wanted Mum here. I wasn't expecting her to take over so completely, though. She makes me feel as if I'm a child again, rather than Aalish's mother."

"We'll talk to her when we get home," Hugh said. "We've both been letting her do everything since the baby arrived. Maybe if we ask her to back off a bit, she'll agree."

Grace shrugged. "We have to do something. I won't have her ringing me to demand that I bring the baby home, not when the baby is my baby, for heaven's sake."

"She demanded that you bring Aalish home?" Bessie asked.

"Not exactly demanded, but she was pretty insistent," Grace replied. "I probably would have made a joke of it if I weren't so tired and so overwhelmed by everything."

"Maybe we should get Aalish home," Hugh suggested. "I think you and your mother need to talk."

"You aren't getting out of it that easily," Grace told him. "All three of us need to talk, although I think you're going to have to change the baby first."

"She needs changing?" Hugh asked.

"Not yet, but she probably will soon," Grace replied.

She got to her feet and took Aalish back from Hugh. He grabbed the car seat and together they managed to get the baby safely buckled inside. Aalish was vocal with her disapproval as they worked.

"Sorry about the noise," Grace said as Hugh picked up the car seat and they headed for the door.

Bessie had also stood up, and while the couple were securing the baby in her seat, she'd filled a small bag with chocolate chip cookies. "It's up to you whether you want to share them with your mother or not," she told Grace as she handed her the bag.

Grace laughed. "She probably needs some sweetening up after that phone call, but Hugh may have them all gone before we get home."

Bessie let the little family out of the house and then sat back down at the table with John and Doona.

"It feels quite empty in here now," Doona remarked.

"It's certainly a good deal quieter," Bessie laughed.

"Right, let's talk about motive and means and opportunity," John suggested. "I know we did all of that recently, but it can't hurt to go over everything again."

"I'll just put the kettle on," Bessie replied.

She was halfway to the sink when another loud noise filled the room. John frowned and then pulled out his mobile. He looked surprised when he checked the display.

"Hello?"

"Yes, speaking."

Bessie watched as John's face went pale. "Can you clarify that, please? In laymen's terms."

Several minutes passed and Bessie could tell from the expression on John's face that whatever he was hearing wasn't good news. All thoughts of tea were pushed aside as she sat down next to him and rested a hand on his arm.

"I'm not home right now, but I can be in ten minutes," he said eventually. "I'll ring you as soon as I'm with the children." He dropped the phone into his pocket as he got to his feet.

"What's wrong?" Bessie asked.

"That was Harvey," John replied, sounding shocked. "Sue has taken a turn for the worse. He doesn't know if she's going to make it, and he wants me to have the children ring her so she can talk to them one more time."

Bessie gasped as Doona stood up. "I'll come with you," she told John. "The children are going to need all the support they can get."

"Do you want me to come, too?" Bessie asked.

John looked at her for a minute and then shook his head. "I'm hoping Harvey is overreacting. He gave me a lengthy medical report that meant nothing to me before he said simply that he thinks she's beyond any further treatment. I don't know what to think, but I'll worry about that later. For now, I need to get home to the children."

"Do you want me to drive you home?" Doona asked as they headed for the door.

"It isn't far, and I probably need something else to concentrate on anyway," John said. "Just follow me, okay?"

"Sure," Doona agreed.

Bessie watched as they walked to their cars and then drove away. She was left feeling rather helpless, her heart aching for Thomas and Amy. Still, maybe Harvey was overreacting. Perhaps Sue would recover, and the whole scary situation would have a happy resolution.

Feeling too wound up to sleep, Bessie curled up with Onnee's next letter. It was short and talked a great deal about how difficult pregnancy was proving to be. They'd moved into a larger flat, but were still looking for a house to purchase. Faith's name wasn't mentioned once.

Bessie was yawning when she finished the letter. While she was tempted to continue, wondering about Faith, she knew she was too tired to transcribe the difficult handwriting properly. Instead, she carefully put everything away and headed for bed.

While she was tempted to ring Doona to find out what was happening with Sue, she knew that she was simply being nosy. Doona would tell her what she could when she had the chance. Bessie was sure that she'd never be able to sleep, not with both Sue and Phillip's murder on her mind, but she was asleep as soon as her head touched her pillow. The next morning she was very aware that she'd had a number of unpleasant dreams, but they faded quickly as she showered. After a bowl of cereal with milk, she went out for her walk, determined to walk to the new houses and back.

She hadn't gone far past Thie yn Traie when she changed her mind. If she saw Hugh or Grace, she might be tempted to say something to them about Sue, and it wasn't her place to pass that news along. She walked for a short while longer and then turned around when she was still some distance from the new houses.

A light rain was starting to fall when she reached the steps to Thie yn Traie. She'd only gone a few additional paces when she was surprised to hear someone calling her name.

CHAPTER 12

"*A*unt Bessie?"

Elizabeth Quayle was making her way down the stairs from Thie yn Traie.

"Be careful," Bessie shouted, wincing as Elizabeth jumped from one rickety staircase to the next. "The stairs are slippery when they're wet," Bessie reminded the girl. Bessie knew firsthand how dangerous they could be, too, as she'd fallen, or rather been pushed, down them herself.

"I'm fine," Elizabeth laughed as she leapt to the ground, ignoring the last several steps. "How are you?"

"I'm quite well, thank you," Bessie told her. "I did forget my umbrella, though, which is unfortunate."

Elizabeth laughed again and then opened the large umbrella she was carrying. "I have one, but I didn't think to open it," she said. She got closer to Bessie, holding the cover over both of them.

"What are you doing up so very early?" Bessie asked.

The girl blushed. "I don't always lie in until midday," she said. "Okay, I often lie in until ten or eleven, though." She giggled and then shrugged. "Today I'm working. It's nearly Christmas and suddenly everyone wants to have parties and special events, and I'm almost overwhelmed."

"Your new business is doing very well, then."

"It is, almost too well. I've no time for anything else. I had planned to go across for a few days to visit some friends, but I've had to cancel, which was disappointing."

Bessie wondered whom Elizabeth had been planning to visit. Andy Caine was at culinary school across. He and Elizabeth had spent quite a lot of time together during his recent summer holidays and Bessie knew he'd been coming back to the island much more regularly lately than he had in the first year of his studies. Andy was a hard-working young man who had recently come into a completely unexpected fortune. Bessie thought he was a good match for Elizabeth, a rather spoiled girl who'd have her own fortune one day. "That's a shame," Bessie said.

"Yes, well, never mind. I mustn't complain. This year, for the first time ever, I'm actually going to buy presents for my parents with money I've earned myself. It's weirdly liberating, even though neither of them actually needs anything."

"Congratulations."

"Thanks. I should have started working years ago, of course, but I was a spoiled brat who didn't appreciate all of the advantages I've had in life. I have to say, though, I don't think I was ever as bad as some of my clients. The demands that I get are incredible. People seem to think that if they throw enough money around they can have anything they want."

"Oh, dear."

"But I didn't rush down here to see you to complain about anything," Elizabeth said quickly. "For the most part, life is good, and my little business is turning out to be much more successful than I ever dreamt. Andy will be home for Christmas, too. What more could I want?"

Bessie grinned. "You and Andy are still together, then?"

"I'm not sure what we are, actually, but that's okay, too. We've survived him being away for the last several months and now we get to spend Christmas together. He has to go back for a few more classes and exams, but then he'll be done in February. I suppose the real test of our relationship will come when he's back on the island for good, but I really don't want to talk about him. I always feel as if things are going far too well and if I talk about it, everything will go wrong."

"So what did you want to talk to me about this morning?"

"Oh, yes, of course," Elizabeth laughed. "I was reading in the paper about Phillip Tyler's death. It's so very sad."

"You knew Phillip?"

"A bit. You know Mum is always going along to charity events. I believe she supports every single charity on the island, at least a bit. She hates going to the events, even though Daddy loves them. Whenever he's busy or away, I usually go with Mum so she doesn't have to go alone. That's probably where I got the idea for my business, actually. I've been to an awful lot of events that were clearly arranged by amateurs."

"I suppose our local charities can't really afford to hire you to help, either."

"Oh, I'm doing a lot of volunteer planning for local charities. In fact, I'm up early today to spend some time with a local charity, helping them plan their next fundraiser. I don't charge good causes for my time, and I do my best to get them good prices for catering and whatever else they need. The big parties I do for my mother's friends and mine pay me well enough that I can afford to be generous with my spare time."

"Whether you can afford it or not, it's still very kind of you," Bessie said, patting the girl's arm.

Elizabeth blushed. "It's something that Andy and I talk about a lot, actually. When he gets back and opens his restaurant, he wants to find a way to help with the catering side of things for the charities that I help. But that's another conversation for another day. I can witter on, can't I?"

"What did you want to tell me about Phillip?" Bessie asked.

"Oh, nothing particularly, I just wanted to talk about him, I suppose. I know you're involved in the investigation and I heard that you even found the body. It's all rather horrible, really."

"It's very sad, yes. What did you think of Phillip?"

"He was rather quiet and very focussed, although he kept changing jobs, which meant his focus changed all the time, if you see what I mean."

"I'm not sure that I do."

"I remember meeting him at some event for one of the island's children's charities. He spent ten minutes talking to Mum and me about how crucial it was for the island's children to get the right start in life. They were raising money for a literacy programme, I believe. Anyway, a few months later I saw him at another event. It was for one of those charities that raises money for disaster relief overseas. He was passionate about how desperately our money was needed to save lives after some flood or famine, I forget which."

Bessie nodded. "He did change jobs several times, I believe."

"The last time I saw him, he was working for yet another charity. Mum got a long spiel about supporting medical research for children's cancer. His stories were heartwarming and I know Mum wrote a big cheque on the spot."

"I suppose, when you work for good causes, you need to shift your passion as you change jobs."

"I suppose so, but I found it odd. I even asked him, at the party for that cancer charity, about a natural disaster that had happened recently, one that I knew his former employers were trying to support. He gave me a blank stare, as if he was completely unaware of the situation." She shook her head. "I don't know. I just felt it was odd how completely he'd switched from one cause to another. Maybe it's just me, but if I spent a year of my life trying to drum up support for a good cause, I'd still follow their efforts, even if I moved on to a new job."

"I've never really thought about it," Bessie admitted. "I don't get invited to a lot of charity events, of course, but I've learned a bit about good causes through Christmas at the Castle. Everyone I've spoken to there seems completely devoted to his or her particular good cause.

Most of them are volunteers, though. Perhaps it's different if you're actually employed by the charity."

"Maybe. I just thought I'd mention it to you," Elizabeth replied. "I suppose I'm contrasting Phillip with Oliver in some ways. He's completely and utterly devoted to The Liliana Fund."

"But he started The Liliana Fund. It was his idea from the start."

"Yes, I know," Elizabeth sighed. "I know all about The Liliana Fund, in tremendous detail."

"Really?"

"I met Oliver at one of his Liliana Fund events. It's only in the last couple of years that I've started going with Mum to more things. My older brother used to take Daddy's place when Daddy was away, but now he's invited to just about everything on his own accord, so I've stepped in. Anyway, I met Oliver at some party a few years ago."

"And he told you all about The Liliana Fund?"

Elizabeth flushed. "Not really, not at the party, anyway. We only talked for a few minutes at the party, but that was long enough for him to ask for my number. I was, well, flattered, really. I hadn't been on the island for long and I didn't know many people. Oliver was handsome and charming."

"So he rang you?"

"He did, the very next day, which was also flattering. We had dinner together a few nights later."

"And that's when he told you all about his charity?"

Elizabeth laughed. "I'm telling this story badly. No, that first night we talked about me, mostly. He wanted to hear every last detail about my life, and he seemed to hang on my every word. I'm sure he must have been bored to bits, but I told him all about my family, my friends, all the universities I'd been to, et cetera, ad nauseam. He pretended to be fascinated."

"Pretended?"

"I may be being unfair, but I don't think so. We went out again a few nights later. Now it was his turn to tell me about his life. I got to hear all about his wonderful mother, Liliana, and about how much she'd suffered when she fell ill. He brought me to tears as he explained how he'd founded his charity to try to make certain that no one would suffer as badly as she had during her illness. It was all very moving, really."

"So why do I hear cynicism in your voice?"

"Because the evening ended when he hit me up for a donation," Elizabeth sighed. "I thought we were really connecting and getting to know one another. He thought I was a soft touch."

"Oh, dear."

"The joke was on him, really, because at that point I didn't even have a bank account in my own name. I could have asked Mum to write him a cheque, of course, but I was rather too embarrassed about the whole situation to even consider that. I said something along the lines of not being in a position to help, and then fled the restaurant in a taxi."

"Fled?"

"I felt used and humiliated. Here I was, thinking that he was interested in me as a person, and it turned out he was only seeing pound signs. I was used to going out with men in my same social circle. They all have money of their own and it would never have occurred to any of them to ask me for money for anything. Oliver was something of a rude awakening."

"I'm sorry."

"It was a long time ago," Elizabeth shrugged. "I haven't actually seen Oliver since, although he does send his assistant around to pester Mum for donations from time to time."

"Dylan?"

"Yes, that's the one. Mum isn't fond of him, but she's too nice to tell him to leave her alone."

"I didn't realise that Dylan visited donors."

"We may be the only ones that Oliver doesn't deal with personally. I think he's still angry with me for fleeing from our dinner."

"He should be embarrassed for treating you that way."

"Whichever, he seems to be avoiding both me and Mum. Dylan rings about twice a year and invites her to lunch. She usually goes, although I think she turned him down the last time."

"Why?"

"She said something about him turning up the pressure on her to make a larger donation. Mum gives generously, but she gives to many different good causes, which means they have to share her generosity. Once in a while a particular cause or a particular fundraiser will push her to give more to them than she feels she should. Usually, at that point, she stops giving to that particular cause."

"Perhaps I'm better off having never had money," Bessie speculated.

Elizabeth laughed. "You'd be far more selective in whom or what you supported. Mum can't say no, but I suspect you wouldn't have that difficulty."

Bessie grinned. "You may be right about that. I do give to a few good causes on the island, but usually anonymously, and I never give very much money at a time, either."

"Anyway, I don't know if anything I've said will be helpful, but I know you'll want to pass it all along to Inspector Rockwell."

"Yes, I will," Bessie agreed, wondering if John would still be overseeing the case or if he was busy with his own personal matters now. "Can you tell me anything else about Phillip, Oliver, or Dylan?"

"As I said, Mum isn't fond of Dylan. I've only met him a few times, but I didn't care for him, either. He acts as if he's rather thick, but I think it's truly that, an act. I think he's a good deal brighter than he lets on, although I can't imagine any reason behind his behaviour."

"He never asked you out?"

"Not in so many words. The first time we met, he gave me a look that suggested that he might be interested, but I ignored it. He made a point of including me in the invitation to lunch that he extended to my mother, as well, but I declined. I suspect Oliver may have told him about our disastrous dinner at some point, because Dylan has never specifically included me in an invitation since."

"Specifically?"

"I mean, he always suggests to Mum that she might want to bring a friend or two with her to lunch. I'm sure he's hoping for additional prospects, really, but Mum usually asks me if I want to go along."

"And you haven't seen Oliver at all since that abandoned dinner?"

"Actually, I did see him once fairly recently. He was walking on Laxey Beach with a woman. I'm not sure who she was, but she was very pretty. I'd walked down from Thie yn Traie to get some fresh air and exercise."

"When was this?" Bessie asked, feeling excited.

"Maybe September?" Elizabeth made the answer a question. "It was after the summer rush at the holiday cottages, but there were still guests staying at some of them, so I believe it was September."

"Did you speak to him?"

"No," Elizabeth blushed. "When I realised who it was, I turned around and walked the other way. They were strolling along the sand and talking. I spotted them when they were at about the midpoint of the holiday cottages. As I said, when I recognised him, I turned and began to walk towards the new houses. I walked well past them, as well, before I turned around. By the time I got back to Thie yn Traie, they were gone."

"Interesting," Bessie said. There was no way she could ask Oliver what he'd been doing on Laxey Beach back in September, but she was curious.

"I do know Nicole Carr, if it matters," Elizabeth said casually.

"It is such a small island," Bessie replied. "How do you know Nicole?"

"She works at Noble's. I met her when Daddy was having some health issues. She was one of the nurses who took care of him after his minor surgery."

"What did you think of her?"

"She was efficient, but not especially pleasant. I hate to say anything bad about her, really, because everyone at Noble's took such good care of Daddy, but she was one of my least favourite nurses. I can't fault her for the care she gave Daddy, but she never seemed especially happy or even content with her job. I don't know if I'm making sense or not."

"I think I know what you mean."

"Some of the nurses seemed to truly love nursing and took a real interest in Daddy. Some of them just seemed to be going through the motions. Nicole definitely fell into the latter category."

"Did you know anything about her at the time?"

"No, not at all, but I have to say I wasn't surprised to learn that she'd cheated on a former boyfriend. She seemed, well, cold, I suppose is the best word."

"What about Liam Kirk? Do you know him at all?"

Elizabeth made a face. "I made the mistake of taking a tour of his gym when we first moved to the island. Daddy hadn't found a house yet, so we were staying at a hotel, and their fitness facility was horrible. I went looking for a gym that I could join for a few months, until Daddy found a house and had a gym installed there."

"Why was it a mistake?"

"It wasn't the sort of gym I wanted and Liam was creepy."

"In what way?"

"He leered at me and kept encouraging me to try different machines, and then using that as an excuse to touch me under the guise of helping me with the machine or the weights. It was unpleasant, but never quite obvious enough that I could legitimately object, if you know what I mean."

"Do you remember when this happened? Before or after he got married?"

"I'm not sure. I could probably work it out, but I don't see why it matters. He'd have behaved the exact same way, married or not. If I went there again today, I'd get the same treatment from him."

Bessie shook her head. She didn't understand men, but she believed Elizabeth's assessment of Liam. "We've talked about a lot of people. Can you see any of them killing Phillip?"

Elizabeth shook her head. "I can't imagine anyone killing anyone under any circumstances," she sighed. "Maybe my imagination isn't very good, but the idea of actually trying to physically injure another human being is simply foreign to me."

Bessie patted her arm. "I hope that never changes."

"I do, too."

"Do you know Harry Holt?" Bessie asked as the man's name popped into her head.

"Harry Holt? I don't think so. Should I?"

"He was Phillip's closest friend when he lived on the island. They went to university together. I didn't know if you'd ever met him."

"I don't believe I have. Maybe it isn't that small of an island after all," Elizabeth laughed.

"Perhaps not."

"And now I must dash. I'm going to be late for my meeting, but it was worth it to chat with you." Elizabeth gave Bessie a quick hug and then dashed away, racing up the steep steps.

"Do be careful," Bessie said under her breath, afraid if she called out to her that Elizabeth might be distracted and slip. She watched as the girl reached the top of the last flight of stairs and then disappeared from view.

The rain was still falling, although so lightly that it was almost more of a mist. Bessie hadn't walked more than a few steps when her name was called again.

"Bessie," a loud voice boomed across the beach. "Hello."

Forcing herself to smile, Bessie turned and began to walk towards the last holiday cottage. Maggie Shimmin was standing under a large umbrella on the cottage's patio.

"Good morning," Bessie said when she reached the woman.

"It isn't a very good one, though, is it?" Maggie replied. "This rain is playing havoc with my back, for a start. It isn't just my back, either. My knees are aching, my head hurts, and I'm quite certain I'm brewing something, as well."

"You should get in out of the rain, then."

"Aye, I would if I could. The police still won't let us in our cottage, though. Even though it's ours and they ought to have the case solved by now. I told Thomas I've half a mind to ring the chief constable myself and demand that they release the cottage."

"I'm sure they'll release it as soon as they possibly can."

"I wish I had your confidence," Maggie scowled. "They know we aren't using the cottage at the moment, so they've no motivation to get done with it in any hurry. I suppose, all things considered, it doesn't much matter now anyway."

"Oh?"

"We've had our planning application turned down. I thought you'd already know that."

"I'd not heard anything. I am sorry."

"Someone must have objected, I reckon. I'd love to know who it was and why they objected."

"I thought such things were a matter of public record."

"Maybe, but maybe not," Maggie said, winking.

Bessie didn't know what Maggie meant by that, but decided she didn't want to know. "What will you do now, then?" she asked.

"Oh, we're going to appeal, but I don't know that it will do us any good. Once the police give us access, we're going to tear down this cottage regardless. We can't rent it out, not now, not after everything that has happened in it."

"Maybe you could use it for storage, or you and Thomas could stay here during the summer months. It would save you a lot of time and effort running back and forth."

Maggie stared at her for a minute. "I'm not staying in there," she said, nodding towards the cottage. "People have been murdered in there."

And yet you complain because holidaymakers don't want to use it, Bessie thought, biting her tongue.

"It wouldn't be at all suitable for storage, either," Maggie told her. "Although maybe we could build a storage shed here if we can't get permission to build a larger cottage."

"I'm not sure that would be very attractive."

"We could design it to look the same as the other cottages, but without all the interior walls. It would be a lovely huge space to store all of the things that we need down here."

"Or you could just use the cottage that's already here," Bessie suggested again.

Maggie shook her head. "It's not at all suitable."

It seemed that Maggie was more spooked by the second murder

than she had been by the first, Bessie thought. "Well, good luck to you and Thomas," she said. "I hope you can get permission to do something."

"We've been given permission to tear the cottage down and rebuild a new one exactly the same," Maggie sighed. "There seems no point in doing that, though, does there?"

"It would give you another cottage to hire out."

"Yes, but I don't know if it would be enough to break the curse."

"Curse? You can't be serious."

Maggie flushed and looked at the ground. "I don't know what to think. That last cottage has been nothing but trouble since we first built the cottages. First there was that horrible accident with that couple from across, then a murder, and now a second murder. How many awful things have to happen somewhere before you decide the place is cursed?"

"A good deal more than three," Bessie said firmly. "I don't believe in curses, although I will admit that you've had a run of bad luck with that cottage. Still, if you start thinking about the number of murder investigations I've been involved in lately, you may start to think that I'm cursed as well."

Maggie pressed her lips tightly together.

She truly does think I'm cursed, Bessie thought, feeling amused by the idea. "Anyway, I should be getting home," she said.

"Going to ring John Rockwell and tell him everything that Elizabeth Quayle told you?" Maggie asked.

"I don't see why that's any of your business," Bessie said.

Maggie laughed. "We all know you tell Inspector Rockwell everything that you hear. He couldn't do his job half as well if he didn't have you telling him everything that's truly happening in Laxey."

"John is excellent at his job and he doesn't need my help," Bessie said tartly. "I do share some of the things that people tell me with him, certainly, especially when he's investigating a murder. I hope you'll agree with me that we all want murderers found and put behind bars as quickly as possible."

"Yes, of course. Anyway, I'm sure Elizabeth had a lot to say about

Oliver Preston. She chased after him quite shamelessly for several weeks when she first arrived on the island."

"Really?"

"They met at one of his fundraisers. Thomas and I were there and I couldn't help but notice the way she pushed her telephone number on him with suggestions that he really ought to ring her soon. I'm sure poor Oliver thought he was going to get a big donation from the family, but I don't think it worked out that way."

"I wouldn't know."

"No? Elizabeth didn't say? She's probably embarrassed about her behaviour back then, especially now that she and young Andy Caine are a couple. I keep waiting to hear that they've split, but with him off-island, it's impossible to find out anything."

"Do you have your tickets for Christmas at the Castle?" Bessie changed the subject.

Maggie blinked at her and then chuckled. "I know, I know. You and Mary Quayle are unlikely friends now, so you won't talk about Elizabeth. Fair enough, I suppose. For the record, yes, I do have tickets for Christmas at the Castle, but I'm not certain we'll actually attend. A lot depends on how Thomas is feeling, you understand."

"Of course. Please give him my best."

Maggie nodded. "And now I must go and get some work done. I can't waste all day chatting with you, you know." She spun on her heel and quickly disappeared around the cottage.

Bessie sighed and then turned towards home, half expecting someone else to interrupt her. She didn't mind long chats on the beach most days, but after two of them, in spite of the umbrellas she'd shared, she felt soaked through. She stopped just inside her door and watched as water dripped off her clothes. It took her half an hour to change, hang up her wet things, and dry her hair. When she was done, she sank into a chair and sighed.

Ringing John held little appeal. While she wanted to share what she'd learned from Elizabeth with him, she was afraid of what he might have to tell her about Sue. As she dithered over whether to ring or not, she suddenly remembered the new shop assistant in the shop at the top of the hill. She'd promised to bring her some books to read and she'd completely forgotten.

The girl had said she usually read romance, a genre that Bessie didn't much enjoy. Still, she found a few paperbacks scattered across her shelves when she went to look. As she hadn't known she had them, she didn't much care if she ever got them back again. They were exactly what she needed to lend to the poor shop assistant. She added a few copies of some of her favourite mystery novels. She often bought duplicate copies of real favourites specifically to lend. After putting the books into a bag, Bessie looked outside.

"Still raining," she sighed. A walk in the cold rain sounded more appealing than ringing John though, so she put on her waterproofs and her Wellington boots and headed up the hill.

"Oh, goodness," the shop assistant exclaimed when Bessie handed her the bag. "I can't possibly…"

"Of course you can," Bessie interrupted. "You may not even want to read any of them, but you're welcome to read them all. If you particularly enjoy any of them, feel free to keep them, otherwise, you can donate them to a charity shop or give them back to me and I'll lend them to someone else. I'm Bessie Cubbon, by the way."

"I'm Sandra Cook, but are you quite sure about the books?"

"I'm positive," Bessie said firmly.

Bessie did a quick bit of shopping while Sandra looked through the books. Bessie grabbed a few packets of biscuits, a couple of tins of soup, and a fresh loaf of bread. When she got back to the counter, Sandra was already reading.

"That didn't take long," Bessie laughed as the girl quickly shoved a scrap of paper into the book to hold her place.

"I love to read," Sandra said in a low voice.

"I do, as well."

"I can't thank you enough."

"You already have." Bessie took her purchases and headed for the door. "I'll stop back in a few days with more," she told her, fairly certain that all of the titles she'd brought today would be finished with by then.

"Oh, thank you," Sandra called, already reopening the book she'd started.

Feeling as if she'd done her good deed for the day, Bessie walked home in the rain. When she opened her door, her phone was ringing.

"Hello?"

"Bessie, it's John."

"I was going to ring you later," Bessie said. "I talked to Elizabeth Quayle this morning. She had some interesting things to say about Phillip and the others. I also wanted to ask you how Sue is doing."

John sighed. "Sue is holding on at the moment. The kids are upset, but also confused and angry. I'm both of those things and many more, but there's very little I can do from here."

"I'm sorry."

"Tell me what Elizabeth said before I tell you why I rang, then," John invited.

Bessie did her best to repeat the conversation. Once she was finished, she told him Maggie's version of events as well.

"Interesting," John said when she was done.

"But why did you ring?" Bessie asked.

"I want you to repeat your conversation with Dan Ross for me again, please."

"Dan Ross? Why?"

"He was hit by a car last night. It was a hit and run," John told her.

Bessie gasped and felt a chill run up her spine.

181

CHAPTER 13

"*Y*ou don't think it was anything to do with Phillip's murder, do you?" Bessie demanded.

"I don't know anything at this point."

"How is he?" Bessie asked nervously.

"He's expected to make a full recovery, but it's going to take time."

Bessie blew out a sigh of relief. "I don't care for the man, but I don't want anything bad to happen to him."

"Can you tell me everything that was said when you spoke to him, please?"

"I'll try." Bessie did her best to remember the conversation. When she was done, she sighed. "I hope his accident wasn't anything to do with Phillip's murder. I'll feel ever so guilty. What did he say happened?"

"He gave a preliminary statement to the constable on duty. Pete is going to talk to him later today. Let's just say that his preliminary statement was about as uncooperative as you'd expect."

Pete Corkill was an inspector with the Douglas CID. If anyone could get information out of Dan Ross, it was Pete. "I hope Pete has better luck," Bessie replied.

"I suspect Dan is hoping to save up anything and everything from the accident so that he can write his own shocking story for the paper's front page," John sighed. "He won't want to tell Pete anything, as there is always a risk of a leak. Leaked news doesn't sell papers."

Bessie sighed. "He's an idiot. If it was deliberate, he could get himself killed trying to sell papers."

"Indeed. I'm sure Pete will point that out to him."

"And be wasting his time doing so," Bessie guessed.

"Most likely."

"Is he allowed visitors?"

"He has a police guard on the door at the moment. Medically, he may be cleared for visitors, but I don't think Pete is clearing anyone."

"Do you think he'd clear me?"

John chuckled. "I can't see Pete saying no to you, actually. You may have better luck getting information out of Dan than Pete will, anyway. I'll ring Pete and see what he says. I'll ring you back shortly."

Bessie put the phone down and began to pace around the kitchen. She didn't care for Dan Ross and she hadn't enjoyed speaking with him when she'd visited him at his office. Actually trying to get permission to see him again was just crazy. Still, a little voice said, if someone tried to kill him because of you, you owe him a visit and an apology. Her mind was still racing when the phone rang again.

"I caught Pete just as he was getting back from talking with Dan. He said something along the lines of 'Bessie is welcome to him,' which I took to mean that the interview didn't go well," John told her.

"Oh, dear."

"As I said, I believe Dan is excited about writing his own story for the front page. I doubt he'll say anything to you, but Pete has cleared you if you want to try."

"I feel as if I owe Dan an apology. I can't help but feel as if the accident is connected to Phillip's death."

"So you think that Oliver killed Phillip," John suggested.

"The attack on Dan makes me feel that way. A lot depends on whether Dan followed up on my story idea or not, though. If he didn't, then his accident has nothing to do with Phillip or me."

"For what it's worth, Dan wouldn't tell Pete anything about

anything he's currently investigating. Pete suggested that he isn't actually doing anything but sitting around waiting for news to happen, but Dan just laughed and told him that he could believe whatever he wanted to believe."

Bessie sighed. "He might have been investigating The Liliana Fund, then."

"Maybe he'll at least tell you that much, if you ask," John said.

"I think I should ring the woman at the paper and tell her to stay away from the idea, too."

"If you truly think Oliver was involved in Phillip's death, that's probably wise."

"I don't know what to think. The only thing I know for certain is that I feel terrible for thinking that I might have done something that led to whatever happened to Dan Ross. If something horrible happens to the good causes woman at the paper, I'll feel even worse."

"Are you planning to visit Dan today?" John asked.

"Yes, right after I ring the paper," Bessie replied.

"I can send a car. Someone will be there in half an hour or less."

"I'm sure your constables have better things to do than drive me around the island," Bessie protested.

"No worries. I'll send Doona. She's sitting at my house, staring at the telephone in case Harvey rings, but she needs a break."

"What if Harvey rings?"

"Then he'll have to ring back or leave a message on my machine," John snapped. He took a deep breath and then sighed. "I'm sorry. I'm incredibly frustrated, but none of this is your fault. I shouldn't be shouting at you because my ex-wife is ill half a world away while her new husband acts evasive and secretive. If I didn't have so much going on here, I think I'd fly out to Africa myself to find out what's really happening."

"I am sorry."

"Never mind. I'll send Doona to you. It will do her good to have something else to think about for a few hours. She'll still be home before the children get back from school. They're doing their best, but they need someone with them, in my opinion, anyway."

"Of course they do."

"Good luck with Dan," John concluded. "Obviously, ring me and let me know how it goes."

"I will do."

Bessie put down the phone and then dug out the name that Dan had given her.

"Ah, yes, good morning. May I speak to Jane Stoddard, please?" Bessie asked when her call was answered.

"I'm sorry, but Ms. Stoddard isn't in the office at the moment," was the reply. "If you'd like to leave a number, I can have her ring you back."

Bessie hesitated. She didn't really want to leave any more messages for the woman. "When do you expect her back in the office?" she asked.

"I'm not certain when she will return. Early January, probably."

"Early January?" Bessie echoed.

"Ms. Stoddard always takes a long holiday at Christmas. I believe she travels to Australia, where she has family."

"When did she leave?"

"Early December."

Bessie frowned. So when Dan had referred her to Ms. Stoddard he'd done so knowing that she was away and wouldn't return until the new year. "I'll ring back in January," Bessie said with a sigh.

When Doona arrived a short while later, Bessie was still angry. "He told me to talk to Ms. Stoddard, even though he knew she was in Australia," she fumed.

"This is Dan Ross we're talking about. I don't understand why you're surprised," Doona replied.

"I know you're right, but I'm still angry," Bessie told her.

"Does that mean you don't want to go to Noble's to see him?"

"I don't know what I want to do. I was worried that I might have accidentally put him in danger, but now I'm starting to think that he deserves whatever he gets."

Doona chuckled. "You don't mean that."

"No, I suppose not. Let's go and talk to him."

Doona led her out to her car and then slid behind the steering wheel. Bessie waited until they were on the road out of Laxey to speak.

"Any news on Sue, then?"

"None, which is worse than bad news in a way. The not knowing and the worrying are exhausting. John isn't sleeping. The children can't focus on anything and I feel completely caught in the middle of it all and totally helpless."

"John said that Harvey told him that she was really ill."

"That's part of the problem. We only know what Harvey is prepared to tell us, which isn't much. Sue spoke to the children briefly last night, but only to tell them that she loves them and misses them. According to Harvey, she isn't fully aware of how unwell she actually is, and she keeps fading in and out of lucidity."

"My goodness. The poor woman. I can't imagine falling ill so far away from home."

"It was her choice to travel to Africa, and from everything I've heard, she's been more than happy to keep extending their stay, as well." Doona sighed. "I should be more sympathetic towards her, but I'm seeing firsthand what her actions are doing to the children. It's horrible."

"Are they at school?"

"I hope so. I drove them both there this morning, but it wouldn't surprise me to learn that one or both of them sneaked out, really. As I said, neither of them can focus on anything at the moment. They're probably wasting their time even being there."

"It may be better for them to be there than to be sitting at home, though."

"It probably is. They both have some good friends at school, at least. At home they just sit and stare at the telephone."

"Is Harvey meant to be ringing back at any particular time?"

"He said he'd ring back tonight, but he didn't give an exact time. I assume he'll ring sooner if anything happens."

Bessie swallowed hard. "I feel so sorry for Thomas and Amy."

"I'm more worried about John, actually. He's, well, I've never seen him like this. The divorce was hard on him, but this seems worse."

"Do you think he's still in love with Sue?"

"I'm sure he still loves her, even if he isn't in love, if you know what I mean. I sort of understand, because I know how devastated I was when Charles died. We'd been separated for two years and I was trying to get a divorce, but that didn't mean that I didn't still have feelings for him. Sue and John were married for close to fifteen years. Whatever she did, however much she hurt him, they had a long life together, not to mention two children. I understand why he's upset, but that doesn't make it any easier to see him suffering so much."

"Did Harvey say exactly what's wrong with her?"

"No, he was almost deliberately vague, which is making John even crazier. Harvey is a doctor. He keeps talking in all sorts of medical doublespeak that John can't decipher and when John asks him to simplify, he just says that Sue is gravely ill." She glanced at Bessie. "I probably shouldn't tell you this, but John has rung and spoken to the local police in the area where Harvey and Sue are staying."

"The police? Does John suspect foul play?"

"I don't know. I think he's just feeling frustrated and ringing the police is something he can do from here. There isn't much else he can do, after all."

"What did the police say?"

"Nothing yet, really. They've promised to visit and talk with both Sue and Harvey. They're meant to be ringing back in the next day or two as well, which is one reason why I need to be there when the children are home. John doesn't want them to know that he's contacted the police, obviously."

"John can't possibly think that Harvey did anything to hurt Sue, can he?"

Doona shrugged. "As I said, I'm not sure what he's thinking. I don't know that he knows what he's thinking, if you follow my meaning. I think he's just reacting and doing what little he can do to try to work out what's happening. If Harvey won't answer his questions, then maybe the local police can learn something that will help John understand the situation."

"If I can help in any way, please let me know. I'm still happy to have the children overnight one night if you and John want to go Christmas shopping."

Doona muttered a curse word under her breath. "We still have to do a lot of shopping, but I don't know when we'll find the time."

Bessie pressed her lips together. The situation with John and Sue was almost impossible and she felt completely unable to help. Doona sighed and then switched on the radio. As the car filled with Christmas music, Bessie wondered if John and his children would be able to have a happy Christmas this year.

"Here we are," Doona said a few minutes later. "I'll let you out at the door and then find a parking space. You know how difficult that can be around here."

Bessie nodded. Doona pulled to a stop near the hospital's entrance. As she drove away, Bessie walked into the building's spacious foyer. John had told her where to find Dan, so she didn't bother stopping at the information desk. Instead, she headed straight for the lifts at the back of the space.

A few moments later she was walking down a long corridor. A uniformed police constable was sitting on a chair outside the last room. He stood up as Bessie approached.

"May I help you?" he asked.

"I'm Elizabeth Cubbon. I'm here to see Mr. Ross."

The man frowned and then looked around. "I'm afraid the patient in this room isn't receiving visitors," he said.

"Inspector John Rockwell in Laxey was going to clear it for me to see him."

The constable shook his head. "I'm sorry, but I wasn't given any instructions about visitors."

"Bessie?" a voice said from behind them.

Bessie turned around and smiled brightly at Helen Baxter, her friend who was a nurse at the hospital. "Helen, what a lovely surprise."

"I do work here," Helen laughed. "Is there a problem?"

"I came to see Mr. Ross, but the constable wasn't expecting me," Bessie explained.

"Did John arrange it?"

"He told me he had."

"Let me ring Pete," Helen suggested. She pulled out her mobile phone and pushed a single button on it. A moment later she began a whispered conversation with whoever had answered her call. As Helen slid her phone back into her pocket, a loud noise came from the constable's pocket.

He dug out his phone and frowned at it. "Yes?" After saying "yes, sir" many times, he put the phone away and frowned at Bessie. "I'm to let you in to see Mr. Ross. I'm not happy about it, though. I shall be keeping a very close eye on you and on Mr. Ross while you're here."

"I'd prefer privacy for my conversation with Mr. Ross," Bessie countered.

"Too bad you don't get what you want," the constable snapped.

Bessie glanced at Helen, who sighed and made another phone call. When the constable's phone rang this time, he looked furious.

"Pete's on his way," Helen told Bessie.

"I hope I'm not dragging him away from anything important," Bessie replied. "It will be nice to see him, though."

Pete and Bessie had first met over a dead body some years earlier. Initial dislike had turned to mutual respect during the ensuing investigation. It was Bessie who had first introduced Pete to Helen, and she and John had stood as witnesses to their marriage not that long ago. While Helen was still using her maiden name professionally, privately she was Helen Corkill. Apparently, the young constable was unaware of that fact, though.

He dropped his phone back into his pocket and gave the women a triumphant smile. "The inspector said I'm to wait here for further instructions."

"Did he, now?" Bessie asked.

The constable nodded. "That means you can't go inside," he added smugly.

Bessie shrugged. "How are you?" she asked Helen.

"I'm okay," Helen replied.

"Just okay? You don't seem yourself, really," Bessie said, feeling concerned for her friend.

"I'm really tired, that's all," Helen replied. "It's been a busy year, with the wedding and everything. Pete and I have been talking about going away for a short while in January or February. I know we just had a honeymoon, but we were so busy seeing the sights and eating anything and everything that we never really relaxed."

"Where will you go?"

"Nowhere exciting. Maybe just across. We were actually talking about going to that holiday park, the one you and Doona visited last year."

"I'm not sure how much rest you'll get," Bessie told her. "There are a lot of activities."

"But you don't have to do any of them if you don't want to," Helen countered. "We could just go and switch off our phones and sleep for twenty hours a day."

"I suppose I can see how that might appeal."

Helen nodded and then looked up and down the corridor. She took a step closer to Bessie and then lowered her voice. "I shouldn't be telling anyone yet, as it's very, very early days, but I think I might be pregnant."

Bessie gasped and then gave Helen a hug. "I know we talked about it, but you seemed to think that you might have problems," she said.

"We did have problems," Helen replied. "It's taken a while to get here and, as I said, it's very early. Things could still easily go wrong, but I'm cautiously optimistic. I keep thinking that I should switch to part-time or even take some time off, though. I'm exhausted and I feel that I need to do everything I can to look after the baby."

Bessie opened her mouth to reply, but shut it again when she spotted Pete walking towards them. Helen grabbed her arm. "Don't say anything to Pete," she whispered. "I promised him I wouldn't tell anyone until I was past twelve weeks."

As Bessie greeted the grumpy-looking inspector with a hug, she watched the young constable frown and then begin to look worried.

"Inspector, sir, how are you?" he said when Pete turned towards him.

"A bit frustrated at having to come back down here. I'd only just left, you see," Pete replied. "I thought things were well in hand here. What's the problem?"

"This woman arrived and said she wanted to talk to Mr. Ross," the constable said, pointing to Bessie.

"So you asked for her name and checked the list to see if she was an approved visitor, right?" Pete replied.

The constable flushed. "I was told Mr. Ross wasn't to have any visitors."

"Were you now? By whom?"

"The constable who was here earlier, er, Constable Richards."

"I'll have to have a word with Constable Richards, then," Pete said.

The man nodded nervously.

"Bessie, if you'd like to come with me," Pete said. He offered Bessie his arm. She took it and let him lead her into the small hospital room. Dan was lying on the bed, scowling.

"Thank you," Bessie said to Pete. "I'm not sure why the young constable was so difficult."

"He's annoyed because he wants to be out on patrol. Refusing to let you in was him flaunting his authority. He doesn't know that I'm married to Helen or that she'll be reporting everything he does back to me. He'll learn, I hope. I think he has great potential, once he gets over some of his attitude problems."

"How are you?" she asked softly.

Pete grinned, an expression that she'd rarely seen on his face prior to his relationship with Helen. "I'm wonderful. I wish I'd met Helen years ago, but I probably wasn't ready for her then. I don't think things could be any better at home, anyway."

"That's good to hear."

Pete glanced at Dan and then leaned in close to Bessie. "She might be pregnant, but don't tell her I told you. We aren't meant to be telling people for months yet, but I'm starting to feel as if I might burst if I don't share the news."

"Congratulations," Bessie whispered.

"Thanks," he replied.

"Don't mind me," Dan snapped from his bed. "I'm not sure why you're using my hospital room for your secret conversation, but don't worry about me. I'm not trying to listen in or anything."

Bessie winked at Pete and then turned to Dan. "Sorry about that. Pete and I haven't seen one another in a while. He was kind enough to grant me permission to come and visit you, though."

"I'll be outside," Pete said loudly before nodding at Bessie and leaving the room.

"Of course, you'll simply repeat everything I say to him later, won't you?" Dan asked.

"Maybe, if I think it's important," Bessie replied. "I don't generally keep secrets from the police."

"Sometimes there are very good reasons for not telling them things," Dan countered.

"Such as?"

"Such as getting a front-page headline."

"I'd rather be alive and well than worry about such things."

"You make the headlines quite regularly, anyway."

"Unfortunately."

"But what do you want?" Dan demanded. "If you were coming to gloat over my half-dead body, I'm sorry to disappoint you. While the police prefer to suggest to everyone that I'm at death's door, I'm actually doing rather well and could probably have been sent home already if the police would allow it."

"You can't blame them for wanting to protect you."

"I was hit by a hit-and-run driver. Accidents happen."

"You genuinely think it was an accident?"

"As I understand it, you don't drive," Dan replied. "I'm sure you'd happily run me down, given the chance, though."

"Especially after you gave me Jane Stoddard's information without bothering to mention that she's in Australia until January."

"Is that where she goes every December? I did wonder, but I never bothered to ask. Sorry about that."

"Except you aren't sorry at all."

Dan shrugged. "Is that why you came? To shout at me for sending you to Jane even though she's away?"

"That's part of it, certainly. You can make a proper apology by giving me the name and phone number of whoever is doing Jane's job while she's gone. I'd still like to see a story about some of the island's charities."

"Can't help you. Jane turned in all of her articles through Christmas before she left. If anything happens in her department that's considered newsworthy, it will get assigned to a reporter with some time to spare. It's too close to Christmas now for the sort of series you're talking about anyway."

"Did you follow up on my idea at all?" Bessie asked.

"Not really. I may have asked a few questions of a few of my sources, but I didn't launch a proper investigation. That's really Jane's department. I don't want to step on any toes."

"And you don't think there's any connection between your questions and your accident?"

Dan stared at her for a minute and then began to laugh. "Is that why you're here?" he asked after he'd regained his composure. "Do you really think someone tried to kill me because I asked a source a few innocuous questions about The Liliana Fund? I've heard of people who think the entire world revolves around them, but I'd never pegged you as being one of them."

"That's a no, then?" Bessie asked.

Dan chuckled. "It's a no. It was an accident, probably kids who'd stolen a car and gone for a joyride. The car was found on the next street, wiped completely clean of any prints. That's the work of kids who watch too much television. The chances of the police getting usable fingerprints from a car are tiny, really."

"If you're happy it was an accident, I won't take up any more of your time."

"It may not have been an accident," Dan told her. "Right now, as we speak, I'm investigating three different stories. There are a few things happening in one particular government department that are starting to feel a bit like corruption. I've spoken to several people about a few issues and the first article expressing my concerns will be hitting the paper tomorrow."

"I'll have to make sure to get a copy," Bessie told him.

Dan laughed. "Even if you don't, you'll soon hear the story. I'm expecting it to be the talk of the island after tomorrow."

"Are you suggesting that someone from the government tried to run you over?"

"Not at all," Dan waved a hand. "I'm just pointing out that I'm involved in a number of important stories, all of which are much more significant than whatever is going on at The Liliana Fund. Did you know that one of the island's most high-profile couples is having difficulties? I won't mention any names, but if I tell you that they've had seven children in the past decade, you'll know who I mean."

Bessie nodded. The couple had moved to the island about ten years earlier, buying a huge mansion near the southern coast. She was his third wife and as Bessie understood it, they were planning on having a dozen children together.

"He's having an affair, and it isn't his first. What I found surprising is that she's also cheating. I'm not sure how she has time, with seven children at home. Rumour has it that he's going to be demanding paternity tests on the last three children in the new year."

"You can't be suggesting that either of them tried to kill you."

"No, he has more than enough money to have hired someone to do the job. She'd probably have had to borrow from him or her lover, one or the other, but I've no doubt she could get her hands on plenty of cash in a hurry if she wanted it."

"You can't be serious," Bessie said.

Dan shrugged. "Again, just an example of the sorts of stories that I'm covering. As I said, they're important stories."

"Phillip Tyler was murdered."

"Yes, of course, but you can't seriously believe that anyone involved with The Liliana Fund had anything to do with that. I mean, there may be a few question marks about where the money that

Oliver is so good at raising goes, but murder? The man has dedicated his life to helping others."

Bessie shrugged. "I'm sorry for bothering you."

Dan glanced around the room. "I've an even bigger story," he said in a loud whisper. "I'm about to blow the lid off a huge drug-smuggling operation on the west side of the island. There are several prominent island residents involved, including some with the police and the local government. The story is going to make my name here and get me what I've been after for the last ten years."

"Which is what?"

"A job with a big national newspaper across, of course. You didn't really think that I wanted to stay on the island forever, did you? I can't imagine that. The island is just a stepping stone on my way to better things. I just have to keep Harrison Parker from stealing my headlines."

"Harrison Parker?"

"He just moved to the island a few months ago," Dan explained. "He's young, only a few years out of uni, and he's ambitious. He'd stab me in the back if he thought he could get a good story out of it."

"Maybe he was driving the car that hit you," Bessie suggested.

Dan frowned. "I never thought of that." After a minute, he shook his head. "No, he wouldn't actually do anything that could land him in any trouble, but I'm sure he's furious that he missed out on seeing it happen. He jumps and runs whenever he hears a siren."

"Maybe I should have given my story idea to him."

Dan shook his head vigourously. "No, no, no. Don't encourage the man. He's ruthless and relentless. As I said, there may be a few small issues with The Liliana Fund, but Harrison would turn them into big issues and he'd destroy Oliver along the way. None of us want that to happen."

"What sort of issues?" Bessie asked.

"Oh, just a few little question marks over where the money goes, that's all," Dan shrugged. "I asked Oliver for a list of the grants he made last year and he was a bit evasive. When I suggested that it might be time for someone to go through his records, he was almost hostile. I'm sure it's nothing. He's just used to having complete control over the fund and not having to answer to anyone."

"Could he be diverting money to his own accounts?"

"He has to file a full accounting of everything the charity does every year. The government keeps a close eye on such things."

"So why did he get hostile with you?"

"Maybe his records aren't as thorough as they should be," Dan suggested. "He's been doing this for a long time now. I suspect whatever government department is responsible for checking his reports probably simply rubber stamps whatever he submits. Maybe he knows he's been a bit sloppy lately with a few things."

"Or maybe he's stealing money from The Liliana Fund."

Dan chuckled. "You'd like that, wouldn't you? Then you could blame him for Phillip's murder. The problem is, you like Phillip's family, so you won't even consider them as possible suspects. Whenever you're involved in a murder investigation, the killer always turns out to be someone you don't like. That's rather convenient, anyway."

"Are you suggesting that the police are sending innocent people to prison simply because I don't like them?" Bessie demanded.

"I just think you tend to focus far too narrowly on the suspects you aren't friendly with and never consider anyone who used to eat biscuits in your kitchen."

Bessie flushed. "That isn't fair," she said tightly.

"Fair or not, that's how I see things," Dan replied.

"I came to apologise, just in case anything I did led to your accident. As you've dismissed that idea, I'll simply wish you a speedy recovery and be on my way," Bessie said, turning towards the door.

"If you ever meet Harrison Parker, don't tell him anything," Dan said from the bed.

Bessie didn't bother to acknowledge Dan's words. Instead, she swept out of the room and quickly walked down the corridor towards the lifts.

CHAPTER 14

$\mathcal{P}$ete and Helen were standing together near the nurses' station.

"Did he tell you anything interesting?" Pete asked.

"Not a thing," Bessie replied. "Apparently he's investigating several different things at the moment and there are a long list of people who might want to stop him. He seems convinced that what happened to him was an accident, though."

Pete frowned. "I'm not, but he won't answer any of my questions, which makes the investigation much more difficult than it should be."

"Are you keeping him here, under lock and key, for the foreseeable future?" Bessie asked.

"That's mostly going to be up to him, really. His doctor reckons he'll be fit for release tomorrow. I'd like to persuade Dan to stay here for another day or two beyond that, but I can't force him to do so."

Bessie sighed. "I'd hate for anything to happen to him, even though I find him thoroughly disagreeable."

Pete nodded. "My job is to protect everyone, even the, um, disagreeable people."

Helen laughed. "Very good," she said. "By the time the baby comes, you won't be cursing at all."

"I thought we weren't talking about the baby yet," Pete replied.

"We aren't, not with anyone except Bessie," she told him.

Pete nodded. "I'll walk you out," he offered Bessie.

Helen made a noise.

"What's wrong?" Bessie asked.

"Oh, nothing, it's my lunch break, that's all. I thought maybe Pete and I could have lunch together," she replied.

"You go and have lunch together. I'm perfectly capable of finding my own way out. Doona is waiting for me in the lobby, anyway. She's probably getting anxious because she wants to be at John's when the children get out of school."

"That's a right bloody mess," Pete said.

Helen shook her head. "Language," she said in a teasing tone.

"I'm right, though," Pete replied. "Things just keep getting messier and John is stuck in the middle of it all."

"He's lucky to have Doona's support," Helen suggested.

"I hope he realises how lucky," Pete added.

Bessie agreed and then boarded the lift. She'd only taken a few steps across the lobby when she heard her name being shouted.

"Miss Cubbon? Wait, please."

The man who was rushing towards her was a total stranger. His dark brown hair fell casually around his face, some of it flopping into his brown eyes. Bessie guessed that he was in his early twenties. He reached her side and then gave her a beaming smile as he brushed his hair from his eyes.

"Miss Cubbon, I've been waiting ages for an excuse to speak with you," he said.

"Really?"

"I'm Harrison Parker. I've only just moved to the island recently, having taken a position as an investigative reporter with the *Isle of Man Times*. Obviously, I've done my research on the island, and you are near the top of the list of people I'm anxious to meet and get to know now that I'm here."

"I can't imagine why."

"Now, now, don't be modest," he said with a chuckle. "Even

without all of the recent difficulties that have been popping up all around you, you've led a fascinating life and you know the island, or at least your little corner of it, better than anyone. Having you as a source for information would be invaluable."

"I've no interest in being a source for you," Bessie told him flatly.

"That's entirely up to you, but whatever, I would like to speak to you about a number of things."

"I'm not interested in answering any questions."

"I was hoping to learn more about the island's history, though. I'm told you're an expert on old wills. I'd love to write an article about that for the paper, but even more, I'd simply love to learn more about the subject for my own edification."

"I've given papers at various conferences on the island which have been published. I suggest you try reading those."

Harrison grinned at her. "You're a tough woman to befriend, aren't you? Let me try a different approach. I know you and Dan Ross have had, well, let's say a difficult relationship. I also know he's here and that you came to visit him. Why?"

Bessie shook her head. "I'm not answering any questions."

"I reckon it must have something to do with Phillip Tyler's murder, which suggests that you think Dan's accident had something to do with the murder. What did you ask Dan to investigate when you came to his office the other day?"

"I didn't ask Dan to investigate anything."

"You left a note for Jane Stoddard, suggesting that she profile some of the island's charities. The Liliana Fund was on the list that you gave her. Phillip Tyler used to work for The Liliana Fund. Connection?"

"I have to go." Bessie took a few steps away from him.

"I'm going to take that as a yes," Harrison called after her. "I think I need to go and speak to Oliver Preston. I'm sure he'll be quite interested to learn that you think he's up to something criminal."

Bessie felt her cheeks blaze, but she kept walking. Replying to him would be like adding fuel to the fire. Doona was sitting near the door, using her phone.

"I was starting to worry," she told Bessie.

"I'll tell you everything in the car," Bessie replied. "I know you need to get back to Laxey."

"I don't, actually. John just texted. He's taken the afternoon off, so he's already at home. I think he wants some time alone with the kids, although he's invited me to join them for dinner later."

"Pete said it was all a mess."

"Pete's right, but when did you see Pete?"

"Before I saw Dan. The constable at the door wouldn't let me in."

"I thought Pete cleared your visit."

"Apparently the constable didn't understand that."

Doona sighed. "I do think the Douglas area constables need better training. John had to spend ages working with our newest constable. He worked in Douglas for six months before he came to Laxey, but he was almost as bad as a new recruit."

"I wouldn't have minded so much if it were just bad training, but this young man had something of an attitude problem as well."

"Ms. Moore? What can you tell me about John Rockwell's former wife? She's honeymooning in Africa, isn't she?"

Doona looked confused as Harrison Parker joined them. "Who are you?" she asked.

The man introduced himself, handing Doona a business card as he announced his name.

"Nice to meet you," Doona said as she shoved the card into her handbag. "We must be going." She stood up and headed for the door at a rapid pace with Bessie on her heels.

"The public have a right to know if one of the island's senior police inspectors is too distracted by his personal life to do his job adequately," Harrison shouted after them.

Doona stopped in her tracks and took a deep breath.

"Don't say a word," Bessie hissed in her ear. "He'll only use it against you."

Doona took another breath and then nodded slowly before continuing on her way. They were in the car before either of them spoke again.

"He's horrible. He makes Dan Ross seem almost nice," Doona said.

"I wouldn't go that far, but he is pretty bad. He interrogated me when I got off the lift."

"If I'd seen it, I would have rung security for you. What did he want you to tell him?"

"He wanted to know what I'd talked to Dan about when I visited his office and whether I thought that conversation led to Dan's accident."

Doona sighed. "What's worrying is that he may be quite a bit smarter than Dan."

"Dan said he was ambitious. Maybe he won't stay on the island for long."

"We can but hope. But where are we going? I don't have to be back in Laxey until six. Do you want to do some shopping, since we're in Douglas?"

"I wouldn't mind a trip to the bookshop," Bessie replied.

A few minutes later, Doona found a parking space in the garage for the town centre. "I need a few things from the chemist and probably a dozen other places as well," she told Bessie. "I can meet you in the bookshop in about an hour if that suits you."

"That sounds good," Bessie agreed.

She walked down the busy street that was lined with shops, looking in windows and studying displays. Christmas was right around the corner and there seemed to be a sense of urgency among the shoppers. A man carrying a six-foot-tall stuffed giraffe hurried past her, while a woman struggling with large bags that seemed to be full of pillows rushed along in the opposite direction. After sticking her head into a few shops and doing nothing more than browsing, Bessie was nearly at the bookshop when she spotted a familiar face in the crowd.

Oliver Preston was walking quickly towards her. Bessie stepped back from the bookshop doorway, ready to greet him. She wanted to speak to him before he talked to Harrison Parker, ready to tell him about the idea she'd shared with Jane Stoddard. Before he reached her, however, Oliver turned and disappeared down one of the small alleys between the shops.

Feeling as if that was slightly odd, Bessie moved towards the book-shop door again. As she reached to open it, she stepped backwards again. *Where could Oliver have been going?* she wondered.

As she walked towards the alley, a little voice in her head reminded her of her conversation with Doona. She'd learned from her mistake, she reminded herself. Pulling her phone from her bag, she rang Doona.

"I just saw Oliver disappear down the alley across from the book-shop," she said when her friend answered. "I'm going to see where he went."

"Don't be silly. Wait for me," Doona said quickly. "Stay right where you are. I'm just waiting in the queue to pay."

"I'll be here," Bessie promised.

The alley was short, more of a courtyard for the shops on either side of it. There were four doors that opened off it. Oliver could have gone into any of them. Bessie stood where she was, trying not to look as if she was staring into the empty alley. A moment later one of the doors swung open. Bessie gasped as she recognised Dan Ross. He was still meant to be in hospital. He glanced back and forth and then went back inside.

Doona had to be getting close, Bessie thought as she began to creep forward. If Dan and Oliver were talking, she didn't want to miss the conversation. There was a large crack in the window next to the door that Dan had opened and closed. It had been covered with card-board, but that did little to muffle the sound.

"…to meet me," she heard.

"I was more than happy to meet you," was the reply. Bessie was fairly certain it was Dan's voice.

"I heard you were in hospital, though." That had to be Oliver, Bessie decided.

"I was. I signed myself out."

"Good to know that you weren't too badly injured, then. I was told you were hit by a car."

"Yes, that's right. I'm fine, though."

"Good."

A short silence followed. Bessie shifted and then looked over at the alley's entrance. Where was Doona?

"What's that?" Dan asked suddenly.

"This? Nothing," Oliver replied.

"It's a knife."

"Yes, it is. I brought it with me for protection."

"Protection from what?"

"You, of course. You've been harassing me, threatening to write a story about how I'm stealing money from The Liliana Fund if I don't pay you off to keep quiet."

"I've been doing no such thing."

"I can't afford to pay you, though. I take a very meagre salary from the fund. I wish I could afford to devote every single penny to helping others, but I have to eat."

"Of course you do," Dan replied, his voice shaking slightly.

"I have to have a car, too, of course," Oliver continued. "Did you see my new car? I thought I deserved something new as I've been working so much harder lately."

"Good for you."

"Yes, it is good for me. I bought a flat in London last year. Property prices are insane, of course, but it's a good investment for me. Perhaps I should have looked further afield, though. London isn't all that far away, really."

"No, but it's a great city."

"Of course it is. I've always wanted to live there, but it's very expensive. I was always a hard worker, but I never made a lot of money. Once my mother fell ill, I realised that there were other things that were more important than money. Starting The Liliana Fund gave my life purpose and meaning."

"Yes, of course. Everyone knows how devoted you are to your work." Bessie thought Dan sounded less nervous now. Maybe Oliver had put the knife down.

Oliver laughed. "That's me, devoted to my work. I was, too, you know. When I started out, I truly thought that I could make a difference. I genuinely wanted to help people. I raised as much money as I could and I gave every penny away to people who needed help. It was very fulfilling."

"I know I'm not as generous as I should be," Dan said. "Let me write you a cheque for the fund."

"You can't buy your way out of here, if that's what you're thinking," Oliver replied.

Bessie spotted Doona as she arrived at the alley's entrance. She waved, but then put her finger to her lips. Doona raised an eyebrow and then slowly walked over to join Bessie.

"What do you want?" Dan demanded.

"I want you to understand," Oliver replied. "No one seems to understand."

"I'm sure I will."

"Maybe."

"What's going on?" Doona hissed in Bessie's ear.

"Oliver is talking to Dan," Bessie whispered back. "Now hush."

Doona frowned. The silence inside the building seemed to drag on endlessly. Eventually Oliver spoke again.

"That first year, I didn't take a salary. I lived off my inheritance, the money that my mother had left me. It wasn't a huge amount of money, but it was more than I'd ever had at one time in my life. I may have been a bit more extravagant than I should have been, really."

"I should write an article about you and your mother," Dan said. "What do you think? We might even be able to get the front page in the lead-up to Christmas. We could pull a few heartstrings and get you a bunch of new donors for The Liliana Fund."

"After that first year, when my inheritance ran out, I started paying myself out of the fund," Oliver continued as if Dan hadn't spoken. "I took a modest salary, no more than what I'd been making before I'd started the fund."

Doona was busy on her mobile phone during the silence that followed Oliver's words. Bessie looked at her questioningly. Doona held up the phone to show Bessie that she was texting. "John," she mouthed. Bessie nodded, wondering if Doona was telling John about the conversation they were overhearing or if the texts were about Sue.

"I really need to get to my office," Dan finally broke the silence.

"I still have more to tell you, though," Oliver protested.

Bessie took a step backwards as the handle on the door in front of her rattled.

"Please unlock the door," Dan said.

"When I'm done," Oliver replied. "I was explaining. It's important to me that you understand."

"Go on, then." Dan sounded impatient.

"We didn't award many grants in that first year, you know. I wasn't certain how much money we'd be able to raise or if the money would keep coming in after the initial burst, so I was very cautious with my funding. The letters, though, they were heartbreaking. Our application was very clear about what sorts of things we'd fund, but we still received requests for medical treatments, usually experimental ones. I turned those down, no matter how poignant, but that still left hundreds of appeals for everything from books to trips to wigs to food. The decisions were almost impossible."

"This would make a good story, actually," Dan said.

"Eventually, I developed a list of criteria that I began to use to help me make my decisions. Each letter was awarded points based on their request, their level of need, and a dozen other things, all of which were subjective, of course. By the end of the second year, I'd given away about two-thirds of what I'd planned to give away. That left a big chunk of money in the bank, just sitting there. At the same time, my car started giving me difficulties. It was an older car, and the repairs would have cost more than the car was worth. It was easy enough to write myself a few letters, letters that clearly met my criteria for funding. I made half a dozen grants, just enough to replace my car with a reliable secondhand vehicle. I told myself that I needed the car for work. It was necessary so that I could continue to do the good things that the fund was doing."

"You should have simply given yourself a larger salary."

Oliver laughed. "I'd already done that. I'd done some research into what charity heads were paid and I bumped up my salary accordingly. I was very careful to keep it in line with what others on the island were making, of course. The last thing I wanted to do was draw any attention to myself. As it was, I didn't sleep for a week when my accounts went to the auditors. I was certain they were going to recognise my, um, creative accounting, let's say, but they didn't. I don't know that they did much more than rubber-stamp everything, really."

"I'd like to believe that they're more thorough than that," Dan remarked.

"Whatever, by the end of that year I'd realised that I'd be much more capable of doing my job if I had a new car. My fundraising efforts were proving more successful than I'd dared hoped, so it seemed only fair that I should have some reward, as well."

"And you've been stealing from The Liliana Fund ever since," Dan concluded.

"Not stealing!" Oliver snapped. "I should be allowed to have a nice house and a nice car and a holiday or two every year, even if I do work for a charity."

"Of course."

"The fund brings in far more money than we need to give grants to the people who meet my criteria, anyway. I'm still funding everyone who does that."

"What percentage of last year's grant recipients were real people, then?"

"I don't know. Maybe half. As I said, I funded everyone who met my criteria. It isn't my fault if hundreds or thousands of other people have to be turned down. I'm doing my best."

"Of course you are."

"That sounded somewhat sarcastic."

"It wasn't meant as sarcasm. Put the knife down, okay? Hey, I don't blame you for helping yourself to a bit of the money. You're still doing great things for a lot of people and you're getting to have a nice life yourself. It's no less than you deserve."

"You do understand. Phillip didn't."

"No? I don't suppose it matters now."

"No, it doesn't. If he'd done as I'd asked him, he never would have caught on anyway. He loved meeting the people that we'd helped. It was incredibly annoying, really. One of the reasons I usually fund people in the UK or beyond is so that I don't have to meet them."

"I can understand that."

"Anyway, when Phillip decided to move across, he took copies of the letters from some of the people we'd helped during his years with the fund. It was all an ego trip for him. He'd turn up and introduce himself and get thanked a million times, as if he'd actually had anything to do with the funding decisions. That was all my doing, you understand."

"I'm sure it's the most difficult part of the job."

"It is, yes. Anyway, he copied a bunch of letters, but I insisted on going through them before he left. He'd chosen several that I'd actually written, so I had to pull those, obviously. If he'd stuck to the letters I'd approved, he never would have discovered what I was doing."

"But he didn't?"

"He told me later that he'd found a few copies of some other letters in his paperwork when he unpacked. He reckoned he must have forgotten to get my approval for them before he left. He also didn't bother to ask once he'd found them, I should add. Those were the people he couldn't find, of course."

"Because you'd made them up."

"Some of them were completely imaginary, but others were real people. I simply borrowed their identities for my letters. I tried to mix things up a lot so that if the auditors ever did find anything they might not realise the extent of the issue."

"I'd love to hear more about how you managed all of this."

"I don't think it matters. You aren't going to be doing anything similar."

"I'm awfully tempted, after talking with you. It sounds an easy way to make a lot of money."

"It took me a while to set up a small network of people in the UK and abroad who help. I have to pay them, of course, but if I ever do get caught, they should get the blame. It can't be my fault if The Liliana Fund was targeted by a number of fake applicants, can it?"

"That's genius."

"Phillip didn't know what to think," Oliver continued. "He didn't want to believe that I'd done anything wrong, but he'd met someone whose identity I'd borrowed in one of my letters. She'd never heard of The Liliana Fund and was in perfect health."

"Oh, dear."

"Luckily for me, Phillip was dumb enough to ring me to ask about it, rather than going straight to the police. I managed to persuade him to come back here so that we could talk in person. I told him I could explain everything and hinted that I was doing certain things for a greater good. He wanted to believe me, of course. He'd worked for me for two years and never suspected a thing, after all."

"So you suggested he come back to the island to see you?"

"It was nearly perfect," Oliver chuckled. "He was obsessed with not seeing Nicole again. He insisted that we not tell anyone he was coming. He even begged me to find a place where we could meet in total privacy. He didn't want to see anyone or for anyone to ever know he'd been here. I looked around a couple of different locations, but that cottage on the beach seemed perfect."

"It was too bad someone killed Phillip before you were able to meet with him, then, isn't it?"

"What do you, oh, I see what you're doing. You don't want to hear this part because you think that once I've told you, I'll kill you, too."

"You wouldn't do that, or rather, you shouldn't. I told the police where I was going and who I was meeting. They'll be here any minute."

Oliver laughed. "You didn't tell anyone where you were going or why. I promised you the story of a lifetime. You wouldn't risk that for anything."

"I'm all about getting a good story, but even I wouldn't meet a murder suspect in an empty building without backup."

"I suppose they'll find your body, then," Oliver said.

Dan muttered something under his breath that Bessie hoped she'd misheard. Even considering the circumstances, such language was inappropriate.

Doona touched her arm. "We need to get out of the way," she whispered.

They'd only taken a few steps backwards when Bessie heard Dan scream. A second later, he hurled himself out the broken window, landing in a heap on the ground right in front of Bessie and Doona. Before Bessie could react, the alley filled with police officers.

Pete looked worried as he entered the alley. When he spotted Bessie and Doona, standing to one side, he smiled and nodded. A few minutes later, Dan was taken away on a stretcher.

"Did you get Oliver?" Bessie asked when Pete finally joined them after half an hour or more.

"We did. Thanks to Doona, we had constables at every door and window. The first constable opened the door to the room the two men were in just as Dan jumped out the window. Oliver had nowhere to go."

"Is Dan going to be okay?" was Bessie's next question.

"He managed to knock himself out somehow. He may have hit his head on the window frame or else he banged it when he landed. Whichever, he was pretty groggy when they took him away. I believe he had a broken arm, as well."

"Oliver had much worse planned for him," Doona said with a shiver.

"It took us longer than it should have to put the operation together," Pete said. "If it would have been up to me, we'd have interrupted their conversation a good deal earlier."

"But this way Doona and I got to hear Oliver's entire confession," Bessie pointed out.

"Yes, I'm going to need statements from both of you," Pete replied. "At the moment, Oliver is refusing to answer questions."

"He's been helping himself to The Liliana Fund for years," Bessie said. "I'm sure the auditors will be able to find evidence of it, once they start looking."

Pete nodded. "I need a bit more time here, so I'm going to send you two over to the Douglas station. One of my colleagues there will take your statements and then bring you back to Doona's car. If I have any additional questions, I know where to find you."

A few minutes later a very polite young constable escorted them to his car and drove them to the nearby police station. An inspector Bessie had never met before took her statement and then left her in a small waiting room while he spoke with Doona. They were driven back to Doona's car as soon as Doona was finished.

"I never got to the bookshop," Bessie sighed as Doona pulled out of the parking garage.

"We'll plan a trip down here next week," Doona promised. "I still have to do my Christmas shopping."

"When you were texting John, was it about Oliver and Dan or about Sue?" Bessie had to ask.

"Both," Doona replied. "I let him know what was happening so that he could get the police into position, but he also updated me about Sue."

"And?"

"And she's still holding on. Harvey was angry because the police came to see him this morning. I don't think John was at all apologetic."

"The police didn't find anything suspicious?"

"John hasn't heard back from them yet. He's concerned because Harvey said something along the lines of making certain that the police realise with whom they are dealing, and the value of the difficult work that he's doing in their country."

"Oh, dear."

"The kids got to speak to Sue again, though. Apparently she was talking about all the things she wants to do with them when she gets home. John said she seemed a bit confused as to how old they are, though. She talked about taking them to the park and pushing them on the swings. Amy was very upset afterwards. I'm rather anxious to get over there."

Doona dropped Bessie off at Treoghe Bwaane, not even coming inside to check the cottage, something she always insisted on doing.

"I'm already late for dinner with John and the kids," she said when she pulled to a stop at the cottage. "Do you mind if I don't come inside?"

"Not at all," Bessie said stoutly. "You know I hate when you fuss."

She let herself into the cottage and then waved to Doona to let her know that everything appeared exactly as she'd left it. When her phone rang, she answered it without thinking.

"Ah, Miss Cubbon, it's Harrison, Harrison Parker. I'm working on tomorrow's headline story and I'd love a quote from you. How did you feel when you heard Oliver Preston confess to Phillip Tyler's murder?"

"I didn't, that is, no comment."

"Oh, come on, Aunt Bessie. I know you were there, in the alley, listening to Dan's conversation with Oliver. Give me something."

Bessie simply put the phone down. It rang again immediately, but she ignored it. Harrison left four long messages on her answering machine before it ran out of room to record any more. Once she'd turned the ringer off on the phone, the cottage was lovely and quiet. After making herself some dinner, Bessie curled up with a book about Catherine the Great and read until bedtime.

CHAPTER 15

$\mathcal{T}$he headline on the local paper the next day screamed at Bessie when she visited the shop at the top of the hill. "Seemingly Dedicated Charity Founder Turned Heartless Killer," it read. Bessie put a copy in her basket, along with some chocolate and a few other necessities.

"How are you today?" she asked Sandra.

"I'm good, thank you. I've read about half of the books you lent me. I'll bring the ones I'm finished with here the next time I work so that I can make sure to get them back to you."

"I truly don't need them back, but I'll take them if you don't want them."

"If you're sure, I may keep a few," Sandra replied, blushing. "I really enjoyed a couple of them."

Bessie walked home and then sat down with a cup of tea and the paper. The article didn't tell her anything she didn't already know, except that Dan was still in Noble's but was expected to make a full recovery. The article was credited to Harrison Parker, something that Bessie suspected would upset Dan almost as much as nearly being murdered.

Christmas at the Castle kept Bessie busy for the next few days.

Doona rang her with regular updates on Sue, telling her each day that there was no change. Bessie was pleased to see John's car parked next to her cottage one afternoon when she arrived home from Castletown.

"Do you know the owner of that car?" Mark asked.

"It's Inspector Rockwell's car," she told him.

"In that case, I won't worry," Mark laughed.

Before Bessie could open the door, John had emerged from his car and crossed to Mark's. He opened her door for her and helped her out.

"I rang to let you know that I was coming, but you weren't at home," he told Bessie after she'd thanked Mark for the ride.

"Christmas at the Castle opens tomorrow. I thought I was going to be in Castletown all evening, but everything is ready. We actually ran out of things to do."

"That's good news, right?"

"Oh, yes, of course. Last year things were considerably more difficult."

John nodded as Bessie let them both into the cottage. "I won't stay long," he said. "I just wanted to have a quick chat with you about Oliver Preston."

"Let me put the kettle on," Bessie suggested. "I've been baking American Christmas cookies all week, in between trips down south. You'll have to take some home to the children, too."

"I'm sure they'd love that."

"How are they?" Bessie asked as she filled the kettle.

"As good as can be expected, I suppose. Harvey rings daily, but never says much. In his opinion, Sue could hang on for weeks or even months, but he doesn't expect her to recover. I suggested bringing her home, but he reckons she's too ill to travel."

"Are the police still investigating?"

"They are, which is making things increasingly tense between Harvey and myself. He's insulted that I consulted them, and I see his point, but I still have my suspicions."

"Why would he want to hurt her?"

"Maybe he realised that he really isn't ready to be a stepfather, or maybe he decided that he wanted to stay in Africa and Sue argued with him. Maybe he simply got bored with her or got tired of her nagging or hated the way she laughed." John sighed. "Maybe he didn't have anything to do with whatever is wrong with her. My line of work tends to make me see things that aren't always there."

"What's actually wrong with her?"

"An unspecified fever," John said. "She had all of the required vaccinations before she went, but Harvey administered them. None of them given one hundred per cent protection, of course."

"It's all very odd."

"Yes, it is exactly that. I'd really like to fly down there and get to the bottom of what's happening myself, but I can't leave the children or my job to go on some wild quest just because I have unanswered questions."

"Do you think Sue will recover?"

"I convinced the police to insist that she be seen by a local doctor. Harvey is furious about that, too, of course. I haven't had the doctor's report yet. The children are holding on to hope that Harvey is wrong and the local doctor will be able to cure their mother. I'm trying very hard to temper their expectations."

"Those poor kids."

"This close to Christmas it's especially difficult. They'll be on their school holidays soon and I'm afraid they'll spend far too much time sitting around and worrying about Sue when they've no distractions."

"They can come here one day. We can bake cookies and walk on the beach."

"I'll suggest it to them. I'm not making any plans for them as I want them to feel as if they have some say in what's happening in their lives right now."

Bessie nodded. "But you wanted to talk about Oliver Preston," she said as she put teacups for each of them on the table. While they'd been talking, she'd filled a plate with Christmas cookies. She put that in the centre of the table and then sat down across from John. "Why?"

"I've read your statement and Doona's. It's almost uncanny how closely they match one another."

"We've had a lot of practice with this sort of thing."

"Yes, I suppose you have. Dan Ross's statement is broadly similar, but in his Oliver actually confesses to murdering Phillip. That isn't in your statement."

Bessie thought back. "It was clear, from what he said, that he'd killed Phillip, but he never actually said that he had. He was about to, I think, when Dan said something about someone else killing Phillip and that rather changed the subject."

John nodded. "Oliver is denying everything, of course, and Dan is insisting that he confessed. You and Doona may need to testify when the whole thing goes to trial."

"You've found evidence of Oliver's fraud, though, right?"

"We've found evidence of something not right with The Liliana Fund. Oliver is insisting that he's the victim, that unscrupulous men and women were requesting funding and he was naïve enough to believe their stories. It may take a while to pin the whole thing down."

"He's very clever."

"He is, which is why he managed to get away with what he was doing for so long. If Phillip had stuck to looking for the people that Oliver told him to look for, Oliver might never have been caught."

"I feel sorry for all of the people who requested funding and were turned down so that Oliver could drive a new car and have holidays. I can't imagine cheating cancer patients out of money. Is there any evidence that Dylan knew what was happening?"

"Nothing we can prove, yet, but we believe that he was fully aware of the situation. He was being paid an incredibly generous salary for what he did, far more than Phillip had been paid, and from what I've been told, he didn't do much of anything to earn that salary."

"So he was being paid to keep his mouth shut, if nothing else."

"It certainly appears that way."

"Phillip would never have been bought off in that way."

"I suspect you're right. I wish he'd rung the police instead of confronting Oliver on his own."

"That would have been the sensible thing to do."

"While we're talking about being sensible," John said, catching Bessie's eye. "Walking into that alley was a very dangerous thing to do. If Oliver had looked out that window or opened that door, he would have spotted you immediately. He would have killed you without hesitation, you know that."

Bessie nodded. "At the time it didn't feel dangerous. We were on a public street in the middle of the afternoon."

"You were in a rarely used alley well off the main road. I'm sure Oliver chose it because he was confident that he and Dan wouldn't be interrupted there. The buildings on either side of the alley are both mostly empty at the moment, although someone does live in one of the first-floor flats in one of the buildings. He wasn't at home while all of this was happening, though."

"I'll be more careful next time," Bessie promised.

"I hope there won't be a next time. You've been involved in far too many murder investigations lately. Maybe this was the last one, at least for a while."

"That would be fine with me."

The pair talked about Christmas and Thomas and Amy for a short while before John glanced at the clock and sighed.

"I need to get home. Doona took the children to a movie tonight, but they'll be getting back soon. I don't want them coming back to an empty house. We're trying to act as if everything is perfectly normal, even though it isn't anything like normal."

Bessie nodded and then walked John to the door. "I hope Sue recovers and comes home soon."

"I'm more afraid that she'll recover and decide to stay out there," John replied. "She's not acting at all like the woman I knew and loved. That woman always put Thomas and Amy first."

"I'm still not sure how Dan got into the town centre so quickly," Bessie said as John reached for the door.

"Apparently, after he spoke with you, he rang Oliver. Oliver suggested that they needed to meet in person immediately. I gather he promised Dan the biggest story of his life if he could be in Douglas quickly enough. Dan was in a taxi five minutes later."

"I hope he's recovering from his injuries."

"As I understand it, he's doing well physically. He's more than a little upset about everything that happened with Harrison, though."

"Has something happened with Harrison?"

"You know he got the byline for the article on Oliver's attempt to murder Dan. Oliver is threatening to sue the paper over that, by the way, but Harrison only reported exactly what happened, even if the headline was a bit misleading."

"He called Oliver a murderer."

"Yes, but in the article he made sure to use words like 'suspected' and 'alleged.' Whatever, one of the national papers in the UK picked up the story and let Harrison write a series of articles for them. By the end of the week, he had a job offer from them. He's moving to London in the new year."

"I won't be sorry to see him leave the island."

"No, neither will Dan, but apparently Dan thinks the job should be his, as he should have been the one to write the article. The problem was that Dan was drifting in and out of consciousness while Harrison was writing the story."

"How did Harrison even get the story?"

"Ah, apparently he was following you."

"Me?" Bessie asked angrily.

"Yes, but when he saw you in the alley, he went around to the front of the building and let himself in with some handy lock-picking tools. They've been confiscated now, after the police found him hiding in an otherwise empty airing cupboard in the hallway outside the room where Oliver and Dan were talking. Luckily for Harrison, the walls in the building were thin and he managed to hear every word that was said."

"Does his version agree with mine and Doona's?"

"His had a few, well, let's call them creative flairs," John said dryly.

Bessie laughed. "That doesn't surprise me."

"No, but it makes his statement far less useful." John opened the door and then turned back around and pulled Bessie into a hug. "I want you to be more careful next time," he told her. "You're important to me."

"I will," she promised. "Let me know if you want me to have the children here for a few hours or even a few days."

"I'll ring you," he replied before he walked back out to his car. Bessie watched as he drove away and then shut and locked the door. She'd forgotten to pack up cookies for the children, she realised, when she saw the still full plate on the table. Instead of putting them away immediately, Bessie sat down and nibbled her way through a cookie, sipping her tea and letting herself relax. It had been a long day and Christmas at the Castle was going to make for a busy weekend.

GLOSSARY OF TERMS

House Names – Manx to English

- **Thie yn Traie** - Beach House
- **Treoghe Bwaane** - Widow's Cottage

English to American Terms

- **advocate** - Manx title for a lawyer (solicitor)
- **aye** - yes
- **bin** - garbage can
- **biscuits** - cookies
- **bonnet (car)** - hood
- **boot (car)** - trunk
- **car park** - parking lot
- **chemist** - pharmacist
- **chips** - french fries
- **cuppa** - cup of tea (informally)
- **dear** - expensive
- **estate agent** - real estate agent (realtor)
- **fairy cakes** - cupcakes

- **fancy dress** - costume
- **fizzy drink** - soda (pop)
- **fortnight** - two weeks
- **holiday** - vacation
- **jumper** - sweater
- **lie in** - sleep late
- **midday** - noon
- **pavement** - sidewalk
- **plait (hair)** - braid
- **primary school** - elementary school
- **pudding** - dessert
- **skeet** - gossip
- **starters** - appetizers
- **supply teacher** - substitute teacher
- **telly** - television
- **torch** - flashlight
- **trolley** - shopping cart
- **windscreen** - windshield

OTHER NOTES

The emergency number in the UK and the Isle of Man is 999, not 911.

CID is the Criminal Investigation Department of the Isle of Man Constabulary (Police Force).

When talking about time, the English say, for example, "half seven" to mean "seven-thirty."

With regard to Bessie's age: UK (and IOM) residents get a free bus pass at the age of 60. Bessie is somewhere between that age and the age at which she will get a birthday card from the Queen. British citizens used to receive telegrams from the ruling monarch on the occasion of their one-hundredth birthday. Cards replaced the telegrams in 1982, but the special greeting is still widely referred to as a telegram.

When island residents talk about someone being from "across," they mean that the person is from somewhere in the United Kingdom (across the water).

ACKNOWLEDGMENTS

Thank you readers, for staying with Bessie for so many books.

Thanks to my editor, Denise, who has been trying to help me with my grammar since the first book.

Thanks to Kevin for the wonderful photos that grace my covers.

And thanks to my beta readers who help in a million small ways.

AUNT BESSIE VOLUNTEERS

RELEASE DATE: SEPTEMBER 19, 2019

Aunt Bessie volunteers to help Manx National Heritage clear out years of accumulated rubbish at Peel Castle.

Elizabeth Cubbon has been known as Aunt Bessie for most of her life. She's acted as an honourary aunt to most of the children who've grown up in Laxey over the past fifty years or more. She's also well known for being a helpful volunteer with Manx National Heritage, the group charged with preserving and publicising the island's rich history.

Aunt Bessie volunteers to take a quick look.

When Mark finds what looks like a skeleton in one of small towers in the castle walls, Bessie reluctantly takes a peek. A quick call to the police has Inspector Anna Lambert on the scene a short while later.

Aunt Bessie volunteers to help the police work out the identity of the skeleton.

Bessie knows people all over the island. It doesn't take her long to compile a list of women who left the island at the right time and never returned. Now the police just have to work out which woman never got any farther than St. Patrick's Isle, the tiny island where Peel Castle sits.

Bessie and the police need to work out the identity of their skeleton, but that isn't all. They also want to know how she died and how her body ended up at Peel Castle. Equally puzzling is how it managed to remain undiscovered for over thirty years.

ALSO BY DIANA XARISSA

Aunt Bessie Assumes

Aunt Bessie Believes

Aunt Bessie Considers

Aunt Bessie Decides

Aunt Bessie Enjoys

Aunt Bessie Finds

Aunt Bessie Goes

Aunt Bessie's Holiday

Aunt Bessie Invites

Aunt Bessie Joins

Aunt Bessie Knows

Aunt Bessie Likes

Aunt Bessie Meets

Aunt Bessie Needs

Aunt Bessie Observes

Aunt Bessie Provides

Aunt Bessie Questions

Aunt Bessie Remembers

Aunt Bessie Solves

Aunt Bessie Tries

Aunt Bessie Understands

Aunt Bessie Volunteers

Aunt Bessie Wonders

The Isle of Man Ghostly Cozy Mysteries

Arrivals and Arrests

The Quinton Case

The Rhodes Case

The Isle of Man Romance Series

Island Escape

Island Inheritance

Island Heritage

Island Christmas

ABOUT THE AUTHOR

Diana grew up in Northwestern Pennsylvania and moved to Washington, DC, after college. There she met a wonderful Englishman who was visiting the city. After a whirlwind romance, they got married and Diana moved to the Chesterfield area of Derbyshire to begin a new life with her husband. A short time later, they relocated to the Isle of Man.

After more than ten years on the island, it was time for a change. With their two children in tow, Diana and her husband moved to suburbs of Buffalo, New York. Diana now spends her days writing about the island she loves.

She also writes mystery/thrillers set in the not-too-distant future as Diana X. Dunn and middle grade and Young Adult books as D.X. Dunn.

Diana is always happy to hear from readers. You can write to her at:

Diana Xarissa Dunn
PO Box 72
Clarence, NY 14031.
Find Diana at: DianaXarissa.com
E-mail: Diana@dianaxarissa.com

Made in United States
North Haven, CT
06 November 2023

43689072R00134